NOT MUSHROOM FOR DEATH

A RIGHT ROYAL COZY INVESTIGATION BOOK 3

HELEN GOLDEN

DREW BRADLEY PRESS

COPYRIGHT

DEDICATION

To my parents, Ann and Ray.

You have always been there to support me in whatever way I needed. I am so grateful for your love and care.
Oh, and I'm sorry I was so awful between the ages of fifteen and nineteen!

NOTE FROM THE AUTHOR

I am a British author and this book has been written using British English. So if you are from somewhere other than the UK, you may find some words spelt differently to how you would spell them. In most cases this is British English, not a spelling mistake. We also have different punctuation rules in the UK.

However if you find any other errors, I would be grateful if you would please contact me helen@helengoldenauthor. co.uk and let me know so I can correct them. Thank you.

For your reference I have included a list of characters in the order they appear, and you can find this at the back of the book.

1

MID-AFTERNOON, THURSDAY 1 OCTOBER

"Oh my giddy aunt!" Perry Juke whispered to Lady Beatrice, the Countess of Rossex. "Luca's actually here."

She followed his gaze across the giant marquee, past the stage, and into the opposite wing. *Oh my gosh, he's getting ready to go on.*

Luca Mazza bounced on his feet just offstage while a harassed-looking producer attempted to fit a microphone to the collar of his chef jacket. As she put her hand on his shoulder to stop him moving, he raked his unruly brown hair up onto the top of his head, and wrapping it around his fingers to form a bun, he wound a hair elastic over it to keep it in place.

"He must have made a miraculous recovery then," Lady Beatrice said quietly, turning back to her friend. They had all been convinced Luca, having spent the last two days ill in bed, wouldn't be well enough to perform the demonstration this afternoon.

Perry nodded, his blond fringe falling into his eyes. He swept it away. "Simon will be relieved. He was dreading having to go on stage with Seb if Luca failed to show up. They only had a chance to do one brief run-through earlier."

Tucking her long red hair behind her ears, Lady Beatrice looked back across the tent where Luca was now in deep conversation with Sebastiano Marchetti. She could tell from the way Seb was rubbing his clean-shaven chin with his thumb and forefinger that he wasn't happy. Perhaps he was trying to persuade Luca not to go on stage.

Just to Seb's left, Simon Lattimore stood, his hands on denim-clad hips, a frown etched into his tanned forehead as he stared at the two chefs. He must be worried too. Simon turned his head and looked over towards her and Perry. In her peripheral vision she saw Perry raise his arm and wave at his partner. Simon responded with a grin.

Standing on Simon's other side, a slim blonde woman looked over and frowned. Lady Beatrice recognised her as Fay Mayer, Luca's girlfriend. As Fay returned to staring at her boyfriend, who was now swivelling his torso from side to side, Seb looked up. His blue eyes scanned the wing where she and Perry were standing until he caught Lady Beatrice's eye.

Feeling she should give her beau some gesture of support, Lady Beatrice raised her hand and gave him a thumbs up.

Seb smiled and blew her a kiss, then resumed talking to Luca. Their conversation ended with Luca clapping his hands together and nodding his head vigorously. With a brief shake of his head, Seb switched on his own microphone and walked onto the stage.

A wave of energetic clapping rang around the massive tent. Sebastiano Marchetti broke into a grin. "Thank you, thank you. *Grazie, grazie.*" Shouting to make himself heard above the noise of the greeting, he waved his hands to signal for the audience to stop.

Lady Beatrice couldn't help grinning too. *They really love him.* She knew how hard he'd worked to get the Fenn House Food and Wine Festival up and running despite his concerns about Luca's illness. *He deserves this.*

The noise died down, and one hundred and forty pairs of eyes gave their complete attention to the tall chef standing before them.

"Ladies and gentlemen, thank you very much for coming today and joining us for this first demonstration of the festival." There was a sprinkling of applause, and Seb bowed his head for a few seconds until it died down. "We have a packed schedule for you over the next four days, and I hope you'll enjoy everything we have to offer…"

"He's very good with a crowd, isn't he?" Perry whispered in her ear. "But then I could listen to him talk all day long with that deep, sexy Italian voice of his."

Lady Beatrice turned and rolled her eyes. "Shh!" she said, putting her forefinger to her lips.

Of course, he's right. Seb's voice was something she found enthralling. And, although she wouldn't admit it to anyone, she sometimes found herself not listening to the words he spoke but simply allowing herself to be serenaded by the tone and camber of his voice. Was that normal? *Shouldn't I be hanging on his every word?*

After just over a month of casually dating the charismatic and popular chef, she was still unsure of her feelings about their very public budding 'relationship'. It was all so new with Seb, she was reluctant to even call it a relationship. For her, they were just two people getting to know each other. The press might be building it up to be the hottest romance of the year, but she refused to be pushed into speeding things up beyond her comfort zone. *A handful of dinner dates and some time spent lounging around a pool in the sun does not a couple make!*

She also hated the attention they got from Seb's fans and the press. It was nothing new to her. As a member of the British royal family and the daughter of a princess, her life had always been under the microscope however unwelcome the intrusion was. But even so, it was much worse now when she was out and about with a famous chef. Everywhere they went. Everything they did. It was all fodder for social media and the newspapers. On the plus side though, Seb was charming and entertaining. And although she was still getting to know him, when they were on their own or with friends, she enjoyed his company. *But is it enough to endure constant public scrutiny for?* The jury was still out. She sighed and returned her gaze to the handsome chef on stage.

"...and so now, without further delay, let me introduce you to your host for our first demonstration."

A rumble of excitement came from the audience seated in the stands. Looking over to the wing opposite, Lady Beatrice saw Luca Mazza pumping his arms and shaking his head from side to side as if he was a sprinter about to bend down and settle himself on the starting blocks.

"He's an amazing chef, a fellow Italian, and I'm proud to call him my friend." Seb swept his right arm out to the side. "Please welcome Luca Mazza."

Luca bounded onto the stage to a roaring round of applause.

The two men hugged and patted each other on the back. Then Luca broke free, and moving to the centre of the stage, he took a deep bow.

Seb backed away from the stage and into the wings, his gaze remaining on Luca's back the whole time. A good-looking man sporting a red bandana passed by, and Seb grabbed him by the arm and whispered into his ear.

Is he asking him to keep an eye on Luca?

Luca's speech dragged her attention back to the stage. "Ladies and gentleman, thank you very much for your warm welcome. I have a treat in store for you this afternoon. But first let me introduce you to my good friend and sous chef for this demo, Ryan Hawley." He extended his arm out, and the chef Seb had been talking to walked on stage to rousing applause.

"Now, *he's* worth the entrance price alone," Perry said over her shoulder.

Turning, she grinned at him. "Perry! Don't make me tell Simon that you're having impure thoughts about another man."

Perry tilted his head to the side. "I can look, can't I? And don't think I didn't see the way your eyes followed him across the stage. I'm not the only one looking."

Feeling heat rush into her cheeks, she slapped him playfully on the arm. *How did he notice that?* She returned her gaze to the demonstration.

The two men, having turned away from the audience, walked towards a large stainless-steel unit sitting halfway along the stage. As they arrived, Luca swivelled around to face the crowd while Ryan began collecting ingredients from the bench and fridge behind them.

"So today we are going to make for you two dishes," Luca told them. "The first is chicken breast stuffed with basil pesto and served with sautéed mushrooms, garlic, and tomatoes." Murmurs of approval rose from the crowd. "And the second" —the audience leaned forward in their seats— "is... a secret!" They let out a sigh. The cheeky Italian chef grinned at them. "You'll see soon... I promise. But let's start now."

The two men got to work — Luca putting the pesto ingredients into the blender, and Ryan throwing slithers of garlic, chopped mushrooms, and fresh tomatoes into a large frying pan and shaking it.

The rich sweet smell wafted over to the wings. Lady Beatrice inhaled deeply, her tummy rumbling in response. *I hope they bring the leftovers back here.* She looked across to see how Seb was doing, standing next to Simon. Both men had their arms folded as they watched the stage with hawk-like concentration.

"Is it me, or does Luca look like he's flagging already?" Perry asked her.

She glanced back at the stage just in time to see Luca bend over and wipe his forehead with a tea towel attached to his apron tie as he picked up the frying pan. His face was the colour of the tomatoes that had been on the bench behind him a few minutes ago.

"He doesn't look too good, does he?"

The words were barely out of her mouth before Luca staggered forward, tossing his frying pan back onto its ring, where it landed teetering on the edge. Jerking his head up, Ryan leapt towards the pan and grabbed it just as it was about to slide off. Seb and Simon appeared on the stage, running towards Luca.

But they were too late to catch him.

Luca collapsed into a heap behind the unit, his microphone picking up the thud as he hit the ground.

A WEEK EARLIER, THURSDAY 24 SEPTEMBER

The Society Page online article:

Lady Beatrice and Sebastiano Marchetti Together at Fenn House

Lady Beatrice (36), the Countess of Rossex, and Sebastiano Marchetti (38), known to his legion of fans as Chef Seb, are spending time together at Fenn House, her uncle's, King James's, private house in Fenshire while they both work there on separate projects.

Lady Beatrice, alongside her business partner Perry Juke (34), the long-term other half of the author and celebrity chef Simon Lattimore (39), are managing the refurbishment of ten guest suites and four sitting rooms. This is phase one of a five-year project to update the interior of the Jacobethan-style Fenn House, which was rebuilt in 1829 and has 784 rooms, including 15 state rooms, 18 royal apartments, 60 guest bedrooms, 156 staff bedrooms, 88 offices, and 65 bathrooms.

Meanwhile, Chef Seb is the main organiser of the Fenn

House Food and Wine Festival that starts on Thursday 1ˢᵗ October and is being held close to the visitor's centre in the twenty-five-thousand-acre estate. Expected to be the largest food festival in the UK, there will be food and drink stalls from all around the country, as well as big names from the world of food hosting cooking demonstrations during the four-day event. These include Luca Mazza (38), the television star of Get Your Cook On; *up-and-coming Ryan Hawley (30), a regular on BBC's* Sunday Roast; *Simon Lattimore, winner of last year's* Celebrity Elitechef; *and Finn Gilligan (32), Head chef at The Flyer in Mayfair. Renowned food critic Fay Mayer (30), Luca Mazza's girlfriend, is hosting a panel discussion about food sourcing on the Friday.*

Lady Beatrice and Sebastiano Marchetti have been dating for a month, and it's the first relationship the countess has acknowledged in public since her husband James Wiltshire, the late Earl of Rossex, died in a car accident fourteen years ago. The new couple recently returned from a holiday in Mauritius, where they stayed in a private villa belonging to legendary singer Erick Barber and his husband Ricardo Barry, who are long-time friends of the countess.

3

LATE AFTERNOON, MONDAY 28 SEPTEMBER

"Daisy, get off that chair!" Lady Beatrice scolded her West Highland Terrier, who immediately jumped down and went to sit in her bed, her tail wagging. *She looks like butter wouldn't melt in her mouth.*

Perry Juke, standing by her side, chuckled. "She's just trying it out for comfort, aren't you, Daisy?" The little white dog tilted her head to one side and wagged her tail even more furiously.

"Indeed," Lady Beatrice said dusting down the seat of the plush navy-blue armchair where Daisy had been sitting. "But she knows she's not allowed on the furniture, Perry. I don't know where this naughty streak has come from. I can normally bring her with me without worrying, but these last few weeks, she's been..." She couldn't quite think how to describe the change in Daisy since they'd started the refurbishment at Fenn House. *Clingy? Wary? Unsettled?* Yes, that was it. She seemed unsettled. Not her usual relaxed self.

"Not herself?" Perry offered.

"Indeed. That's it. Do you think she's ill?"

Perry shook his head. "No. I just think the changes in her

life are making her feel a bit insecure."

"Oh, listen to you, Mr Dog Whisperer! How do you mean?"

"Well, normally you take her everywhere with you, but recently, you've been going out more without her."

Lady Beatrice stopped in front of him and leaned her head to one side, frowning. "Have I?"

"Well, you went on holiday for almost a week to Mauritius to live it up with your new *lurve* interest, gorgeous Sebastiano."

Lady Beatrice rolled her eyes. Perry sounded like a newspaper headline. And there had been plenty of them during the brief trip she and Seb had taken a few weeks ago to get to know each other better. The security team at the home of Erick and Ricardo had tried their best, but it had taken less than twenty-four hours for the paparazzi to find out they were there. After that, she and Seb had been confined to the villa. And although she'd relished the chance to relax after the events at Fawstead Manor had come to a dramatic conclusion only days before they'd flown out, she hadn't felt truly at ease, aware that their holiday was the centre of attention back home in the popular press. Sam, her thirteen-year-old son, had kept her updated with what he was up to at boarding school on a daily basis, and Perry had supplied her with almost hourly photos of Daisy in various sleeping positions captioned 'Aw bless' with a red heart emoji. But although Seb had been great company, she'd disliked being so far away from them all and had not been able to wait to get home.

Looking at Daisy now curled up in her bed, the gentle rise and fall of her chest occasionally disturbed by a paw flicker as she dreamt, Lady Beatrice wondered if she'd traumatised her little dog by going away for so long. *Don't be silly, Bea. She was with Simon and Perry.*

"But she was with you and Simon, and she loves being with you two. You didn't mention that she played up or anything."

Perry reached out and patted her arm. "Don't worry, Bea, she didn't. She was as good as gold. But it must've been a bit unsettling for her. And then you've been very busy since you got back. Popping up to London for odd days to see Seb and not wanting to bring her here while we've been moving things around."

An icy shiver ran up her spine. Lady Beatrice raised a hand to her heart and gasped. "I've been neglecting her, haven't I?" *Oh, Daisy, I'm so sorry.*

Perry shook his head. "I didn't say that, Bea. I just think she needs a bit of time to get used to it, that's all."

Poor Daisy. Lady Beatrice didn't want to be that person who spurned their friends and family (and pets) when a man came into their life. "What can I do to make it easier for her, do you think?"

"Why don't you begin taking her with you when you go to see Seb? See how that works."

She blushed. "He has a thing about dog hairs on the furniture in his flat." She'd been surprised the first time he'd invited her up to London to stay and had asked her not to bring Daisy. He had a cleaner who came in every day, after all. But she'd wanted to respect his wishes and had reluctantly agreed. *You need to compromise to make things work, don't you?* Lady Bea sighed. But there was a bigger problem than just dog hairs…

"And anyway, I don't think she likes him."

"What do you mean?"

She shook her head and shrugged. "Daisy. She doesn't seem to like Seb much."

There, now I've said it out loud. It was something that had been bothering her for weeks. Daisy, normally keen to greet and receive a fuss from anyone, kept her distance from Seb. And Seb, unlike most people Daisy met, hadn't fallen for her charms. Instead, he complained she was food-obsessed and warned Lady Beatrice she shouldn't encourage her little dog by feeding her human food. He was probably right. *But Daisy isn't a dog-food kind of girl.*

"Well, now you mention it, Simon and I have noticed. And it appears to be mutual."

Lady Beatrice moved over to Daisy's bed and sat on the floor beside it. Stroking the wiry white fur of her most adored companion, she whispered, "Daisy, I'm so sorry. Have I abandoned you for a tall and handsome Italian?" Daisy, her tail going like the clappers, lunged forward and licked her mistress. Lady Beatrice laughed and wiped her face with her hand as she stood and dusted herself down. She moved over to the sideboard where she picked up a sample of wallpaper. "Okay, we have work to do if we want to watch Simon do his rehearsal." Walking to where Perry stood, she held up the flamboyant *Christian Lacroix* botanical mural against the wall and tilted her head. *Yes, I think this will be perfect.* "What do you think?"

Perry clapped his hands, smiling. "Love it!"

"Great, we'll go with this then." Taking the teal paint swatch Perry handed her, she lifted it up and placed it next to the wallpaper.

Perry moved closer to study the combination. "So how *is* love's young dream? Are wedding bells on the horizon?"

"Oh my gosh, no!" It rushed out of her with no thought. *Marriage?* She shook her head. "We barely know each other."

She was still struggling to trust Seb completely. Maybe it was the way he lapped up the attention she shied away from.

During their recent holiday, he'd still wanted to explore the local area even though they would have been followed everywhere by the press already camped outside the villa. *He seems to court public attention.* And that couldn't be any further from what she wanted.

And as much as she disliked acknowledging it, she was still intensely annoyed by the parting comment made by Detective Chief Inspector Richard Fitzwilliam the last time she'd seen him. "*I would hate for you to get used by him.*" Her hackles were rising even now just thinking about it. Working for the Protection and Investigation (Royal) Services, PaIRS for short, Fitzwilliam's job was to find and investigate threats to the royal family, not to make comments on her love life. *So impertinent!* And especially when he'd so clearly made a mess of his own. A smile tugged at the corner of her mouth as she recalled how he'd told her he was in the doghouse with his sister Elise after he'd ended his short-lived relationship with her friend. But his words were still haunting her a month later. *Is Seb using me to get publicity?* She'd thought so back in August when they had only been on a couple of dates and the press had seemed to know of their every move. She'd even confronted him about it, accusing him of feeding information to the papers. The heat rose in her cheeks as she recalled the embarrassment of having to backtrack and apologise to him after her mother's revelation that it was she who owned and provided much of the information to *The Society Page.*

Just as well he forgave me. But recently, that nagging doubt had come back. She'd deliberately kept her mother in the dark about many of their plans and yet, the press had still found them…

Shaking his head at the teal sample she was holding, Perry said, "Too blue. Don't you want to get married again?"

She shrugged, fiddling with the rings on her right hand. "I've not really thought about it, to be honest. I'm quite happy with me, Sam, and Daisy, and I don't see me wanting to change that anytime soon."

"But when you fall in love, everything changes. Rather than not being able to imagine that person in your life, you can't imagine your life without them."

She smiled sadly. She'd felt that way about her husband, James. They'd known each other all their lives, their parents having been family friends. She'd never known not having James in her life and had not expected to ever have to be without him. That was until fourteen years ago when his car accident had cruelly taken him away from her and their unborn son.

Will I ever feel like that about anyone again? "So do *you* want to get married?" she asked as she flipped through half the swatches, trying to find a darker version of the previous option, as Perry did the same with his set.

Perry's face lit up. "Yes. Definitely. Without a doubt. Totally," he said, his blue eyes shining.

She laughed. "Is that a yes, then?"

He pulled a face at her.

She stopped and looked up, frowning. "So how do you know?"

"I knew from the first moment I saw Simon that I wanted to spend the rest of my life with him."

Wow! She couldn't claim that kind of reaction to her first remembered meeting with James. But then she had been only two years old at the time. "That's amazing. So why aren't you guys married already, if you're so sure?"

Perry sighed. "I don't know if Simon wants to get married again."

Again!? "What? Simon was married?" Her voice had risen a pitch.

Perry smiled. "Yes." He slapped his hand to his chest and raised the other to his brow, leaning back in mocking shock. "And to a woman!"

What? She couldn't believe that Perry and Simon had kept this nugget of information from her for all this time. She dropped the wallpaper sample and paint cards back on the sideboard and, grabbing two chairs, pulled them towards her, sitting down on one and holding the other out for Perry. Daisy jumped up at the noise and moved to sit by Perry's chair. "Tell me all about it," Lady Beatrice demanded, crossing her legs and leaning back.

Perry shook his head as he sat down next to her. "It's not my story to tell. He was a rufty-tufty police officer back then. Let's just say he felt under pressure to do what was expected of him. Anyway, my point is, I think it may have put him off marriage." His expression grave, as he stared at the floor, his hand resting on Daisy's head.

Oh, Perry. A prickle erupting at the back of her eyes, she reached over and squeezed his arm. "Simon loves you so much. You can see it in everything he does. I think if you asked him, he would rush to say yes."

Perry turned and looked at her, a crimson tide spreading up his neck. "I couldn't do that, Bea. I know *I* would say yes, but I don't know that *he* would, and I'd never be able to cope if…" He shook his head and bent to stroke Daisy for a few seconds, then raised it again, a grin replacing his frown. "Anyway," he added, "I'm old-fashioned about it. He should be the one to ask *me*."

She smiled and patted his arm, then let go. "Come on, Doris Day. Let's agree on what colour we're going to paint the walls. Then we can go and watch Simon's rehearsal."

4

EVENING, MONDAY 28 SEPTEMBER

Click, click, click.

"Lady Beatrice, this way!"

"Countess, over here!"

Click, click, click.

Her heart beating out of her chest, she shielded her eyes from the bright flashes of artificial light invading the back seat of the Bentley as they pulled up outside the front of The King's Hotel. Simon took her elbow and helped lift her forwards as she placed one foot on the kerb and found a firm footing. Perry moved to the other side of the car door as she took a deep breath and shifted her weight, pushing herself upright. *And breathe…*

Click, click, click.

"My lady, here!"

"Are you here to see Chef Seb, your ladyship?"

Click, click, click.

Trying to filter out the cacophony surrounding her and concentrate on the entrance to the hotel lit up in the dark ten metres ahead, she took another deep breath. She dropped her arm by her side as she inched forward, sandwiched between

Simon and Perry. Although she could feel the adrenaline rushing through her body as they proceeded towards the large glass door that had just opened before them, the presence of her two friends made her feel less vulnerable tonight.

I know I should be used to this by now.

The press' obsession with her and Seb's blossoming relationship invaded their every meeting, creating a circus around her that she'd spent her whole adult life trying to avoid. Of course, total anonymity wasn't an option. Indeed, when she and her husband James had undertaken public duties after their marriage and until his death a year later, she'd been tolerant of the attention they had received from both the public and the press. It had been part of their job as working members of the royal family to be photographed and written about. The benefit that the good causes and charities they supported gained from the publicity far outweighed the personal discomfort she'd felt of being constantly scrutinised. But after James's death and all the speculation that had surrounded it... *Stop it, Bea.* She swallowed and focused on the door ahead of her.

Click, click, click.

"Mr Lattimore, this way!"

"Lady Rossex, over here!"

"Can we have a photo before you go in, please?"

Click, click, click.

They finally reached the glass porch, the entrance just inches away. *Turn. Wave. Smile.* The lights were blinding.

Click, click, click.

She turned back, and the three of them entered the lobby. The door slammed shut as they headed for the restaurant to meet Seb. *And breathe...*

An hour later, putting down her knife and fork, Lady Beatrice wiped her mouth with a napkin and placed it on the side of her plate. Studying the sizeable dining area in the hotel with its high vaulted ceiling and dark wooden beams, she was grateful that Seb had arranged for an area of the room to be screened off for the use of the hosting chefs and production staff staying here. He had just told them a catering tent was being erected tomorrow on-site at Fenn House to provide somewhere for the crew and talent to eat during the day. He'd assured her their backstage passes would allow her and Perry to use the facilities too. *I can't wait.* As the press couldn't get backstage at the festival, it would allow her to move around freely, the cast and crew having got used to seeing her by now.

Sitting opposite her, Perry, a look of sheer pleasure on his face, made joyful noises as he spooned up the remains of the port jus that had accompanied his duck. Next to him, Simon studied the menu. *No doubt contemplating the dessert options.* Seb, who had left a half-eaten plate of food in front of him, sat next to her with his head down, studying his mobile phone.

"So how did your rehearsal go, Seb?" Simon asked as he placed the menu down on the table. "Sorry I didn't get time to come and watch."

Seb looked up from his phone. "It went smoothly, *grazie.* Finn was on point, and we didn't have any issues. How did you get on with Marta as your sous chef?"

"She's incredible. I can't believe she agreed to help me. I'm grateful to you for that."

Seb shrugged. "No problem. My chefs always jump at the opportunity to get away from their restaurants for a few days. Not to mention, the exposure it brings them to be featured at an event like this."

Lady Beatrice's body jerked involuntarily as Seb placed a hand on her knee under the table. She whipped her head around and met his gaze. He smiled. "All right, *bella*?"

She exhaled. *Why do I always do that?* She looked down at his left hand resting in her knee. A white scar, the result of slip with a sharp knife while cutting into a lobster, so he'd told her, showed up against his tanned skin. She shifted her leg slightly, still not used to the tactile nature of the drop-dead gorgeous man sitting next to her. She was more comfortable being hands-off in public. The tension left her when he removed his hand and went back to his phone. She looked up and caught Perry's eye. He was grinning.

Simon raised his hand and waved. "There's Luca. I wonder how he got on today?"

A slim olive-skinned man with a mane of bushy curly hair waved back. He had his other hand on the small of the back of a petite blonde as they wound their way over to the table.

"*Ciao*," he said as he appeared by Simon's side.

"*Ciao*, Luca," Seb replied while Simon said, "Hi."

"I don't think you've met everyone here, have you?" Seb asked, turning to her and Perry. "This is Lady Beatrice, the Countess of Rossex. Beatrice, this is Luca Mazza, the executive chef at Nonnina and his girlfriend Fay Mayer, the food critic."

Lady Beatrice recognised them both from various television cooking shows that Simon insisted she and Perry watch with him. "Pleased to meet you both," she said. Smiling, she reached over Seb and held out her hand.

Fay gave a polite smile in return as she said hello, while Luca grabbed Lady Beatrice's fingers in both hands and kissed them, bowing. "Enchanted, my lady. Seb has told me so much about you."

Her cheeks burned as she withdrew her hand. *What is it*

with these Italian men? They're so… hands on.

"And this is Perry Juke, my partner in crime and in life," Simon said, chuckling and turning towards Perry. Fay nodded in Perry's direction while Luca bowed his head.

"So how did your rehearsals go today, Luca?" Simon asked.

"A bit rushed, eh, Seb? But it went well in the end. I'm pleased with the dishes I've chosen. Even though we've more rehearsals tomorrow and Wednesday, I'm glad we've, as you say, 'nailed down' this first one. I'm very excited about opening the show."

Seb nodded. "Well, ticket sales are doing really well. In fact, I think most of the demos are sold out. It's going to be busy."

Luca smiled. "That's great. I'm really pleased for you, *amico.*"

"I can't wait to have a look around the site properly in the morning," Perry said, his eyes shining bright.

"You mean sample all the food and drink?" Simon nudged his partner and smiled.

Perry laughed. "Of course!"

"And are you staying for the rest of the week, Fay?" Simon asked the woman with small pink lips and heavily made-up eyes.

She shook her head. "I have to get back to London tonight, but I'll be here for the start of the festival. I'm hosting a panel show on Friday morning." Fay looked at her watch. "I'm sorry to be rude, but we need to eat, Luca, or I won't get home until the early hours," she said, hooking her arm through his.

"Of course, *cara*. Nice to meet you, my lady." He winked at Lady Beatrice as he allowed his girlfriend to steer him towards the other side of the restaurant.

5

LATE MORNING, TUESDAY 29 SEPTEMBER

Pushing her sunglasses up her nose, Lady Beatrice smiled as she took in the hive of activity going on around her. With less than forty-eight hours to go before the public descended on them, everywhere she looked, stall holders were assembling their stands and preparing to display their goods. The balmy late summer was set to last for a few more days, and the vendors were laying out chairs, tables, and parasols for sun-seeking crowds with deep pockets. There was a noticeable buzz about the place that gave her a short adrenaline rush. She raised her hand and itched the back of her head. The black bobbed wig shifted slightly, and she removed her hand swiftly to avoid disturbing it any further.

She and Perry headed towards a cordoned off area of massive white marquees dominating the landscape, looming over the festival site like the Himalayas. As they reached the barrier, a security guard stepped forward, and they showed him their passes. He nodded, and after consulting a sheet on his clipboard, he directed them to the furthest one of the four demonstration tents.

Forty minutes later, Simon walked off stage and joined them in the wings. Followed by a petite woman with dark hair arranged in a neat plait running down the middle of her back. He stopped in front of them, smiling. "Hello, you two, this is a pleasant surprise."

"We thought we'd come and see how you were getting on, love," Perry said, returning his partner's smile.

Simon dragged his fingers through his short light-brown hair and sighed. "Don't ask. I thought I'd timed it just right, but we've overrun, and now we've got to figure out a way to shave at least five minutes off the whole thing."

He turned to look down at the woman standing just behind him as she said, "Don't worry. We can make up a batch of tortellini beforehand, and once you've shown the audience how to make a few, I'll bring them out. That should save us both some time."

"Great idea, Marta. That should just about do it." He turned back, then raised his hand to his throat. "Sorry, guys. You haven't met Marta before, have you?" Perry and Lady Beatrice shook their heads. "Well, this is Marta Talaska-Cowley. She's head chef at Squisito, Seb's brasserie in Piccadilly, and has been strong-armed into acting as sous chef for my demonstrations."

Marta pursed her red lips together and shook her head. "That's not true. I'm very happy to be here and take part in whatever capacity."

"Thank you," Simon said as he patted her arm and continued, "Marta, this is my better half Perry Juke, and believe it or not, under that ridiculous black wig and sunglasses is Lady Beatrice, the Countess of Rossex."

Marta's thick black eyebrows rose as she studied Lady Beatrice.

Is my wig ridiculous? Perry had told her it looked quite realistic, and certainly when she'd looked in the mirror, she'd thought the combination of the wig and the glasses meant that even her mother wouldn't recognise her. Lady Beatrice pulled the large glasses away from her face and perched them on top of the wig.

"It's very good," the woman finally said, a smile lighting up her face. "I would never have recognised you without your long auburn hair."

Lady Beatrice returned Marta's smile, then looked over at Simon and smirked. *It may be ridiculous, but it works.* "Thank you, Marta. I'm just trying it out, ready for when the public arrives on Thursday. If it works, I'm hoping it will mean I can move around the site hassle free."

The sous chef nodded, then untied her apron and pulled it off, revealing a pair of baggy jeans and a chef's jacket that looked three sizes too big for her. "If you will excuse me, I want to make a call before I'm needed again."

"Yes, of course. See you later." Simon turned to them. "She really has been such a help, especially since they've had to rearrange the rehearsal schedule because of Luca."

"Why, what's he done?" Perry asked.

"He's not done anything. He's ill. So we've all had to move our slots around."

"Will he be okay?" Lady Beatrice asked. *Poor Seb, that must be inconvenient for him.* Reorganising all the demo slots would be hard work.

Simon nodded. "It's nothing serious, apparently. Just something he ate at dinner at the hotel last night that didn't agree with him. I'm sure he'll be fine by tomorrow."

6

LATE AFTERNOON, TUESDAY 29 SEPTEMBER

Seb: *I'm so sorry, bella, but I need to cancel dinner and work here at the hotel instead this evening rearranging tomorrow's schedules. I'll make it up to you, I promise. xx*

Bea: *Please don't worry, it's fine. I've had a busy day so I'm all right with a quiet night in. How is Luca? x*

Seb: *He's still suffering. I've told him to rest and drink plenty of water. You could come to the hotel later maybe and stay? xx*

Bea: *No. We've been through this. It's not appropriate right now for me to be seen staying with you at the hotel. Plus, I can't bring Daisy and I've been neglecting her lately. Sorry. x*

. . .

Seb: *Well, if your dog is more important than me...*

Bea: *Don't be silly. I'll see you tomorrow. Can we have lunch together? x*

Seb: *Okay, but it's not the same. I miss you. xx*

7

LATE MORNING, WEDNESDAY 30 SEPTEMBER

"I like this one," Perry said as he pulled forward a small gold side table with walnut inset on the top. Daisy gave it a thorough sniff, then sat down beside it.

"Indeed. I like it too. If we use it in the Yellow Room, then we'll need to stick to an art deco theme throughout the room. We'll use gold as our yellow hue. You know, glamorous with geometric patterns. Golds, reds, glass, and lots of mirrors. Do we have anything like that?" Lady Beatrice's footsteps echoed on the stone floor as she walked over to join Perry on the other side of the basement room at Fenn House, where a randomly placed collection of furniture, objects, and furnishings made it look like a pop-up antique store.

"Well, there's these two," Perry said, pointing to a pair of large circular gold-rimmed mirrors leaning up against the back of a captain's table. "They would work."

She nodded and pointed. "And how about that bar trolley console? That would fit too." Spotting another couple of items that fitted her criteria, she walked back to the entrance where she'd left her phone and a pad of stickers, Daisy trotting behind her. Picking them both up, she was on her way back when her mobile vibrated.

Seb: *Morning. Are you still able to make lunch? xx*

Bea: *Yes. Say 12:30? How's Luca? x*

Seb: *Not so good. I've tried to persuade him to go to the hospital, but he says no, he's fine. xx*

Bea: *Oh no, I thought he would be better by now. Can't you insist? x*

Seb: *He says he's feeling better than yesterday, but he doesn't look it. What can I do? You know us Italians - stubborn as mules! I'll check back on him later. See you for lunch. xx*

"What's wrong?" Perry said, walking over to meet her and Daisy in the middle of the room.

Lady Beatrice, still staring at her phone, looked up as he spoke. "It's just a text from Seb checking up on lunch plans. Oh, and Luca is still ill but refuses to see a doctor."

Perry shook his head. "Typical man. We like to complain when we're not well, but we won't voluntarily see anyone who could make us better."

Lady Beatrice rolled her eyes. "Well, I just hope he's okay

for tomorrow, or that'll really throw a spanner in the works for Seb and the rest of the chefs."

Perry nodded.

"Okay, let's get on. I'm getting hungry. Have these" — she handed Perry a wad of stickers— "and anything you see that you think might work for this art deco bedroom, stick a yellow one on. You take that pile. I'll look at the stuff over there."

"Seb!" A cry from the entrance of the catering tent in the grounds of Fenn House made them all look over as a stocky grey-haired man made his way across the spacious marquee towards their table, waving. Lady Beatrice popped the last piece of her tuna melt panini in her mouth as she recognised the sun-tanned man as Seb's agent Malcolm Cassan. Following behind him was a woman Lady Beatrice had also met previously, Mal's personal assistant Klara. The woman, her brown straight hair bouncing off her shoulders, wore a yellow dress splattered with bright red flowers. She looked like a walking vase.

"She'd work well in the Yellow Room," Perry whispered across to Lady Beatrice, smirking.

Lady Beatrice suppressed a giggle as Mal's voice got louder.

"Seb!"

Sighing heavily beside her, Seb put down his sandwich and grabbed a napkin.

"I'm glad I've caught you, old chap." Mal's cheeks were light purple when he stopped at the table and put his hand on his hip, inhaling noisily. "I wanted to ask you—"

Seb cut him off. "Mal, you know Lady Beatrice, but I

don't believe you've met the author Simon Lattimore, who won last year's *Celebrity Elitechef*? And this is his partner Perry Juke. Simon, Perry, this is my agent Malcom Cassan and his PA Klara Damas."

"Oh no, sorry," the man blustered, itching the side of his grey beard. "How rude of me. Mr Lattimore. I'm familiar with your work, of course." He beamed at Simon. "My wife's also a big fan, you know."

"Thank you. It's always good to know that someone is reading my books." Simon pushed his empty plate away and returned the man's smile.

Mal chuckled and, turning around to the woman wearing large red glasses behind him, said, "Card, please, Klara." Klara scrambled in her laptop bag and pulled out a handful of business cards, offering them to him. Mal plucked one from her palm and spun round, his arm outstretched towards Simon. "Please don't hesitate to call me, Mr Lattimore, if I can help you with anything. If you're going to do more of these demonstrations, then you really need someone to represent you to make sure you get properly compensated for your time. And then, of course, there are television opportunities that—"

"Mal!" Seb's voice rose above the man's babbling. "You wanted to talk to me?"

"Oh yes. Yes. I wanted to ask you to have a word with Luca. Ambrose and I are worried that if he continues to take this line about wanting more money and five-star hotels, he'll screw it up for all of us and will put the whole deal in jeopardy." Taking a white handkerchief from his trouser pocket, he wiped his forehead. "And I don't need to tell you how much—"

"*Si, si.*" Seb nodded. "I'll talk to him as soon as he's well enough."

"Oh, yes, I heard he was ill. Nothing serious, I hope?" Mal raised his bushy eyebrows.

"No, I don't think so. Just something he ate at the hotel on Monday night that has disagreed with him."

"At the hotel?" Mal frowned. "But we all ate at the hotel on Monday night. Is anyone else ill?"

"Not that I know of, but—"

At Klara's short cough, they all turned to her. "Er, I had a bit of a dicky tummy yesterday," she informed them, a tide of dark pink creeping up her neck. "So…" She shrugged, her eyes fixed on Seb.

Seb looked away from her and carried on as if she hadn't spoken. "There were many people eating at the hotel that evening, so it's impossible to know if anyone else has been taken ill."

Lady Beatrice cringed. *That was rude.* She leaned back and looked around Seb at the woman partly obscured by Mal's hefty frame. Klara chewed her lip and rubbed the corner of one eye with a finger as she gazed at Seb's profile. *Poor woman. She didn't deserve to be spoken to like that. She was just trying to help.* Klara looked up, and their eyes met. Lady Beatrice smiled, but the other woman grimaced and quickly looked away.

"Well, when he's well enough, Seb, please tell him to behave and leave the wheeling and dealing to us. I'll talk to Ambrose when I see him and—" Klara tapped him on the shoulder, and he spun around. "What?" he barked.

"He's over there," she mumbled, pointing to a large man with short curly brown hair sitting by himself over by the entrance. Lady Beatrice had seen him in the hotel restaurant a few nights ago.

"Right-o. Well, I'll catch him now. I'll talk to you later" —he leaned towards Seb— "about that other matter." Then he turned on his heels, and with Klara scurrying behind him, he headed towards the door.

"Sorry about that," Seb said to Simon, refilling his cup. "Mal can act like a buffoon sometimes, but he's very good at what he does. I can recommend him if you want to do more television shows and public appearances. He's well worth the money."

Simon smiled. "Thanks, Seb, but right now, apart from these few local shows, I've no intention of doing more. I'd rather be writing than in front of the camera."

"Who's Ambrose?" Perry asked, turning back to face them.

"He's Luca's agent," Seb replied, taking a sip of coffee.

Perry leaned forward and grabbed the pot of coffee from the middle of the table. "And is it normal for your agents to be here when you do shows and stuff?"

Seb shook his head as he put down his cup. "Not always. But they're in the middle of trying to secure a deal with the BBC for a show for me and Luca, so they want to be close by. Mal is good like that."

"Ooh, that sounds exciting. Tell us all about it," Perry said, returning the coffeepot to the middle of the table and grabbing the cream.

"Perry!" Simon turned to him. "Seb probably can't talk about it at the moment."

Perry raised his hand to his mouth and mumbled, "Sorry."

Seb smiled slowly and leaned in. "It's top secret, but as long as you promise not to spread it around..." he whispered.

Perry nodded and pulled his thumb and forefinger across his lips. "Mum's the word," he whispered back.

Seb grinned at him and said in a low voice, "Well, the working title is *The Two Italians,* and the plan is for me and

Luca to travel the country in a tour bus, stopping in remote places and showing the locals how to cook Italian food."

Perry clapped his hands together. "Ooh, I like the sound of that."

"And Luca is being awkward, is he?" Lady Beatrice asked.

Seb turned and shrugged. "It's nothing, *bella*. Luca's asking for a bit more money than they're offering and doesn't want to live full-time on a tour bus. I'm sure they'll work something out."

No wonder Mal is concerned. Could Luca's demands ruin the deal as Mal suggested? "And if they don't, will you lose the show?"

Seb placed his hand on hers. She shivered. "They've told Mal they want me more than they want Luca, so I don't think so. If we can't find a solution that works for Luca, then we'll just have to find someone else to take his place."

Perry squeaked and pointed to Simon.

Seb laughed. "Maybe. Would you be up for that, Simon?"

Simon smiled and shook his head. "As I said, I'd rather be writing, and I have publisher deadlines to meet in the next few months."

Seb nodded and picked up his coffee again. "Of course. Not to worry. There are plenty of young chefs who would kill for a chance to get that kind of television exposure." Looking over Simon's shoulder towards the door, he continued, "Talking of young chefs keen to find fame and fortune, I spy Marta heading our way."

"Hi, everyone," Marta said as she approached the table. Although she smiled, it didn't quite reach her eyes, and her voice cracked a little as she said to Seb, "Chef, can I have a word, please?"

Seb nodded and rose. "Excuse me, but I need to get on."

He turned to Lady Beatrice. "I'll contact you later, *bella*, when I know what's happening with Luca."

Seb: *I'm sorry, I cannot see you tonight. Luca is still ill and I need to arrange a back-up plan in case he can't do the opening demo tomorrow. xx*

Bea: *That's fine. My sister has asked me over for dinner tonight, so I will say yes now. Sorry this is creating so much work for you. x*

8

LATE EVENING, WEDNESDAY 30 SEPTEMBER

Lady Beatrice turned the key in the door of her apartment and let Daisy run in ahead of her. She dropped the key on the sideboard by the door in the hallway and moved to the dressing room. She'd had a lovely evening with her sister Lady Sarah Rosdale, her brother-in-law John, and her niece Lottie. With being so busy working at Fenn House recently and spending time with Seb, she'd not seen as much of her sister as she was used to. It had been marvellous to catch up.

Her sister had been itching to know more about how her relationship was progressing with Seb, so while John had gone up to make sure twelve-year-old Lottie had been getting ready for bed and not chatting online with her friends, Lady Beatrice had told her sister all about her concerns that Daisy didn't like Seb, her growing mistrust of Seb because he seemed to love the attention from the press they'd been getting, and her shock at how rude he'd been to his agent and his agent's PA that afternoon. Sarah had suggested that maybe Lady Beatrice should take a step back and slow things down with Seb while she made sense of her feelings towards him.

Now, plaiting her long hair and putting on her sleepwear,

she mulled over what her sister had said. *Is Sarah right?* Did she need to put the brakes on with Seb? She sighed as she turned off the light in the dressing room and moved into the bedroom. She turned on the bedside light and placed her mobile phone on the charger pad. Smiling, she gently rolled Daisy into the middle of the bed and pulled back the covers. But just as she reached out to turn off the bedside light, a beep sounded from her phone.

Seb: *Goodnight, tesoro. I wish you were here with me. Your dog is very lucky. xx*

Lady Bea swiped away the message and typed 'what does *tesoro* mean in Italian?' into her phone browser. *Darling?* Her heart sank. It sounded so… serious. Too much like their relationship was further on than it was.

She sighed as she dropped the phone onto the bed beside her and pulled her knees up to her chin, the covers creating a tent over her lower body. This wasn't what she wanted. *What am I going to do?* She reached out for Daisy curled up beside her, resting her hand on the small dog's head. Seb was pushing them too hard, too fast down the road to coupledom. *I don't think I'm ready.*

She stroked Daisy's head with her thumb, smoothing the dog's hairy white eyebrows as Daisy's eyes fluttered behind her lids. Life had been so much simpler before she'd met Seb. Admittedly, the press' attention surrounding Alex Sterling's death at Francis Court back in April, the first case she, Perry, and Simon had been involved with, had been fierce. But it had soon died down when the case had been solved. And when the rumours started by *The Daily Post* not long after, concerning the existence of a letter to her from her husband James, written just before his death fourteen years before, had been proven to be without foundation, she'd been mostly left in peace to enjoy her new working life with Perry, managing refurbishment and renovation projects.

She removed her hand from Daisy's warm fur and tugged on the end of the auburn plait resting over her shoulder, raising it to her face. But since Simon had introduced her to Seb last month, during their second murder investigation — this time at the country home of a friend of her mother's— she'd been swept down a path that had taken her back into the spotlight. And now she felt she was on a runaway train, desperately running up and down the corridors looking for the emergency brake.

How can I slow him down without hurting his feelings? She sighed. She knew she'd have to tackle it with him in person; that was only fair. *But when? Now? After the show?* She huffed, and lowering her knees, she picked up her phone again.

Bea: *How is Luca? Will he be well enough for tomorrow afternoon? x*

Seb: *He says he's feeling much better now and is sure he'll be well enough to do his demo. I'm not convinced, and Marta is worried about him. I have a contingency plan ready just in case. xx*

Bea: *I'll have my fingers crossed for you. Goodnight. x*

9

MID-MORNING, THURSDAY 1 OCTOBER

Inside the catering tent in the private, sectioned-off area beside the showground, Lady Beatrice blew on her steaming black coffee and took a sip. *Ouch!* She quickly returned the cup to the table and picked up a glass of water. Her stomach fluttered. Was it the excitement of having dashed through the crowd in disguise on their way here, hoping the wig would stay in place? Or was it the build-up to the first show taking place in just a few hours? Even the normally calm Simon was shredding a paper napkin opposite her. The large marquee, full of staff and production crew, had a buzz about it that was energising. She raised her hand to her chest. *I feel like I'm about to go on a first date.*

"So are you two taking this afternoon off still?" Simon asked.

Sitting next to him, Perry nodded. "Yes. We decided we wanted to be here for the opening show and then for both of your first demos."

Simon placed his hand over Perry's. "Well, thank you. I really appreciate it."

Feeling Seb move beside her, Lady Beatrice instantly

tucked her hands under her thighs. As she looked up, she spotted a young man dressed in a blue hoodie, jeans, and grubby trainers making his way over to them. She recognised him as Finn Gilligan, Seb's head chef at The Flyer and sous chef for his boss during the festival demonstrations.

"Chef." The pale young man stopped in front of Seb, his lips tight but his eyes shining. "Any news yet on Luca?"

Seb shook his head as he lowered his cup to the table. "No. I don't know if he'll turn up or not, Finn. So prepare yourself to switch to doing my demo for me if I need to step in for Luca. I've asked Marta to help you as she's not needed until later to support Simon here."

Finn nodded enthusiastically at Seb. "Sure," he said, his strong Northern Irish accent making the word sound like a steam train starting up. "I can do that, no problem. I'll find Marta now."

Lady Beatrice smiled at Seb as Finn left. "It's good you've got a robust backup plan."

Seb nodded. "The great thing about chefs like Finn is that they're used to things not going to plan during a busy service, so they can adapt quickly when needed." He picked up his coffee again, and wrapping both hands around the cup, took a big mouthful.

She removed her hands from beneath her and glanced over at Perry, who smirked. *What?*

Then glancing at his watch, Perry turned to Simon, still grinning. "Have we got time to go now? It's only two minutes from here. It'll be worth it, I promise." He pressed his palms together and raised them to his mouth.

Simon grinned back and nodded. "All right, but we need to be quick."

Perry was out of his chair like a shot. Simon rose at a more leisurely pace. Laughing, he addressed Lady Beatrice and Seb. "I promised Perry we'd visit the dessert stall he's been obsessed with since he saw it a few days ago. Do you want to come too?"

Nodding, Lady Beatrice began to rise.

Seb looked up from his phone and shook his head. "I have to run through Luca's show with Ryan just in case I need to step in."

"Indeed. Well, we'll come and find you—" Halfway out of her seat, Seb put his hand on her arm.

Looking down into his face, she met the piercing gaze of his blue eyes. "Can we have five minutes before you go, *bella*?" he asked.

Her stomach dropped. *No! Because you have a serious face on and look like you want to 'talk'.* Her skin itched where his hand was touching her, and she wanted to pull away. But she couldn't. Instead, she plastered a smile on her face and said, "Yes, of course." She turned to Perry and Simon, now hovering by the side of the table. "I'll catch you up." They nodded and left as she sat down again.

Seb's hand moved down her arm and grabbed her fingers. "Are you all right, *bella*? You've been very quiet lately."

No. I'm not all right. I'm not sure I want to do this anymore. You're getting clingy. The press are everywhere we go... You grab me when I least expect it. You sulk when you don't get your own way. And you were really *rude to poor Klara the other day and... my dog doesn't like you.*

"Yes, I'm fine. Just busy, you know, what with Sam coming home this weekend and all the work we're doing up at the house. I feel like—"

"I know." Seb squeezed her fingers together. "It's crazy right now, isn't it? I don't know if Luca is going to turn up or not. And what happens if the public don't show up as expected? What if they don't spend money and the stall-holders aren't happy?" He shook his head as he reached out his other hand and sandwiched hers between both of his. "I understand, *tesoro*. I really do," he said, nodding his head.

How did asking me if I'm okay become all about you? Lady Beatrice coughed and tugged her hand out from his, reaching for her now cold coffee and raising it to her lips. She unclenched her teeth and let the liquid pass down her throat.

He leaned further towards her, and she held onto her cup even tighter. His coffee breath hit the side of her face. "But we must make sure we still find time for us, *bella*. Let's have lunch together later, just the two of us. We can talk about our plans for when the show is finished. I thought maybe we could go to Miami. A friend of mine has a villa in Bal Harbour. I could ask him if we can borrow it for a few weeks."

What? I have a project to finish, and then Sam will be off for half-term. Then we have to prep the Drew Castle job. And anyway, I don't want to go to Miami with you... A sudden coldness overcame her, and she almost lost her grip on her cup. *I don't want to go away with him.* As the realisation hit her, she felt paralysed. For a few seconds, she couldn't speak.

"*Bella*?" Seb's deep tone filtered through her cloudy brain, and she blinked at him, his brows heavy as his forehead creased up. "Are you all right?"

Get a grip, Bea. She focussed on his blue-eyed gaze. "I'm sorry, I can't do lunch. I have a call scheduled with Sam."

Seb leaned back in his chair and crossed his arms. "But you talk to him every night. Why do you need to talk to him at lunchtime too?" His pinched expression wiped away his handsomeness in a second, leaving him looking like a disgruntled rat.

Am I supposed to be on rations when talking to my son?

"It's a joint conference with his housemaster. We do them once a month. It's checking on his progress and—"

"Well, how about dinner then?"

She sighed. They needed to talk. But now clearly wasn't the right moment. *He's not listening.* She needed to find a time when he wasn't so distracted with worry about the show. Maybe dinner tonight after a successful day? She smiled. "Yes, dinner would be great."

She rose and picked up the bag containing her wig and sunglasses as he grabbed her other hand and leaned towards her. "Thank you, *bella*," he whispered as he kissed her fingers.

10

EARLY AFTERNOON, THURSDAY 1 OCTOBER

"Are you sure you don't want this last one?" Perry asked, pointing to a box emblazoned with *Too Sweet to Share* on the front lying on the sideboard before them in the Yellow Room in Fenn House. Inside, a single slice of luscious dark-red velvet cake rested.

"The mind is willing, but the body says no," Lady Beatrice replied, grimacing. She held her stomach. *I'm so full!* The chocolate brownie had been delicious, as had the carrot cake. But she was now bordering on that line between happily satisfied and feeling sick.

Perry shrugged, a smile pulling at the ends of his mouth. "Okay. I'll take one for the team and finish it." He carefully lifted the fat wedge made up of reddy-brown sponge sandwiching a thick layer of cream cheese icing and topped with an even plumper blanket of the same, then took a giant bite.

Lady Beatrice watched him as he moaned with pleasure. *Where does he put it all?* Perry's slim six-foot-one frame didn't look like it held a gram of excess fat, and yet, she seemed to spend her whole life watching him eat. *And it's not like he works out.* As he frequently commented — why would you want to get all hot and sweaty unless the reward was more than a cold shower and unattractive bulging muscles? She shook her head as he popped the last chunk into his mouth and licked his fingers.

"Umm, so that was probably the best cake I've ever had."

"Well, when you've stopped stuffing your face, can we look at these plans again and see if we think the layout will work now that we've seen the room in person?"

He nodded, and after wiping his hands on a napkin, he dropped it into the box and closed the lid. "Yes, of course. Oh, how did you get on in the teacher-parent conference, by the way? Is Sam doing okay?"

"He's doing really well in physical education, science, and maths, but not so good in English, geography, and art. Sam says they're not exciting enough!"

Perry shrugged. "Well, he has a point. I hated geography at school."

Lady Beatrice rolled her eyes. *Boys!*

Perry continued, "I bet you can't wait for him to get back on Saturday. Can he come with us and see the show?"

Lady Beatrice smiled. "You just try to stop him! He's so excited and has apparently been bragging to his food club at school about all the famous chefs he's going to meet. He's spending Saturday with James's parents, but he'll be with us all day Sunday."

Perry raised an eyebrow. "So will you introduce him to Seb this weekend?"

She sighed. "I don't think I'll have much choice. Sam's dying to meet him."

She wished her son wasn't quite so keen to meet the famous Chef Seb he'd seen on television. She would much rather keep them away from each other until she was more certain of her feelings about Seb. She didn't want Sam to get his hopes up. Her mouth feeling dry, she grabbed her take-away cup and took a sip of lukewarm coffee.

"What's wrong?" Perry asked, gazing at her with concern. "I've noticed you've been quiet around Seb these last few days. Is everything all right?"

Should I tell him about my concerns? Lady Beatrice looked at her friend's face. A large frown wrinkled his normally smooth brow. Perry had been so excited at the start of her relationship with Seb. Would he be disappointed if she now told him she was having second thoughts about continuing? *Only one way to find out…*

"Er, not really."

Perry gasped, then steering her towards an old sofa that hadn't yet been moved into storage, he took her by the shoulders and sat her down. "Tell me everything," he said as he perched on the edge of the settee beside her and placed his hands on his knees.

"I'm just not sure this relationship is for me, Perry. I know he's handsome and charming and I should be flattered that he wants to be with me, but he's going way too fast. He's already talking about another trip away together after the show. Oh, and he's started calling me darling in Italian." She shook her head. "It's all too much too soon." She felt a little breathless as anxiety bubbled up inside her. "And…" She shook her head.

"And what, Bea?" Perry's eyes shone bright as he crossed his legs and moved one arm so it rested along the back of the sofa.

She let out a deep sigh. "There are things about him that are rather bothering me."

"Like what?"

"Well, for a start, did you hear how he spoke to his agent's poor PA yesterday?"

"Who? Do you mean the mousey girl with a crush on him?"

Really? She frowned. "How do you know she has a crush on him?"

"From the way she's fixated on him, hanging on his every word." He grinned. "Either that or she's planning to kill him. It's the quiet ones who are the most dangerous." He tapped the end of his nose.

"Indeed. Well, anyway. He was really rude to her. She was trying to contribute to the conversation, and he cut her off and carried on as if she hadn't spoken."

Perry nodded. "Yes, I thought that was uncalled for."

"And plus," she continued, "he constantly talks over me. I don't think he listens to half of what I say. He pouts when I say I'm busy with Sam or have other plans. And, as you've seen, Daisy doesn't like him."

Perry shrugged. "Well, they do say dogs are a better judge of character than people are."

She huffed. *Great, thanks!*

Perry raised his hand to his chest. "Sorry, Bea, I'm not helping much, am I? So is there anything about him you *do* like?"

"Yes, of course there is!" she replied indignantly.

"Like what?"

Heat burned her cheeks. "Well, to start with, he's attractive. It's been good to get that physical attention from someone."

A smile tugged at the corners of Perry's mouth.

She cleared her throat. "But it's not enough, is it? I'm more than happy with that side of things when we're on our own, but when we're in public, he keeps grabbing me. I hate it!"

Perry smirked.

"What's so funny?"

"Sorry," Perry said, lifting his hand to his face. "It's just I couldn't help notice you jumped out of your skin when he put his hand on your knee at dinner the other night, and this morning when we were having coffee, you sat on your hands. What's going on?"

Is there something wrong with me? Perry and Simon were always touching each other. It looked sweet when they did it. James hadn't been one for big public displays of affection, but she recalled how he had gently guided her into a room with his hand resting on the small of her back. That had felt nice. And occasionally, if they had been seated next to each other at a formal dinner, he'd reach for her hand under the tablecloth and give it a quick squeeze. It had been subtle. It told her he was aware of her. They were in it together. *But when Seb does it to me, it feels...*

"It feels possessive. Like he's staking his claim on me." A hot sensation ran through her body. "Is it me, Perry? Am I being overly English and uptight about it?"

Perry pulled his arm back, and uncrossing his legs, he reached out and took her hand (which felt very natural to her), saying, "Don't be silly. If that's how it makes you react, then I think it's a reflection of your feelings towards him."

"How do you mean? You and Simon are very tactile. Don't you feel like he's being possessive when he grabs you?"

Perry dropped her hand, and giving a short laugh, he shook his head. "He doesn't grab me, Bea. He reaches out and touches me. It feels affectionate, not possessive. But then I love him, and I'm happy for others to see that we're together. I think that's your issue with Seb."

Is he right? Was her reaction to Seb because she didn't want to be associated with him as a couple? She sighed. With so many thoughts going through her head, how was she ever to make sense of it all?

"Bea, you seem to have a long list of reservations about him, and the only positive you've come up with is that you find him attractive, which no, to answer your question, isn't enough. So if you're not happy, then you must end it. And sooner rather than later."

"But won't that make it awkward for Simon? After all, he's Seb's friend, and he introduced us."

"Simon wouldn't want you to be this unhappy. And anyway, I wouldn't say Seb is a friend of Simon's. He's more of a colleague. Simon will support you in whatever you decide to do. As will I."

She smiled to herself. *I am so lucky to have these wonderful men in my life.* "All right. I'll find the right time to talk to him and tell him how I feel." A chill ran up her spine.

"Crikey. Look at the time," Perry cried as he sprung up. "We need to get a wiggle on if we're going to make it to the opening demonstration on time."

11

MID-AFTERNOON, THURSDAY 1 OCTOBER

Watching Luca Mazza and Ryan Hawley moving around the stage together, Lady Beatrice marvelled at how they were like a well-oiled machine, each knowing their role but also aware of the other person at all times. She looked across the stage to the opposite wing from where she and Perry were watching to where Simon and Seb stood, their eyes glued to the stage. *Are they still worried about Luca?* He seemed to be doing fine to her. Hopefully, with this first demonstration over and Luca back to full strength, Seb would be less distracted and she could talk to him about slowing things down between them.

"Is it me, or does Luca look like he's flagging already?" Perry asked her.

She glanced back at the stage and studied the red-faced man who was sweating profusely. "He doesn't look too good, does he?" she agreed, her eyes now transfixed on the stage.

Suddenly, Luca staggered forward. Ryan ran towards the stove to save the pan the chef had hastily returned to the heat, grabbing it as it teetered on the gas ring. Rushing from the wings, Seb and Simon appeared on stage, running towards Luca.

But they were too late. Luca Mazza collapsed and hit the ground. *Thud!*

The audience gave a combined gasp.

"Is he dead?" Perry Juke whispered to her. "I can't see if he's moving or not!" They both craned their necks around a metal pillar obstructing their full view to take a closer look at what was happening on stage.

Simon and Seb had now reached Luca, who laid in a crumpled heap behind the bench. Simon crouched down and talked to Luca while Seb walked around to the other side of him and knelt by the fallen chef.

"He appears to be responding to Simon," Perry told her.

"Ladies and gentlemen." Ryan Hawley had walked in front of the kitchen counter and was now approaching the edge of the stage. "Please don't be alarmed. Luca will be fine. He hasn't been feeling too well the last few days…"

Behind the counter, Simon and Seb had hooked their arms under Luca's armpits and tried to lift him.

"…but he bravely insisted he wanted to carry on because he didn't want to let you down by not appearing as promised, so—"

They now had Luca upright, and with their support, he was standing. Albeit unsteadily.

A smattering of applause started, and as more and more joined in, the whole tent was filled with clapping and cheering as Simon and Seb helped Luca off the stage.

Lady Beatrice let out a breath as she turned to Perry. "Oh my gosh. Thank goodness for that."

Perry nodded, grinning.

Looking past Ryan, still at the front of the stage waiting for the noise to subside, she peered across the stage into the wing opposite. Luca sat on a chair, Fay and Simon holding his arms to keep him upright, and two figures in green jump-

49

suits crowded round them, talking to the confused-looking chef.

Seb, standing next to a woman with a clipboard, wrapped a chef's apron around his waist as the two talked urgently. When he finished fastening the ties, she handed him a microphone, which he hooked around his ear. He nodded at her as he switched it on and walked onto the stage.

"Thank you, everyone," he said as he moved to join Ryan. The crowd settled down, and he continued, "As Ryan explained, Luca will be fine. The paramedics are with him now, and he's conscious and talking." A collective sigh filled the marquee. "So, although I'm not much compensation for Luca Mazza—" He grinned, and the audience laughed. "Ryan and I will carry on and do our best to recreate what Luca was going to show you this afternoon."

Seb put his arm around Ryan's shoulders as they turned around and walked back to the demonstration counter to a thundering round of applause.

"He handled that well," Perry whispered to Lady Beatrice. She nodded as she peered into the wings to see what was happening with Luca. The paramedics had a portable trolley beside where Luca was sitting, and with Simon's help, they guided Luca towards it. Staggering sideways like someone who was drunk, Luca gently manoeuvred into position. Once they had him swaying on the edge of the cart, one man swung Luca's legs up, and the chef fell onto his back. Simon straightened up as the other paramedic released the brake on the trolley, and they wheeled Luca down the ramp, Simon following, and out of sight.

Lady Beatrice and Perry looked at each other.

"Fingers crossed, it's nothing serious and they can fix him quickly," Perry said.

She nodded. "Indeed."

Hearing light footsteps on the ramp, she turned to see Simon walking up it to join them.

"Will he be all right, love?" Perry asked as he moved forward to greet his partner.

Simon nodded. "I think so. We told the paramedics he'd been ill for a few days with an upset stomach, and they seem to think he's become dehydrated. They started getting some fluids into him as soon as they got him into the ambulance. They're taking him to the hospital in King's Town. Fay's gone with him."

Perry rested his hand on his partner's arm. "I'm so proud of how you handled the whole situation. But are *you* okay?"

Simon smiled back at Perry. "Yes, I'm fine. Although it's been five years since I left the force, I still find my policeman's instincts kick in whenever something like this arises. It's what they trained me to do," he said as he patted Perry's hand.

Watching the two men together, Lady Beatrice's heartbeat quickened. *Am I asking too much to want what they have?* Didn't she deserve someone who responded to her needs? Redirecting her gaze to the stage where a smiling Seb was talking the audience through what he and Ryan were cooking, she felt her stomach drop. She was fairly sure that Seb wasn't that man. She watched Seb present the final plate to the audience while they *oohed* and *ahhed* at the beautiful presentation. She rubbed her forehead. How was she going to approach this with him now when he was most likely worried about Luca and how they would manage during the next four days without him? Maybe she should leave it until after the festival was finished... A few more days wouldn't do any harm, would it?

The sound of booming applause made her jump as it reverberated around the tent. Seb and Ryan had moved to the front of the stage and were taking a bow. She smiled. They had done a great job in the circumstances, and the audience seemed more than happy with the outcome.

With a final wave to the crowd, Seb hurried towards them in the wings. The smile he'd had plastered on his face for the last forty minutes turned to a grimace as soon as he stepped off the stage, and he immediately whipped out his phone. Ryan, following a few metres behind, stopped beside him. "Any news?" he asked.

Seb was silent for a few minutes as he stared at his screen, then replied, "Fay says they've admitted him to a ward and have started further rehydration treatment on him. The doctor is concerned that the fluids they gave him in the ambulance don't seem to have made much difference." He shook his head. "I'd better get to the hospital." He turned to the chef by his side. "Can you find Finn and tell him what's happened? He should be ready to stand in for me at the next demo with Marta's help."

Ryan nodded. "Yes, of course. I'll help him too," he said as he hurried towards the ramp.

Seb looked around and caught Lady Beatrice's eye. He walked towards her, holding his arms out before him. "I'm so sorry, *bella*, but I must see how Luca is." She nodded, then stiffened when he grabbed her hands and kissed her cheek.

I'm a bad person. He's worried about his friend, and all I can think about is how quickly I can pull away from him. She let out a slow breath through her nose and smiled. "Of course, you must go."

"I'll ring you from the hospital, *tesoro*." He nodded as he dropped her hands, then headed over to Simon. "Thanks for your help. I'll let you know how he is later." Simon nodded and patted him on the back as Seb made his way past them and left the wing.

"I hope Luca's going to be all right," Perry said as the three of them watched the audience leave their seats and file out the back of the marquee, their happy chatter proof they had loved the show despite Luca's collapse.

"I hope so too," Simon said with a deep sigh. "All we can do now is wait for an update."

Seb: *Sorry but I won't be able to make dinner now, tesoro. The doctors are concerned as Luca isn't improving. They're going to run some tests to see if they can work out what's wrong. xx*

Bea: *I'm so sorry, Seb. I hope they get to the bottom of it quickly. What about the show? Will you cancel his demonstrations? x*

Seb: *No. The show must go on. It's what Luca would want. Fay is going to stay with him while I return to the hotel and work with the producers to decide who'll do what. I think we have a long night ahead of us. xx*

Bea: *Indeed. Try and get some rest if you can. I'll speak to you in the morning. x*

12

MID-MORNING, FRIDAY 2 OCTOBER

"Isn't that Detective Inspector Mike Ainsley coming our way?" Perry Juke asked Lady Beatrice as they walked out of the side entrance of Fenn House. "He doesn't look like he's dressed for a day of exploring a food and wine show."

"Plus, he's in completely the wrong place if he wanted to," Lady Beatrice pointed out. "And anyway, isn't that Detective Sergeant Hines with him?"

Perry nodded. "Do you think maybe the police have a watching brief when there's an event on at Fenn House?"

She shrugged. "That must be it. I can't think why else they would be here."

"Mike." Lady Beatrice smiled at the sturdily built grey-haired man in a blue suit walking towards her and held out her hand. "Good to see you. Are you on-site to pick up some delicious food to take back to Fenshire CID HQ? If so, Perry here can recommend an excellent cake stall."

Mike Ainsley laughed as the two men came to a standstill in front of her. Shaking Lady Beatrice's hand and nodding at Perry, he said, "Well, thank you for the offer, my lady. I do have a sweet tooth, so I may take Mr Juke up on that a bit later. But for the moment, we're here in an official capacity investigating the poisoning of Luca Mazza."

"Poisoning?" Lady Beatrice and Perry cried together.

"Yes. Unfortunately, it would appear Mr Mazza has potentially ingested some death cap mushrooms and is very ill as a result. We need to find out when and where he could have eaten them so we can establish if it was through someone else's gross incompetence or if he accidentally ate them himself."

Death cap mushrooms? A heavy feeling settled in her stomach. *But he's a professional chef. How did he not know?*

"Aren't they fatal?" Perry asked, his eyes wide as he gazed at the inspector.

Mike nodded. "They can be if the eater doesn't get help quick enough. Fortunately, a doctor on call when Mr Mazza arrived at the hospital knew he was a chef and recognised the symptoms of death cap mushroom poisoning, so acted quickly to get him treated. They are doing everything they can, but it's not looking good."

Oh my gosh, poor Luca. Lady Beatrice ran her fingers through her long hair. Seb must be beside himself with worry. *That's if he even knows.* She glanced at her watch. He would have only just finished his show.

"So what exactly are you investigating, Mike?"

"Well, the Environmental and Health Authority are up at the hotel where he's been staying. Luca's girlfriend told us he thought it was something he'd eaten on Monday night at dinner that made him ill. They're checking to see if anyone else who was having dinner at the hotel that night has become unwell. And in the meantime, Hines and I are meeting with the show's organisers to find out if it's possible he could've eaten the mushrooms here and to see if anyone else has been ill."

"Can't you just ask Luca what happened?" Perry asked.

Mike grimaced. "Mr Mazza has been unconscious since he arrived at the hospital yesterday. I'm afraid he can't help us."

How could Luca have been well enough to even start his show yesterday? Rubbing her forehead, Lady Beatrice said, "But he appeared so much better yesterday until he collapsed. It seems unbelievable that it could be something he ate as long ago as Monday night. And how could a chef not know he was eating death caps?"

DS Hines, his grey suit hanging off his skinny frame, stepped forward. "That's the problem with death caps, my lady. You're ill for a couple of days, then you seem to be getting better, and suddenly, you go downhill rapidly. And even experienced mushroom pickers sometimes get it wrong as death caps look similar to puffballs when in the button stage. Once cooked and hidden in a sauce, they would be nearly impossible to identify."

Mike nodded in the sergeant's direction. "Eamon here is a bit of an expert on death cap mushroom poisoning. He was recently on a case where a whole family died after eating mushrooms the father had picked in the woods behind where they lived."

"Why didn't they go to the hospital if they felt that ill?" Perry asked.

Lady Beatrice raised her hand to her mouth. Hadn't Seb told her he'd tried to persuade Luca to go to the hospital, but Luca had refused? *Poor Seb. He'll be mad at himself for not insisting.*

"Unfortunately, for most people, there are no symptoms for the first six to twelve hours. Then they get stomach pains with sickness and diarrhoea and think they've got a bug or mild food poisoning," Hines told them. "So they don't go to see anyone about it, and that's when the damage is done. By then, the internal organs are being severely, sometimes irreparably, damaged." He shook his head.

Perry gasped. "Does that mean he'll die?"

Hines frowned. "It's a real possibility."

13

NOT LONG AFTER, FRIDAY 2 OCTOBER

Seb: *Tesoro, I'm off to the hospital to see Luca. He doesn't seem to have improved. Can we meet when I get back? xx*

Lady Beatrice spotted Sebastiano Marchetti sitting alone at a table on the far side of the catering marquee as she, Simon, and Perry entered.

He looks so dejected. She felt a wave of affection for the man, his chin resting in his hands as he stared into space. She quickened her pace and reached him before the others.

"Seb?" she whispered, not wishing to startle him.

He raised watery blue eyes to her face and gave a sad smile. "Aw, *bella.* You came."

He held out his hand, and she took it. *Now isn't the time to withdraw from him. He needs our support.* "Indeed. We came as soon as we got your message to say you were back from the hospital, and it wasn't looking good. How is he?"

Perry and Simon arrived. Perry took a seat opposite Seb

while Simon said, "I'll get the coffees," and headed off towards the serving counter.

Seb dropped Lady Beatrice's hand as she moved round and took the chair beside him.

He shook his head and sighed. "It's not good news. He's looking dreadful, all yellow and drifting in and out of consciousness. They believe he's going into major organ failure," he said in a choked-up voice. "They say there's nothing more they can do." He hung his head and lifted his hands to his forehead.

Lady Beatrice rubbed her hand slowly up and down his back. "We're so very sorry, Seb."

They sat there quietly, no one knowing what to say. Simon returned with a tray holding a coffee pot and cups on it and placed it in the middle of the table. He sat down and poured a black coffee that he slid over to Seb. "Here, drink this, mate."

Seb lifted his head and dropped his hands. Reaching out, he took the cup and raised it to his lips. Simon continued to pour the others.

Suddenly, Seb slammed his cup down on the table, making them all jump. "Why didn't he listen to me?" he cried. "*Testardo come un mulo!*" He banged the side of his hand on the table.

Simon reached over and put his hand over the other man's clenched fist. "You couldn't have done any more for him, Seb. It's not your fault."

Seb exhaled loudly and nodded. "*Non è un bambino.* He made his own decisions." Simon nodded and released Seb's balled hand.

"How's Fay holding up?" Lady Beatrice asked.

Seb shrugged. "She's staying with him while I'm here to

do my last demo for today. Then I'll go back and sit with him while she has a break."

"Are you sure you're up to doing a show in the circumstances? I could do it for you if you want me to?" Simon offered.

Seb shook his head vigorously. "*No, grazie*. I must do it. People have come here to see me, and I cannot let them down. I must go now to prepare. *Lo spettacolo deve continuare!*" He leaned over and kissed Lady Beatrice before striding off towards the exit.

Simon looked at her sadly. "The poor chap needs to keep busy. I would be the same if one of you got ill..."

Bea: *Just saying goodnight. I hope you get some rest. x*

Seb: *Luca's family's flight has landed. They should be here later. Fay and I will stay with him until they arrive. Good night, tesoro. xx.*

14

EARLY MORNING, SATURDAY 3 OCTOBER

Flicking through the photos posted on *The Daily Post Online*, Detective Chief Inspector Richard Fitzwilliam of the Protection and Investigation (Royal) Services, PaIRS for short, drummed his fingers on his desk and frowned. *What does she see in him?* He swiped to the next picture of Lady Beatrice and Sebastiano Marchetti. This one was grainy and had clearly been submitted by an amateur. Taken from behind, the picture showed the pair sitting at a table with two others, whom Fitzwilliam recognised as Perry Juke and Simon Lattimore. Lady Beatrice was leaning into Seb, her hand on his back. The caption read, 'Lady Beatrice comforts her *amore* as news breaks that Luca Mazza is seriously ill in the hospital'. Peering closer at the screen, he huffed. Crocodile tears, no doubt, just to get her sympathy.

He started as the office phone on his desk beeped, and a green button lit up. He closed his browser and picked up the handset. "Yes, Carol?"

"Chief inspector, I have Superintendent Blake on the phone for you," his PA informed him.

Richard sighed. It was never good news when he got a call from his boss.

"Okay, Carol, please put him through."

The phone clicked, confirming the line was connected.

"Nigel, what can I do for you?"

"Richard, we have a problem at Fenn House."

Fitzwilliam frowned. *Isn't that where Lady Beatrice is working on a refurbishment project?* She better not be involved with whatever this problem was. He suppressed a sigh. Who was he kidding? If there was trouble, then she was bound to be embroiled in it somehow. She was like a trouble magnet when it came to murder...

"The doctors have told Mike Ainsley from Fenshire CID that Luca Mazza, one of those chefy types, who took ill at the show there, isn't going to make it."

"You mean he's going to die, sir?"

"Exactly. They think he's eaten death cap mushrooms. He's in multiple organ failure, and it's too late for them to do anything to save him."

Fitzwilliam shuddered. *Not a nice way to die.*

"The Countess of Rossex is on-site at Fenn House doing her decorating thing, and through her beau, Sebastiano Marchetti, was mixing with the victim. I need you to go up to Fenn House and make sure she's in no danger. Mike's heading up the local investigation, and they think the victim ate the mushrooms sometime in the days leading up to the show's opening."

"So it was an accident then, sir?"

If so, why do you need me there? The last thing Fitzwilliam wanted was to go to Fenn House and watch that smarmy Italian, Sebastiano Marchetti, creeping around Lady Beatrice.

"They can't be sure yet, Richard. That's why I want you there. It shouldn't take more than a few days to sort out."

Fitzwilliam suppressed a huff. "Of course, sir. I'll make the arrangements now, and we'll be there later today."

"Good-o. Keep me posted. Oh, and Richard?"

"Yes, sir?"

"This time, see if you can solve this before her ladyship does, will you?" His boss chuckled, then the line went dead.

Slamming down the receiver, Fitzwilliam felt the blood pulsing in his temples. *They all think it's a joke!* He launched himself out of his chair and, stomping across his office, grabbed the coffee pot from a table by the door. He sloshed steaming black liquid into the mug Carol had bought him for Christmas with 'You must be exhausted from watching me do everything' plastered on the side and stormed back to his desk.

Blake should try telling Lady Beatrice to keep her nose out! Knowing her, she'd probably ignore the superintendent the same way she'd ignored Fitzwilliam during the last two cases he'd investigated up in Fenshire. He puffed out a breath. How could they investigate a threat to Lady Beatrice when she kept sticking her royal nose in and putting herself in danger? *I'm the one who needs protection — from her!*

He took a gulp of hot coffee, the heat soothing him some-what, then as he placed the cup down he recalled he was supposed to be having dinner with his sister and her husband tonight. *Blast!* Elise had only just started properly talking to him again after the unfortunate misunderstanding he'd had with her friend, Hayley, a month ago. And now he was going to upset her by cancelling the plans they had at the last minute. Picking up his mobile, he found his sister's number and dialled. *It's all the fault of that snake, Sebastiano Marchetti, and his stupid show.*

15

___

LUNCHTIME, SATURDAY 3 OCTOBER

Lady Beatrice grabbed her phone from the table scattered with lunch debris and looked at the black screen. It wasn't her phone making the noise. *Whose is it?* They'd all been on tenterhooks since they'd heard the news that Luca Mazza was unlikely to live much longer.

Sebastiano Marchetti got up from the table, his phone in his hand. "It's Fay," he said in a shaky voice. "*Mi scusi.*" He walked towards the exit of the catering tent, his phone to his ear.

Lady Beatrice's stomach dropped. *Is this* the *call?* She jumped as another phone beeped.

Perry Juke, sitting opposite her, nudged his partner Simon Lattimore and nodded towards Simon's mobile vibrating its way across the table. Simon picked it up while Lady Beatrice and Perry leaned towards him, not wanting to miss anything. "It's Steve from CID," he told them. "He says the EHA has completed their report on the hotel, and there were no mushrooms used that night in any of the dishes served. EHA has concluded from the information they've gathered, along with the fact that no one else who ate at the hotel that night has reported being seriously ill, that the source of Luca's illness was not from the hotel."

"So it has to have been something he ate earlier on that Monday?" Perry asked.

Lady Beatrice nodded. "DS Hines told us it can take up to twelve hours before the symptoms show. Luca took ill on Monday night, so that would make sense."

"What we really need to do is find out what Luca's movements were on Monday. That way, we can work out when he ate the mushrooms," Perry said.

"We also need to find out where they came from," Lady Beatrice added.

Simon held his hand up. "Whoa. Hold on Batman and Robin. Since when did we agree to investigate?" The phone in his hand made a sound like a bird chirping. "Right, I have to get ready for my demo." He rose, then turning to Lady Beatrice and Perry, said, "Look, Mike Ainsley is here. Let's leave this one to him and his team, shall we?"

Perry shrugged. "I suppose so."

Lady Beatrice nodded. Simon was right — between his shows and their refurbishment project, they didn't really have time to investigate this. "Indeed. You're right. Let's leave this to the professionals."

Bea: *Are you all right? You've been gone a long time. x*

Seb: *On my way to the hospital. Will call you when I arrive. xx*

16

AFTERNOON, SATURDAY 3 OCTOBER

The Society Page online article:

<u>*BREAKING NEWS Television Chef Luca Mazza Has Died Aged 38*</u>

Reports are coming in that 'Get Your Cook On' star, Chef Luca Mazza, has died today aged just 38.

Chef Luca was rushed to hospital in King's Town, Fenshire, on Thursday after he collapsed during a food demonstration at the Fenn House Food and Wine Festival taking place in the grounds of the king's private royal residence, Fenn House. The cause of Luca's death is as yet unknown, but local sources report that his admittance to the hospital was a precaution to treat dehydration after he had been ill for two days with suspected food poisoning prior to his collapse. However, within 24 hours, rumours were circulating that the chef was not responding to treatment, and his family flew in from Italy to be with him.

His girlfriend, food critic Fay Mayer (30), has been by his bedside throughout, and renowned chef Sebastiano Marchetti

(38) has been a frequent visitor to the hospital in between guest appearances at the festival.

We'll update you as soon as more information comes in...

Lady Beatrice watched Simon tilt the plate up to show off his last dish of the demonstration to a rousing round of applause in the show tent. Placing it back down on the counter, Simon held out his arm to Marta, and taking her hand, he walked around the bench and moved forward to the front of the stage with her. The energy in the clapping increased as they took a bow.

She was glad she'd let Perry dissuade her from telling Simon about Luca's death before he'd gone on stage. It had been a dilemma for her ever since Seb had rung her to tell her Luca had died only five minutes before Simon and Marta had been due to start their demonstration. Standing in the wings and clearly distracted with running through their plan, Simon and Marta had been oblivious when Lady Beatrice had called Perry over and told him. A whispered conversation between them had followed, with Perry insisting it would benefit no one to tell Simon and Marta now. It had been his argument that it would only make it harder for them to go on and perform that had finally swayed her. Now, seeing how much the crowd had enjoyed the show and looking at the joy on Simon's face as he took another bow, she knew it had been the right call.

"That went much better than I thought it would," Simon said, bouncing into the wings a few minutes later. A huge grin covering his face. He turned to Marta. "And it's all thanks to you, Marta. You're so skilled. I really couldn't have done it without you."

Marta shook her head as she moved to a side table. "*Nie, nie*. You're the one who's good with the crowds. You make cooking look so easy, they all want to go home and try it for themselves," she said as she picked up her phone and put it in the pocket of her apron.

Simon frowned as he looked at the table. Lady Beatrice rushed forward to meet him. "Well, I think you both did an amazing job."

"Thank you," Simon said as Perry enveloped him in a bear hug.

"I know I say it every time, but I'm extremely proud of you." He looked over Simon's shoulder and caught Lady Beatrice's eye.

"Have you got my phone?" Simon asked as he pulled out of Perry's arms.

Lady Beatrice took a deep breath. *We've got to tell him.*

Perry nodded. "Yes, don't worry, I have it." He took Simon's hand. "I'm sorry, love. But I have bad news."

Simon's face fell, his smile turning into a grimace. "Is he...?"

Perry nodded.

Marta gasped. Lady Beatrice spun around. *Rats!* They'd forgotten that Marta was an ex-colleague of Luca's. And although Seb had told Lady Beatrice that there was no love lost between the two of them, of course, it would still be an unpleasant shock for her.

"Marta, I'm so sorry," Lady Beatrice said, moving towards her.

The woman took her hands away from her face, tears running down her cheeks. "Is it true?" she whispered. "Is Luca really dead?" She took a sharp intake of breath and hiccupped.

Lady Beatrice stopped a short distance in front of her and

nodded slowly. "Yes, I'm sorry. He died a short while ago in the hospital."

Turning, Simon stretched out to take the crying chef's arm. "Marta, I'm so—"

Shaking her head, she moved out of his reach, and muttering, "*Nie, nie,*" she hurtled across the wings and fled down the ramp.

17

LATE AFTERNOON, SATURDAY 3 OCTOBER

As they walked towards the impressive mansion of Fenn House, Detective Sergeant Tina Spicer of the Protection and Investigation (Royal) Services shook her head. "I'm still not one hundred percent sure why we're here, sir. I don't see where the threat to Lady Beatrice or any other member of the royal family is. Am I missing something?"

Good question! It had been the same question his sister had asked him when he had rung her to cancel their dinner plans so he could rush off to Fenshire.

"I don't understand why you need to go all the way up there, Rich, just because a famous chef is ill. I thought it was your job to investigate threats to the royal family. What's that got to do with a food festival?" Elise had asked peevishly.

He'd suppressed his frustration and explained, "Sometimes, Elise, I simply have to do as I'm asked. If my boss wants me there, then I have to trust he has a good reason why he thinks I should be there."

"And what if you just said no?"

He'd sighed. "Well, for a start, I could fairly much guarantee that I'd struggle to get my next promotion."

"Arghhh…" His sister had made a noise like a small person screaming into a gigantic cannon. It had echoed through the telephone line. "You always put your job first!" she'd bleated.

"And you know why, sis? Because I want us to have a better life than the one we had when we were kids. It's why I help you out with the boys' school fees and take us all away on nice holidays."

"And we appreciate it, Rich, we really do. But none of that is important if we never get to see you because you're always working!"

"Come on, not always. I get at least one week a year off," he'd joked, hoping to defuse the situation.

His sister had sighed. "I don't find it very funny, Rich. It's already cost you your marriage, and now you'll die all alone without any friends or family. But at least it will say *He worked hard* on his tombstone. Is that what you really want?" she'd shouted.

"But Elise—" It had been too late. She'd slammed the phone down.

He'd heaved a long sigh. Why couldn't he get anything right when it came to women?

"Sir?" Spicer's enquiry brought him back to the present.

"Sorry, Spicer, no," Detective Chief Inspector Richard Fitzwilliam said to his sergeant. "You're not missing anything. I've been asking myself the same question ever since I got the call from the superintendent." Even when he'd got a second call from Nigel informing him that Luca Mazza had died, it hadn't changed his view that he was wasting his time on investigating the chef's death. *It's most probably a straightforward accident.* It didn't need their skills and expertise. He slowed down his pace. Turning to the slim blonde woman beside him, he shrugged. "I think it's a bit of a stretch to think that Lady Beatrice or, as you say, any other member of the royal family, is in danger because some over-hyped chef ate poisonous mushrooms that he no doubt had picked himself to be 'environmentally forward' or whatever the buzz phrase of the moment is." He sighed. "However, no one likes it when someone dies in a royal home, especially when that person is well known to the public."

He stopped, and rubbing his thumb and middle finger up and down his grey-speckled temples, he looked down at her and said, "Between you and me, I think they just want the investigation concluded as soon as possible, so they've brought us in to help Fenshire CID wrap it up quickly and smoothly."

She looked up at him and nodded. "So you don't think there's anything suspicious about Mr Mazza's death then, sir?"

"I doubt it, sergeant. We need to keep an open mind, of course, but it's most likely that Mr Mazza only had himself to blame."

Spicer shrugged as they began walking again. They continued along the hedge-lined gravel drive and turned left down by the side of the manor house.

"Ah, there he is." Fitzwilliam pointed to a thickset man in a blue suit who had come into view from the other side of the building.

They quickened their pace and met the inspector in front of a set of stone steps leading down to what appeared to be the basement.

"Mike, good to see you again." Fitzwilliam smiled as he held his hand out to the inspector from Fenshire CID.

"Fitzwilliam," Mike Ainsley greeted him, taking his hand and shaking it. "I'll be honest. I was surprised when head-quarters said you were on your way here. But you're always welcome, you know that. As are you, DS Spicer." He nodded and smiled at the woman dressed in a black suit and a baby blue T-shirt before him.

Fitzwilliam shrugged. "No more than I was when I got the call, Mike. Hopefully, it's straightforward and it won't take more than a few days to resolve."

"Let's hope so. The victim, Luca Mazza, was an up-and-coming young chef who was already a household name through a television cooking show he had a regular slot on. So as you can imagine, there's a lot of press and public interest in his death. And that's on top of the normal pressure from Gollingham Palace when anything nasty happens at a royal residence. They want the investigation concluded as soon as possible." Mike held one arm out to his right. "Shall we walk and talk? I want to show you where you'll be based while you're here."

Fitzwilliam nodded, and they fell into step with the inspector as they moved away from the house and followed him through a stone arch leading to the formal gardens.

Mike filled them in on the Fenn House security and access arrangements as they quickly passed the beginning of the green laurel hedging defining the garden's shape and through a small wooden door to their right.

They approached a series of connected low buildings with a faded plaque proclaiming *Fenn House Security* screwed to the wall just before the first door.

"This is the old security block and not used much these days. The king has recently had a new set of offices reno-vated in the old coach house for the security team, but it's not finished yet, and there's no spare space for us there," Mike told them as he led them along the front of the block, then stopped at the end where a door was half open.

They followed him into a shabby open-plan space

containing two pairs of desks facing each other and separated by a shelving unit topped with an unconnected printer, a box containing various cables, and a pile of files. Over on one side of the room, a whiteboard leaned up against an empty wall, and directly behind the collection of desks and chairs was a glass door with a sticker that said *Kitchen* on it.

Fitzwilliam sighed. *Why do we always end up in the dump room?* Then he checked himself. That wasn't quite true. For their last two cases in this area, they'd been accommodated a short drive away at Francis Court, the home of the Duke of Arnwall and his wife Her Royal Highness Princess Helen. His temporary offices in the Old Stable Yard had been ideally situated just behind the cafe and only a short walk to the Breakfast Room. His stomach rumbled at the thought of the food he had enjoyed in that restaurant. *It's a shame we can't be there now,* he thought, then checked himself again. Being at Francis Court would mean he would be more likely to bump into the duke and princess's interfering daughter, Lady Beatrice, as that was where she not only lived but also where her interior design company was based. No thanks. *This will do just fine.*

"Sorry about the mess. We're still trying to get everything working," Mike said as he sat down in one of the chairs, indicating for them to join him.

Studying the inspector's drawn face and shallow complexion, Fitzwilliam assumed the man hadn't had much of a break since their recent case together had ended last month.

Spicer took the chair at the table opposite him while Fitzwilliam perched on the corner of the desk. "So what do we have so far then, Mike?"

"On Tuesday, Mr Mazza reported that he'd been unwell

overnight. He thought it was something he'd eaten at The King's Hotel, where they're all staying in King's Town, on the Monday night. He was told by his boss to stay at the hotel and rest, which he did on Tuesday and Wednesday. On Thursday, he was feeling better, so he turned up at the Fenn House Food and Wine Festival, where he was due to perform in the opening demonstration at three in the afternoon. About ten minutes into the show, he collapsed on stage. He was taken to the hospital by ambulance and treated for dehydration, but he wasn't responding. A doctor on call in the emergency ward realised the symptoms matched death cap poisoning, and they ran a toxicology report and checked on his liver — a major symptom, confirming it. There isn't an antidote though, and the damage to his major organs was already catastrophic by that time. There was nothing they could do other than make him comfortable and call his family."

"Do we know why he didn't go to the hospital sooner?" Spicer asked.

"Get DS Hines to fill you in, sergeant. He's our expert on death cap mushroom poisoning. But basically, to the eater, it feels like a terrible upset stomach. So unless you *know* you've ingested wild mushrooms, then most people put the symptoms down to food poisoning or even the flu. The ironic aspect of it is that victims feel better after a couple of days, but by then, the damage is done." He shook his head. "A very unpleasant way to go."

"I agree," Fitzwilliam said. "So I assume Mr Mazza didn't realise it was death caps he'd eaten then?"

"Not that we know of. He told everyone he thought it was something he'd had at dinner in the hotel the night before. And unfortunately, by the time we were called in to investigate, he was unconscious. As soon as the hospital informed the EHA, they visited the hotel. The staff confirmed that none of the dishes served that night contained mushrooms. In fact, there were no mushrooms on the premises that day as they were awaiting a delivery."

"So the EHA concluded that the hotel kitchen wasn't the source?" Spicer asked.

Mike nodded. "So that's where we are. We've established that Mr Mazza's demonstration dish contained mushrooms and that he ate the dish during his rehearsal on Monday morning, so that's where we're starting."

That seems the most likely source. Fitzwilliam nodded. "You said he reported feeling ill on Tuesday morning. Who did he report that to?"

Mike opened his notebook. "Er, here we are. He told his boss Sebastiano Marchetti."

Did he now? Maybe creepy Seb had deliberately poisoned the newcomer as he was afraid Mazza would steal his television crown? Fitzwilliam smiled to himself.

Mike continued, "He's a well-known chef and, as I'm sure you're aware, is also the boyfriend of the Countess of Rossex."

"And is Lady Beatrice here?" Spicer asked.

Fitzwilliam knew that Spicer rather liked Lady Beatrice. *I need to keep those two away from each other this time.* He was sure that Spicer had encouraged her ladyship to stick her nose into their previous investigations. *And* he knew that Spicer, like Mike, found the confrontational dynamic between himself and Lady Beatrice amusing. *Well, not this time.* He would make sure she kept her cute royal proboscis out of the case!

"Yes. The countess and Mr Juke are working here at Fenn House on a refurbishment project for the king and queen. Mr

Simon Lattimore is also on-site as he's taking part in the food and wine festival."

Spicer smiled.

Fitzwilliam huffed. *So the troublesome trio are all here, are they? Great!*

18

NOT LONG AFTER, SATURDAY 3 OCTOBER

Head down, following the low hedging that framed the formal gardens, Lady Beatrice headed towards Fenn House, her mind drifting to Seb. *I hope he's finding some comfort being with Luca's family.* She grimaced. How was she going to tell him she wanted to slow things down when he was so clearly devastated by Luca's death...

Someone forcefully cleared their throat, and startled, Lady Beatrice ground to a halt. Raising her head, she was confronted by a man and a woman. She suppressed a groan as she recognised them.

The tall man with short brown hair slightly greying at the temples stared at her grimly while the pretty fresh-faced woman next to him smiled and held her hand out.

"Hello, Lady Rossex," DS Spicer said.

Taking a deep breath in, Lady Beatrice returned the woman's smile and shook the offered hand. "DS Spicer. It seems like only a few weeks since I last saw you."

Spicer laughed. "Yes, my lady." It had, in fact, been only four weeks ago when they had wrapped up the investigation into the murder of her mother's friend's visiting cook.

Her blood pressure rising, she felt Detective Chief Inspector Richard Fitzwilliam's eyes bore into her forehead.

It's no good, Bea. You can't just ignore him.

She swallowed. What could she say to the man who, last time she'd seen him, had told her that her boyfriend was using her and she should dump him? All right, that hadn't been his exact words, but the implication had been clear. *And it's none of his business!* She looked up into the brown eyes of the man who made her madder than any other person she knew. *Don't let him see how much he ruffles your feathers.*

She plastered on her public 'how nice to meet you' smile. "Chief inspector. Here sticking your nose into other people's business, are you?"

He smiled back, but there was no warmth in his eyes. "Yes, Lady Rossex. That's my job. We're here to find out who poisoned Luca Mazza."

Who poisoned him? Surely, it had been an accident.

"But it was an accident, chief inspector. No one deliberately poisoned him."

"And you know this how, my lady?" He smirked and held up his hand. "No. Don't tell me. You and your pals have already completed your investigation, and you're on your way right now to present the facts to Mike Ainsley. Case closed!"

I bet he thinks he's hilarious. She wanted to stick her tongue out at him but knew it would be a childish gesture and likely to make him laugh at her even more. *No, Bea. What's required is a dignified and calm response.* "Well, it wouldn't be the first time me and my *pals* have solved a case for you, DCI Fitzwilliam."

Ever the diplomat, DS Spicer cleared her throat. "We have to consider all avenues of inquiry, my lady. But it looks like it was an accident."

"Unless, of course, your boyfriend killed off his rival for the crown of cheesy television chef of the year." Fitzwilliam chuckled.

What? Was he accusing Seb of being a murderer? Her body tensed. *Oh my gosh, what happens if he frames Seb just to prove a point?*

She wouldn't put it past him. Her arms twitched. *I need to get out of here.* But first she racked her brain for a suitable put-down. "You... you..." She came up blank. "You idiot!" she cried as she turned on her heels and stormed off without saying goodbye.

Classy, Bea! You called him an idiot. She raised her chin to catch some of the chilly breeze on her face to cool down the heat flushing across it. That hadn't been her finest hour.

19

_____

A FEW MINUTES LATER, SATURDAY 3 OCTOBER

Turning left at a large hydrangea bush, its white flowers swaying in the breeze, DS Tina Spicer pulled her jacket closed and buttoned it up. She should have brought something warmer. But she hadn't remembered to check the forecast before leaving and was now concerned that the warm end of September had lulled her into a false sense of security about how hot it would be over the next few days. She hoped they would finish here quickly, so she could get back to Surrey, where there wasn't such a biting wind. The relentless gales, even in the summer, were one reason why, in her early twenties, she'd been happy to leave the Fenshire coast where she'd been born and embrace the muggy atmosphere of London.

Her boss, walking next to her, still chuckled.

Those two are as bad as each other. Normally, she enjoyed the banter between Lady Rossex and Fitzwilliam, often having to fight the urge to laugh out loud as they verbally duelled with each other. But this time, it had got too personal extremely quickly and had been uncomfortable. She didn't know what Fitzwilliam had said to Lady Rossex the last time he'd seen her—Spicer could never predict what her boss would say when he was in her ladyship's company—but whatever it had been, Lady Beatrice was obviously still pretty riled about it. And surely, Fitzwilliam didn't really think that Sebastiano Marchetti had killed Luca Mazza, did he?

Over the past month, Spicer had been devouring the gossip in the press about Lady Rossex and her new beau. *He's gorgeous, that's for sure.* And that voice... A tingle settled in her tummy. For the first time since she'd met the king's niece, she had to admit to feeling a little envious. Her ladyship could keep her big draughty houses and the constant press attention as far as Spicer was concerned, but a charismatic Italian with piercing blue eyes and the power to make you go weak at the knees every time he opened his mouth... Now that was something to go green over.

"Did you see her face?" Fitzwilliam grinned as they passed a bed of brightly coloured chrysanthemums. "I thought she was going to explode."

"Frankly, sir, I'm surprised she didn't slap you!"

"Why? What did I do?" The look on his face was far from innocent.

"Er, you accused her boyfriend of being a murderer!"

He nodded his head and grinned.

"You don't really think that someone tried to kill Luca, do you, sir?"

Fitzwilliam smiled at her. "As much as I'd love to lock up that jumped up so-called Chef Seb and throw away the key. No. I don't think he or anyone else deliberately tried to poison Mr Mazza. I suspect he did that all by himself."

"So why suggest to Lady Rossex that her boyfriend might have done it?"

"Just to see her face, sergeant." He smirked and nodded. "Yes. Just to see her face."

She frowned and shook her head. *This is going to backfire spectacularly.*

"You seem to disapprove of my little game, sergeant?"

"It's none of my business, sir. But you do realise that by winding Lady Rossex up like that, you've now almost certainly guaranteed she'll want to prove you wrong, don't you?"

"And?"

"And now she, Mr Juke, and Mr Lattimore will investigate this case to do just that. Which is exactly what you didn't want, isn't it, sir?"

"Oh, blast!"

20

EVENING, SATURDAY 3 OCTOBER

Lady Beatrice sighed deeply and, picking up her wineglass, took a glug of Malbec, then placed it down on the dining table in the open-plan kitchen of Simon and Perry's home Rose Cottage. "I mean, how could he be so obtuse? Surely he can see that it was an accident?"

Perry leaned across the large wooden surface and, after looking over to where Simon, Sam, and Daisy were peering into the oven, turned, and whispered, "You don't really think he meant it, do you?"

"What? That Seb's a killer?" she cried.

"Shhh, you don't want Sam to hear, do you?"

Oh my gosh. She put her hand over her mouth and swung round to check on her son. *Phew.* He was now engrossed in studying a recipe Simon was showing him with Daisy sitting by his feet.

"Sorry," she whispered as she turned back to Perry. "Why would Fitzwilliam believe that? Luca was Seb's friend. What conceivable motive could he have for killing him?"

Leaning back in his chair, Perry took a sip of his wine. He met her gaze, his blue eyes interrogating hers.

What? Did *he* think Seb was a murderer?

She leaned towards him. "Why are you looking at me like that?"

Putting down his glass, Perry sighed. "It's interesting that rather than saying, 'Oh, Seb couldn't possibly be a murderer', you said, 'Why would he kill Luca?'."

She gasped. *Did I?*

She frowned. The man she'd spent the last month getting to know, the man she'd been... with. He couldn't be a murderer, could he?

Don't be silly, of course not!

She shook her head. "Well, that's because it goes without saying *we* know he couldn't kill anyone. But remember, Fitzwilliam doesn't know him. And I'm sure he doesn't like him either. So he'll be ready to believe that Seb's a murderer."

Perry nodded. "I think we need to talk to Simon about it. But not in front of Sam."

"Indeed," she said as she took another sip of wine.

"Aw, bless him. He's shattered," Perry said as he looked over Lady Beatrice's shoulder. He picked his wineglass up from the dining table and took a sip.

Lady Beatrice craned her neck around, smiling at the sight of her son with a large cookbook open on his lap and one arm resting round a sleeping Daisy nestled by his side. His eyes were closed. He looked peaceful. "He's had a busy day," she said as she turned back to face Perry and Simon.

"And three-quarters of a glass of red wine!" Simon added, grinning.

Perry blushed. "Well, he asked if he could try some."

"A sip, Perry. You didn't need to pour him a whole glass." Simon laughed.

Lady Beatrice leaned over, smiling, and put her hand on Perry's arm. "It's okay. We allow the children to have the odd glass of wine at family meals. No harm done."

Perry smiled at her and mouthed, "Thank you."

"So what were you two whispering about earlier?" Simon asked. "I thought I heard something about Fitzwilliam thinking that Seb killed Luca?"

Lady Beatrice snorted her wine out through her nose. *Oh my gosh. If Simon heard, then...* She grabbed a napkin and wiped her chin.

"Don't worry. Sam was too distracted by what was going on in the kitchen to hear what you said," Simon said, grinning. "And anyway, I have particularly good hearing."

"It's his superpower," Perry added, smiling at his partner.

Coughing, Lady Beatrice took a sip of water and wiped her eyes.

"So am I right? Is that what Fitzwilliam told you?"

She nodded. "He was his typical boorish self," she said in a croaky voice.

"I can't believe he really thinks that. I know what you two are like. He probably just said it to provoke you. Did you say anything beforehand to hack him off?"

Heat crept up her neck. "No, of course not. I was polite, as always."

Simon raised an eyebrow and tilted his head to one side. "Really?"

She looked down at her hand clasped around her wine-glass. "Really," she mumbled.

A noise came from the back of Perry's throat as he slapped his hand in front of his mouth.

She gave him a look.

"Anyway, now that PaIRS and CID are investigating Luca's death, I'm sure it won't take long for them to piece together what happened, and then we can all move on." Simon took a sip of wine. "Hopefully, the public won't find out that he was poisoned by death caps just yet and we'll get through this last day without too much negative attention." He waved his wineglass at Lady Beatrice. "Unless you've told your mother, of course."

She shook her head. She used to tell her mother everything. But now, knowing that anything she said could end up broadcasted to the world via *The Society Page*, she was selective in what she shared with her. *It's such a shame.* "No. I've not seen her for almost a week. She's been away. And anyway, you know how careful I am these days about what I say to her."

Perry and Simon nodded. They'd been just as shocked as she'd been last month when she'd told them that her mother —the king's sister and a well-respected senior member of the royal family—owned and supplied information to the online gossip site that focussed heavily on the royals and their friends and family.

"So does that mean we're not investigating his death ourselves?" Perry asked, his lips pushed out together like someone puckering up for their first kiss.

Simon nodded. "We agreed to leave it to Mike. We said that we were too—"

"Yes, but that was before Fitzwilliam suggested that Seb could have done it," Lady Beatrice jumped in. "How can we leave it to them if Fitzwilliam is going to steer Mike in the direction that it wasn't an accident?"

Simon shrugged his shoulders. "But we don't seriously think he'll go down that route, do we?"

"How can we be sure? Look how stubbornly focused he

was going down his own path in previous cases even when we suggested other options," Perry pointed out.

Simon sighed. "I don't know." He took a slug of red wine. "You two have got your refurbishment to finish, and I really need to get back to my writing. I've spent way too much time away from it with everything going on with the show." He shook his head and put his wineglass down.

"But you said it wouldn't take more than a few days to piece it all together. And Bea and I will do most of the work. Please, love." Perry put his hands together in front of his face and, twisting around so they were facing each other, smiled at him.

"We owe it to Seb, Simon," Lady Beatrice said from across the table. "He's been through enough, what with losing Luca and all the reorganising he's had to do to accommodate Luca's absence. The last thing he deserves is the police on his back."

Simon huffed. "All right! As long as it only takes a few days." He placed his hands on the table and gave them both a stern look. "Same rules apply as previously."

Perry opened his mouth, but Simon put up his hand.

"I know this isn't a murder investigation and that no one is going to get hurt. But it's good practice to treat it with the same discipline. So no withholding evidence or any other type of information from Mike or Fitzwilliam. And if in doubt?"

"Run it past you!" Lady Beatrice and Perry chorused.

"Exactly," he said, now grinning.

21

FIRST THING, SUNDAY 4 OCTOBER

"And this is for Daisy." Nicky, the server in the Breakfast Room restaurant at Francis Court, removed a plate of bacon from her tray and placed it next to Lady Beatrice's coffee. "Cook cut all the fat off, my lady," she said.

Lady Beatrice smiled. It was good to see the staff where she lived were taking Daisy's recently imposed diet as seriously as she was. "Well, please thank Mrs Dunn for me, Nicky." The middle-aged woman nodded and left.

"Here you go, Daisy," Lady Beatrice said, bending down and handing a rasher of meat to the little dog. As she straightened up, her phone beeped. On the screen was an alert saying *The Society Page* had posted a new article.

She sighed. She still felt a certain amount of dread wash over her whenever she read that message even though, now knowing of her mother's involvement, she was certain she didn't need to worry so much. Because she and her mother had a deal. One that Princess Helen had suggested to placate her furious daughter when she'd found out that the source of personal family information being provided to the online newspaper was her mother. Subsequently, they had agreed that if *TSP* was going to report anything original that impacted Lady Beatrice or any of her friends (as opposed to simply repeating what the general press was saying), then she would be informed in advance so she could at least have a heads-up and, if appropriate, the opportunity to respond.

Although not wholly convinced by her mother's 'if you can't beat them, join them' attitude that had prompted her to start *TSP* forty years ago as a young princess being hounded by the popular press and wanting to take back control of her own image and that of her family, Lady Beatrice did at least now accept that Princess Helen was trying to do her best for those she cared about.

Opening the link, she sighed when she saw the headline. *Is the Honeymoon Period Over Already for The Countess of Rossex and Chef Seb?* She sighed. *I fear so…*

The article reported what the popular press was already saying — that because they hadn't seen her with Seb for over twenty-four hours and wasn't by his side during this difficult time like a dutiful girlfriend should be, their relationship must be on the wane.

A thickness invaded her throat. *Am I being a terrible friend by not being there with him?*

Daisy jumped up and bounded across the restaurant to greet Simon Lattimore and Perry Juke, who'd entered through the outside door via the terrace. Lady Beatrice sighed. Thank goodness the staff who ate in the Breakfast Room were used to seeing Daisy and her parents' dog Alfie running free around the house and grounds of Francis Court.

Perry and Simon arrived at the table, Daisy in tow, just as Nicky appeared to take their order. Having requested a full English (Simon) and eggs benedict (Perry), they asked for a fresh pot of coffee and sat down.

"Morning," Perry said.

"Do you think I'm an awful friend?" Lady Beatrice asked.

"Okay, morning to you too. Um, no, I don't," Perry replied.

"Sorry, morning to you both. Simon, do you think I'm a rotten friend?"

"Er, no. What's prompted this?"

Perry clapped his hands. "I know, I know! She's just seen the *TSP* article I was reading as we were walking here. It said the press thinks you're a bad girlfriend because you're not with Seb, holding his hand in his time of need. Am I right?"

She nodded. "But you don't agree?" she asked hopefully.

"Aw, but that's not what you asked, Bea. You asked if we thought you were an awful friend. You didn't ask if we thought you were a bad *girlfriend*!" Simon replied, a smile slowly creeping over his face.

"Because we'd have said yes!" Perry added, grinning.

What? These two men were her best friends and even *they* thought she wasn't doing her duty. She picked up the phone again.

Bea: *I'm sorry if I've not been there for you. Do you want to meet for early coffee?*

Perry frowned. "What are you doing?"

"Texting Seb to see if he wants to meet for coffee. I feel so bad that I've not been there for him."

"Oh, Bea. We were only kidding," Simon cried as he grabbed her hand. "And Perry was just teasing you. The press is being ridiculous, and I'm sure Seb has been too wrapped up in his own grief and looking after Luca's parents to worry about you not being there."

. . .

Seb: *Ciao, bella. I know you have Sam for the weekend, and he needs priority. But yes, coffee would be great. Is 9:30 on-site okay? I need to do some final checks before the show. Will meet you in the catering tent. I'll grab the coffees. xx*

Putting down her phone, Lady Beatrice squeezed Simon's hand before letting it go. "It doesn't matter if you're joking or not. I *have* neglected Seb since Luca died. Would you guys do me a favour and bring Sam to Fenn House later for me? I'm going to meet Seb for a coffee before the show opens to the public."

"Of course we will," Simon said.

"Thank you."

Nicky arrived with their food and more coffee, and they ate and drank in companionable silence. Now and again, Perry dropped small pieces of smoked salmon onto the floor by his feet for Daisy to mop up. Lady Beatrice suppressed a smile. *Does he think I can't see him doing that?*

"Oh, tell Bea what Roisin said," Perry prompted Simon, putting down his knife and fork and pushing his plate away.

"I thought she was coming to the show today?" Lady Beatrice asked.

Simon shook his head as he wiped his mouth with a napkin. "She was, and she was really looking forward to it, but now they want to get the investigation into Luca's death completed as soon as possible. Everyone in Forensics at Fenshire Constabulary has been told to cancel plans and concentrate on the case."

"What a shame," she said. "I was looking forward to seeing her."

Simon nodded, picking up his coffee. "Me too. But that's the job, I'm afraid, and she accepts that. She said they're performing the autopsy later today. But they've had access to the results from the tests the hospital did, and from that, they're confident that he must have eaten the mushrooms on Monday."

"Which we already worked out." Perry lifted his coffee cup to his lips.

Simon also took a sip of coffee. "I know Luca was doing his rehearsal for the opening show on Monday, and it was a mushroom side dish he was showcasing. So I'm going to talk to Ryan, who I think was overseeing the prep. I can only assume that Luca went foraging and added some mushrooms he'd found to the dish. That seems to me to be the most obvious explanation."

"But wouldn't Ryan have eaten them too?" Lady Beatrice asked. "From what I've seen of these shows, the sous chef does most of the tasting."

Simon nodded. "That's a good point, Bea. That's another thing I'll check with Ryan."

Simon turned to Perry. "So with me talking to Ryan, maybe you could try talking to Finn? He wasn't involved with Luca's demo as far as I'm aware, but he might've seen something."

"Sure."

"How about Marta?" Lady Beatrice asked. "Shall I see if she's around too?"

"Yes, you can. If not, we're bound to see her backstage somewhere," Simon replied.

Daisy suddenly woofed and ran towards the back door of the restaurant as Sam entered the room. He patted her on the head, then with her beside him, he waved and hurried towards them.

"Let's not discuss this in front of Sam if we can help it," she whispered. Perry and Simon nodded in agreement.

"Morning, sleepy head." Lady Beatrice pulled out the chair next to her and leaned over to ruffle her son's dark curls.

"Get off, Mum." Sam twisted out of her reach as he took his seat. Daisy settled beside him and closed her eyes.

"Good morning, Sam. Are you going to have breakfast?" Simon asked. Sam nodded, and catching Nicky's eye, Simon waved her over.

"Hello, master Sam." Nicky approached the table, her notepad already in her hand. "What can I get you to drink?"

"Milk, please, Nicky."

"Anyone else?"

"Can we have another pot of coffee, please, Nicky?" Simon requested. "And Sam here would like something to eat. A full English, Sam?"

Looking at Lady Beatrice, Sam said, "Can I, Mum?"

She smiled and nodded. "Yes, darling."

With a grin, Sam nodded at Simon. "Yes, please."

Nicky made a note, and collecting the used coffee pot, she walked back towards the kitchen.

Lady Beatrice glanced at her phone. *Gosh, is that the time?* She needed to leave, or she was going to be late meeting Seb. "Darling, I need to go to the show a little early. Are you all right to stay with Perry and Simon while you eat your breakfast, and then they'll bring you later?"

"Sure, Mum," her son replied. "What about Daisy?"

She'd best leave her here too if she was seeing Seb. "Would you mind looking after her?" she asked the boys. They nodded.

She rose and picked up the lead from the back of her chair

and handed it to Perry. "And don't forget, she needs to be kept on her lead at all times once you leave here."

"Yes, Mum," Perry replied in a child-like voice.

She rolled her eyes and bent down to retrieve two plastic bags from the floor. "And this" —she handed a bag to Simon — "is what Sam needs to wear with what he already has on."

"Oh, is that my disguise?" Sam asked, bouncing in his chair.

"It's just a baseball cap and some clear glasses," she told them.

"Cool," Sam replied.

She leaned in and kissed her son on the cheek, then clutching the other bag containing her wig and sunglasses to her chest, she said, "Right, I'll see you all later."

22

MORNING, SUNDAY 4 OCTOBER

"*Bella!*"

Lady Beatrice smiled as she weaved through the last of the busy tables of staff and crew, heading towards Sebastiano Marchetti, who was rising from his chair. When she arrived, they kissed on both cheeks, and then he lunged forward and hugged her.

Taken aback by the ferocity of his grip, she felt like a buoy being held onto by a drowning man in the middle of an empty sea. *Poor Seb, this has been so hard for him.* Suppressing her instinct to withdraw from his hug (she could only imagine how many people were pulling out their phones right now to capture this moment), she reminded herself why she was here. *Now is the time to be that good friend I promised myself I'd be.* She relaxed into his arms and waited for him to let go when he was ready.

"You look… *sensazione!*" he exclaimed as he held her at arm's length and smiled.

I don't know what that means, but it sounds great.

He, on the other hand, looked less than *sensazione*. The longer-than-normal designer stubble and the dark bags under his eyes told her he'd not had much sleep. She rubbed her hand along his arm as they separated, and he pulled out a chair opposite for her. Dumping her bag on the floor, she sat down, smiling kindly at the tired-looking man before her.

"How are—" she began.

He reached out and grabbed her hands. "I've missed you, *bella*," he said, his blue eyes watery and his voice low. "Promise me when all this is over, you'll come away with me, just the two of us, like when we went to Mauritius."

She studied the man before her, his hands gripping hers so earnestly, and tried to reconnect with the emotions she'd had when they'd first met six weeks ago. Attraction, of course, had been the driving force at the start. His tall, powerful body had made her feel safe and protected. Those twinkling blue eyes had drawn her in and made her feel like the only person in the world that mattered to him. In those first few weeks she'd been surrounded by a mist of happiness and warmth when she'd been with him and she'd believed she was on the road to falling in love.

So what had changed? *Why don't I feel like that anymore?*

"*Tesoro?*" He squeezed her hands, and her heart sank as she looked up. His eyes were pleading with her to say yes.

But how can I when all that will do is lead him on? She sighed. *But am I cruel enough to knock him when he's already down?* "I'll think about it," she said, slowly withdrawing her hands and picking up the takeaway coffee cup he'd put in front of her. "It's just that I'm really busy with the house and things at the moment, so…" She dropped his gaze as she took a sip of warm coffee to soothe her dry throat.

"Of course. I understand." His voice was quiet and lacked energy. As she looked up, he leaned away, his body sagging against the back of the chair.

I'm a bad person.

"So is Luca's family still here?" she asked, desperate to talk about anything other than their relationship.

Seb nodded as he shifted forward in his seat and picked up his coffee cup. "They'll be here for a few more days, I think. The police have told them they've ruled out it being something he ate at the hotel. Now they're looking at where he was in the days running up to him having taken ill."

"Yes. It seems likely it was something he ate here on Monday morning. Maybe during his rehearsal? He was cooking a mushroom dish, wasn't he?"

Seb sat up straight and put down his coffee cup. "Is that what the police think?"

"I don't know. But it would make sense, wouldn't it? It takes between six and twelve hours for the symptoms of death cap mushroom poisoning to manifest themselves. If he started feeling ill during the night, then it must've been something he ate on Monday. Did Luca go foraging, do you know?"

Seb nodded. "He only started recently, but he really got the bug." He raised an eyebrow. "Is that what they think happened? That Luca went foraging that morning and collected some death caps by mistake?"

"It could be, I guess. But surely an experienced chef like Luca could spot a poisonous mushroom and avoid it?"

Seb shrugged. "Normally, I would say yes. But Luca was new to foraging. And also…" He hesitated, and turning his head, he scanned the tent. The breakfast rush was over. The tent was now only half full.

"And?" she prompted.

He turned back to her but said nothing, becoming unnaturally still as he gazed at a point over her shoulder.

She leaned towards him and whispered, "What is it, Seb? What's bothering you?"

He looked up at her, his thick brows pulled into the middle of his face. "I don't like to speak ill of the dead," he whispered urgently. With eyes wide, he lifted his head and ran his fingers through his short dark hair before reaching for his coffee cup and taking a gulp. He returned it to the table, and shaking his head again, he leaned forward. "Something had been distracting Luca lately. I don't know what, but I think maybe he and Fay were having problems." He shrugged. "Anyway, he got sloppy in the kitchen and was coming in late. I had words with him about it a few days before we got here. He said he was sorry and told me he had a lot on his mind."

"Did he say what?"

Seb shook his head. "But he wasn't himself."

"So you think he may have been sidetracked and not paying as much attention as he should've been when he was foraging?"

"*Temo di si,*" he said sadly as he nodded.

She frowned. *Temo what?*

"I fear so, my love," he translated for her.

"I wonder why no one else was ill. Are all the mushrooms that everyone uses kept together, or does each chef have their own supply?" she asked.

"Why are you asking so many questions, *bella*?" A frown appeared on his forehead. "Surely it's up to the police to work out what happened?"

"Yes, but Fitzwilliam is being difficult—"

"Is he the one we met at the tea shop in the village a while ago? The one with the over-excited sister and the toothy girlfriend?"

Lady Beatrice grimaced. She didn't want to be reminded of the awkward meeting they'd had in Francis-next-the-Sea a month ago with Fitzwilliam, his sister, his brother-in-law, and his then girlfriend. She shuddered as she remembered being trapped at the table while Fitzwilliam's sister Elise had gushed about how excited she'd been to meet them all while his girlfriend Hayley had stared at her and Fitzwilliam had ignored all of them except Daisy, appearing as embarrassed as she'd been by the close encounter.

"He's not with her anymore."

"Who?"

"Fitzwilliam. He's not with the toothy woman anymore."

Seb frowned. "And how do you know? I thought you two didn't get along?"

She shrugged. "Anyway, he's here as part of the team investigating Luca's death. I want to work out what happened before he does and prove it was an accident."

"What do you mean, *prove* it was an accident? Of course, Luca's death was an accident!" He'd raised his voice, and the few remaining diners looked over in their direction.

"I'm sure too," she whispered, leaning in. "But Fitzwilliam may take a different view."

He reached out and grabbed her hand. "*Tesoro*, why do you want to get involved? You need to leave it to the police. After all, you just said you're so busy with the house you haven't time to go away with me. Maybe if you left it to the people who are paid to investigate, then you would have time?"

Lady Beatrice bristled. *But I'm doing it for you!* She took a calming intake of breath through her nose. *Let it go, Bea. He's just lost his friend. This isn't the right moment to tell him Fitzwilliam thinks he killed Luca.* She gently removed her hand and looked at her watch. "I'm sorry, Seb. I need to meet Perry and Simon. They have Sam and Daisy with them. Sam's keen to look around the show."

Seb sat back and crossed his arms. "Will I see you later?"

"Yes, I'd like to bring Sam to watch your show if I can."

He shrugged.

She stood up, then bent down to pick up her bag. "Okay. Well, I'll text you later and see how your day is going."

Sebastiano Marchetti nodded, then looking away from her, he picked up his phone.

23

STILL MORNING, SUNDAY 4 OCTOBER

"Ryan, this is Lady Rossex's son Sam Wiltshire. Sam, this is—"

Sam, bouncing by Simon's side in the wings of the demonstration tent, interrupted him. "I know who you are!" Sam's eyes shone as he faced the dark-skinned, short-haired man with a goatee. "We've talked about you in our food club at school. We're going to try one of your recipes next week from the *Sunday Roast* cookbook."

Simon grinned. The young boy was so excited.

Ryan laughed and held out his hand. "Well, nice to meet you, Sam. Which recipe are you going to attempt?"

Sam took Ryan's hand and shook it. "The dill risotto cakes with a fennel and apple salad."

"Good choice. The secret to that recipe is, when you're making the risotto, make sure you wait until the stock is almost fully absorbed each time before adding the next ladleful."

Sam nodded. "Cool."

"Did you want to come on stage and see the layout for my next demonstration?" Ryan asked a beaming Sam.

"Yes, please!" Sam looked at Simon and he nodded. *Thanks, Ryan. I think you've just made his day.* Simon turned and followed Ryan and Sam onto the stage.

"… and this is the mark where we have to be by the end of the first dish so we can show the audience what the finished plate looks like." Ryan looked up as Simon joined him and smiled.

With Sam still investigating the set up on the back bench, his eyes wide as he took it all in, Simon looked around and asked, "Is this the same stage you were on when Luca collapsed?"

Ryan nodded. "Yes. It's also where I'm doing my last show this afternoon." He looked over, and seeing Sam still absorbed in studying the set, he added, "It feels spooky, if I'm honest. You know, knowing that Luca was already dying when he was last on this stage."

"I can imagine. Was it you who prepped the mushrooms for his rehearsal show?"

Ryan frowned. "Yes. And I've thought about it a lot. I'm as sure as I can be that the mushrooms I prepared were fine."

"Were any of them foraged?"

Ryan shrugged. "I'm not a big forager myself, but there were some in the pile I prepped that were a bit muddy. But I've seen death caps twice and none of them looked like the ones on Monday."

"Did you eat any during the demo?" Simon glanced over to where Sam was now taking photos on his phone, looking out from the stage.

Ryan shook his head. "I didn't do it in the end. I had to leave to pick up a fish order from East Sonton, and by the time I got back, they'd finished."

Simon frowned. "That's not good planning, to have you off-site as they're about to do the run-through."

"It wasn't due to take place for another hour, so I would've had plenty of time, but the producers brought it forward." He sighed and slowly shook his head. "I feel very lucky about that. Imagine if they were in that mushroom dish. It would've been me, too, lying dead in the hospital." He gave a shudder.

There but for the grace... "With you not being there, presumably someone else acted as Luca's sous chef? Do you know who that was?" Sam headed towards them. *This will have to be the last question.*

Ryan shook his head. "No. I went straight from delivering the fish to the freezer, into the rehearsal for my first solo show that they'd also brought forward." He cleared his throat. "Will the police need to speak to me, do you think?"

"Probably, Ryan, but it's nothing to worry about. Just answer their questions honestly, and you'll be fine."

24

LATE MORNING, SUNDAY 4 OCTOBER

Lady Beatrice whipped the black wig off her head, and unclipping her long auburn hair, she rubbed her scalp. She still found wearing the wig made her head itch, and any opportunity she had to take it off, she took. *But it's doing the job.* No one had approached her during the festival while she'd mingled with the public around the stalls and the demo tents. She sighed. This was the last day for a while that she'd have to wear it.

Looking in the backstage bathroom mirror, she tried to smooth down her hair as best she could, the static when she'd removed the wig making her look like she'd had an electric shock. *That'll have to do.* She put the wig and the sunglasses in the bag slung across her body and washed her hands. Walking over to the hand towels stacked in the corner of the temporary ladies' cloakroom, she picked one up as the door opened behind her. Hearing a soft whimper, she turned around and saw Marta heading over to the vanity unit on the other side.

Catching Marta's eye in the mirror, she had second thoughts about questioning the chef when she saw, reflected in the glass, the tears streaming down the young woman's face.

I always seem to end up with the crying ones!

Marta looked away from her and, running the tap, bent down and splashed water on her face.

Lady Beatrice, reaching for a towel from the stack nearby, plucked one from the top and, walking across the room, held it out to Marta. The woman smiled and took it from her.

"Thank you, Lady Rossex."

Lady Beatrice smiled. "Are you all right, Marta? You seem upset."

Taking in a ragged breath, Marta gave her a faint smile in return. "Yes. Sorry. It's just been a difficult few days, and I feel overwhelmed sometimes."

"Of course. You've all been so professional in the way you've carried on with the festival even though it must've been hard to focus. I'm full of admiration for you."

"Chef Seb has been determined to ensure the public gets what they came here for." She sighed. "And to be honest, it's been good to have the distraction from thinking about Luca in hospital…" She put the towel up to her mouth to stifle a sob.

Why is she so upset about Luca? Seb had told her the two hadn't got on, and in the end, he'd separated them by moving Marta to another one of his restaurants. Then she remembered Marta's reaction when they'd told her yesterday that Luca had died.

Maybe they hadn't disliked each other as much as Seb believed?

"Did you know Luca well?"

Looking up from the towel, Marta wiped her face, her cheeks turning red. "We used to work together," she mumbled.

Something about the way the woman averted her gaze

made Lady Beatrice question the nature of their relationship. "And were you close?"

She glimpsed watery green eyes before Marta buried her face in her hands and started weeping.

Lady Beatrice reached out to put her arm around the distressed woman's shoulders, but Marta suddenly removed her hands from her face and, shaking her head, cried, "You don't understand. I'm married."

And with that, she barged past Lady Beatrice and fled the room.

———

"Do you think they were having an affair then?" Perry whispered, leaning across the *Too Sweet To Share* cake box resting in front of him on the table they sat at in the far corner of the catering tent.

Lady Beatrice shrugged. "Possibly. It would explain her comment about being married. But it seems unlikely. Seb said they didn't get on, and that's why he had to move her."

"Unless it had all turned sour between them, and that's why they couldn't work together anymore?"

She tilted her head to one side. *Now that would make sense.* But wouldn't Seb know if they'd been having an affair? Kitchens were small places, and surely it would be difficult to hide something like that. "Indeed. That could be it. We can ask Seb when he joins us for—"

"Shhhh," Perry hissed. "Sam's coming back."

Daisy appeared from under the table, her tail wagging.

Lady Beatrice looked behind her and smiled at her son walking towards them. Simon, beside him, was carrying a tray of hot drinks and side plates.

"I've picked up menus for when we're ready to eat,"

Simon said, nodding at the stack of laminated white sheets on the tray he placed in the middle of the table.

Patting the seat beside her, Lady Beatrice smiled at her son as he straightened up after crouching down to greet Daisy. "Daisy, lie down," she said to her little dog. Daisy immediately put her paws in front of her and slid down until she was flat on the floor. Then, head on her paws, she closed her eyes.

"I met Ryan Hawley, Mum. He showed me around his set. You know, where they do the demos and stuff? It was so cool," Sam said as he scrabbled into the chair beside her.

She smiled. "That was very good of him. I hope you said thank you?"

Sam nodded as he reached for a large mug topped with cream and marshmallows. "Is this my hot chocolate, Simon?"

Simon nodded as he lifted an oversized cup of steaming black coffee and handed it to Bea. "Ryan was great. I don't think he's met such an enthusiastic fan before." He grinned as he gave Perry his latte.

Sam giggled. "He's lucky it was just me. The girls in my food club at school would've been much worse!"

Laughing, Lady Beatrice glanced at Perry as she picked up her coffee. He stared down at the unopened cake box, his eyes unfocused, his shoulders drooping. *What's wrong with him?*

He looked up and caught her eye. Then he scratched his nose and, smiling, turned to Sam. "I've something in this box that's yours if you can guess what it is."

"That's easy," Sam said, putting down his drink. "It's cake."

"Ah, but what type of cake?"

Sam frowned and looked at Lady Beatrice. She shrugged.

He turned to Simon, his eyes wide. Simon coughed into his hand. The word 'brownie' was just audible.

Sam grinned at Perry. "Brownie!"

Perry laughed and, opening the box, pushed it towards Sam. "It's all yours, Sam," he said as he turned to his partner and winked.

Lady Beatrice peered inside as it slid across the table. *Why are there only three pieces?* She looked over at Perry.

He shrugged. "Sorry, Bea. I wasn't expecting to see you before lunch, and anyway, they can only fit three in a box."

I'm not surprised. Look at the size of them.

"Mum, do you want half of mine?" Sam said through a mouthful of cake.

She smiled at him. "No, darling, it's okay. I'm going to have a piece of Perry's, aren't I, Perry?"

Perry made a choking noise as he slammed down his coffee and grabbed his napkin. He wiped his mouth, his blue eyes meeting her gaze.

Don't blink; he'll crumble first. Perry blinked. *Gotcha!*

"Yes, I suppose so," he said with a sigh as he stared into the box. "Black forest cake, okay? I really got the white chocolate cupcake for Simon."

She nodded. "Indeed. I'm not a big fan of white chocolate anyway."

Perry removed a giant cupcake topped with an enormous swirl of white chocolate butter cream icing with dark chocolate shards embedded in it and placed it on a plate in front of his partner. Then picking up a knife, he cut the ample dark-brown slice oozing with fruit filling in half. Taking one piece, he lifted it onto a plate and pushed it over to Lady Bea.

"Thank you, Perry." She smiled sweetly at him as she plucked a cherry from the top and popped it into her mouth.

He wrinkled his nose, then grabbing the remaining chunk of cake directly from the box, he took a gigantic bite.

"So I had a chat with one of the producers as Sam and I were leaving Ryan's stage," Simon said. "They've just been told by the police that they need to stay behind after the show finishes today until the police have interviewed everyone. They've had to extend their hotel bookings for at least another night. I don't think they're best pleased."

"Well, I suppose it was that or disrupt the last day of the show," Perry said through a mouthful of sponge.

Simon nodded. "I don't think the production team sees it like that. And I dread to think what the chefs will say."

Lady Beatrice nodded as she stabbed her fork into her slice of cake. *I bet Seb won't be happy if he and his chefs are stuck here for longer than planned.*

25

LUNCHTIME, SUNDAY 4 OCTOBER

The Society Page online article:

Luca Mazza's Family Calls for Urgent Investigation into Chef's Death

Sergio Mazza (68) and his wife Rosetta (62) are calling for the police to take urgent action to find out what caused their son's death. Luca Mazza, executive chef at fine dining restaurant Nonnina in Knightsbridge and popular television food presenter, died yesterday, aged 38. The police have now revealed the cause of death was poisoning by amanita phalloides, *more commonly known as death cap mushrooms. Luca took ill while performing in a food demonstration at the Fenn House Food and Wine Festival on Thursday. He died later in hospital.*

Matteo Mazza (41), Luca's brother and family spokesman, told The Daily Post *that his brother was an experienced chef and regular forager. The family is insistent Luca would not have accidentally eaten the poisonous mushrooms. "Luca had been cooking since he was five years old," Matteo told the* newspaper. "He was an expert on ingredients and produce. For him to not recognise a death cap mushroom is unbelievable to us. We're pressing the police to speed up their investigation into how my brother came to eat the poisonous mushrooms and find out who is responsible for his death."

Sources close to Fenn House say that Fenshire CID and Protection and Investigation (Royal) Services are undertaking a joint investigation into Luca Mazza's death. The PaIRS team is headed up by Detective Chief Inspector Richard Fitzwilliam, who recently investigated the murder of Kelley Lindsell at nearby Fawstead Manor owned by television's Sir Hewitt Willoughby-Franklin.

"I'm not happy, Simon," Sebastiano Marchetti said as he threw himself down on a chair next to Lady Beatrice in the catering marquee.

Raising his voice above Daisy's barking, he continued, "Can they insist we stay? It's okay for me; I was due to be here overseeing the clear up anyway, but my chefs have restaurants to run." He bent down and hollered under the table, "Daisy, be quiet!" The barking stopped. Straightening up, Seb continued, "They can't be away from their jobs for much longer. Can I refuse to let them stay?"

Well, hello to you too! Lady Beatrice frowned as Daisy moved away from Seb and went to sit next to Sam. She could see he was upset, but so far since he'd arrived, he'd blatantly ignored not just her but her son too. Sam was sitting on the other side of her, his mouth open, staring at the chef he'd been dying to meet for weeks. *And he shouted at my dog!*

"I wouldn't recommend it, Seb. They'll be as quick as

they can. And I don't think it'll take long. It's always best to cooperate with them."

Seb shook his head slowly and sighed. "So now I need to find people to replace them with for at least another two services, maybe even more. *Che stress*!"

Lady Beatrice caught Perry's eye, and she wrinkled her nose.

He smiled at her and picked up the menus. "Shall we order?" he asked, handing them around. "That's if you have time, Seb?"

Seb huffed. "I'm not hungry, but I'll have an espresso," he said as he handed the menu back to Perry as if he was the waiter.

If he doesn't start being civil soon, then I'll call him out! Turning to Seb and trying not to glare, she said, "Seb, this is Sam, my son." She leaned back and indicated Sam sitting next to her.

Sam leaned forward, his mouth still open.

Seb placed his forearms on the table and twisted his head towards the youngster. "Ah, Sam, good to meet you at last." He slid his arm across Lady Beatrice and held his hand out to the boy.

Sam didn't move.

"Sam!" Lady Beatrice hissed. "Sorry," she said, turning to Seb. "He's a big fan and a bit star-struck."

Seb laughed and, stretching further across her, took Sam's hand in his and shook it.

Sam closed his mouth. Finally returning the handshake, he grinned at the chef.

Phew, that's better.

"So I hear you like to cook, Sam? Do you have a signature dish?"

Sam opened his mouth, then shut it again as Seb jumped up in his seat. "What's he doing here?"

They all looked in the direction the chef was facing.

An olive-skinned man with short dark hair and thick stubble stood by the entrance, scanning the room.

He looked vaguely familiar to Lady Beatrice, but she couldn't place him. Maybe he was one of the other chefs who Seb worked with?

Seb mumbled, "Luca's brother... please excuse me," before shooting off in the man's direction.

She could see the resemblance now. *What's he doing here?*

"I wonder what he's doing here?" Perry asked as he put down his menu.

"Probably talking to the police. Didn't you see the news?" Simon replied. "Luca's family has apparently been telling the press that Luca wouldn't have made a mistake like picking death cap mushrooms. Therefore, they want a full investigation into what happened. It seems, from reading between the lines, they're looking for someone to blame for Luca's death."

There was a brief silence while they watched Seb and Luca's brother converse by the door, then Perry spoke. "Well, I don't know about you lot, but I'm hungry. Can we order our food now?"

They all made their selection, except for Sam, who couldn't decide between vegetable lasagne and chicken curry. Simon suggested he and Sam should go to place the order to give Sam a little more time to decide.

Lady Beatrice watched the two of them disappear towards the serving counter. "He's amazing with Sam, isn't he?" She turned to Perry, who was still staring in their direction. "Perry?"

Perry started and turned back to her. "Um, yes, sorry. You're right. He's really great with him."

Drawing his eyebrows together, Perry clasped his hands and put them on the table.

Something's not right with him. About to ask, she stopped as she spotted Seb heading back to their table. Daisy made a low-level woof as Seb approached them, and Lady Beatrice quickly moved her little dog over to the other side of the table.

"Daisy, behave, please," she told the white terrier. Her tail wagging while her mistress was speaking, Daisy then sighed and, curling up, closed her eyes.

Sitting down next to Lady Beatrice with a thud, Seb exhaled loudly.

"Everything all right?" she asked.

"That was Luca's brother, Matteo. They've been with the police all morning pushing them for answers about Luca's death. The family doesn't believe Luca would've made a mistake like picking death caps. They think someone else must have foraged them. They want to find out who it was."

"So they can blame someone?" Perry asked.

Seb shook his head. "No, I don't think that's what they're after. I just think they want to clear Luca's name. They're worried that if nothing else comes to light, everyone will remember Luca as the chef who made a stupid mistake that killed him, rather than as the talented and professional chef they believe him to be."

That's an odd turn of phrase. Doesn't Seb agree that Luca was a talented and professional chef?

"And what do you think, Seb?" Simon asked as he returned to the table and sat down opposite.

Lady Beatrice looked around frantically. *Where's Sam?*

"Don't worry," Simon said to her. "He's over there talking

with Ryan and Finn. He's in heaven, and it's only until our food is ready."

Spotting her son chattering away to the two young chefs at a table over by the mock plastic window, she smiled. He was so animated; he was bouncing in his chair.

Perry leaned forward and whispered to her, "I didn't speak to Finn yet. Do you think I should go over now?"

She shook her head. "I'd leave it until later."

Seb was talking to Simon. "Luca got a bit, how do you say—slapdash?—recently. He had something on his mind that was distracting him. He made mistakes at work over the last few weeks…" He shrugged.

Simon nodded. "Did he go foraging on Sunday or Monday, do you know?"

Again Seb shrugged. "Not on Sunday, I don't think. He didn't arrive until late afternoon. But Monday morning, early, maybe? He loved to forage, and the weather was good."

"But surely he'd recognise death caps, wouldn't he?" Perry asked.

Seb sighed. "Yes, I'd like to think so. I've not had a chance to go myself and see what's around in the grounds at Fenn House. But I know they can look very different depending on how old they are and where they grow." He shrugged. "If he wasn't concentrating properly, then maybe he hadn't."

26

EARLY AFTERNOON, SUNDAY 4 OCTOBER

Sam's hand gripped hers so tightly, Lady Beatrice had to wiggle her fingers, forcing him to loosen his hold as they walked out of the catering tent and into the cordoned off area the public couldn't access. "Are you excited, darling?" *As if I need to ask!*

Sam looked up at her and smiled, nodding his head vigorously. "Finn said he's doing a Caribbean-style chicken satay, which is like a fusion dish. Do you think we'll get to taste it, Simon?"

Simon nodded. "Probably. Most chefs let the crew tuck in after the public leaves the tent."

They were now marching towards the third of four demonstration tents ahead of them. Sam's mouth was slightly open as he fixed his attention on the huge marquees.

"Slow down!" Perry cried behind them, holding on to Daisy's lead as she pulled him along, trying to catch up with the others. "These shoes weren't made for running in!"

Sam giggled as they slowed down their pace. "Come on, Perry," he said, "I don't want to miss the start."

"Yes, yes, I'm coming." Perry scampered to get level with them as they headed towards the security men guarding the tent's entrance.

"Simon, Ryan said we can watch his later demo this afternoon from the wings if we want. And after, we can taste the food. Can we go?"

Simon smiled and said, "If your mum says it's okay."

Pleading grey eyes looked up at Lady Beatrice. *Gosh, he looks like his dad.* Lady Beatrice swallowed.

"Can I, Mum?"

She smiled back at her eager son. "Yes, darling."

"I'm sorry, sir, but you can't bring the dog in here." A lanky man in a uniform that looked two sizes too big for him pointed at Daisy. "Health and safety," he added when Perry opened his mouth to speak.

Perry closed his mouth and looked at Lady Beatrice.

Rats! Maybe if I ask Perry nicely... She smiled at him and, putting her hand on his arm, said, "I don't suppose you would—"

"What's it worth?" Perry asked, smiling sweetly back.

"The biggest box they have at *Too Sweet to Share* filled with cake?" she offered. *I think I have him.* Perry hesitated. *Maybe not...*

"Please, Perry?" Sam waded in, coming to stand next to Perry and Daisy. He stroked the little dog's head. "She loves you, don't you, Daisy?"

Daisy wagged her tail and licked his hand.

Lady Beatrice leaned in and whispered, "And we can talk to Finn to save you the trouble."

"Oh, okay!" Perry said with an exaggerated sigh. "But you'd better make sure it's the biggest box they have."

"Indeed." Lady Beatrice leaned over and gave him a peck on the cheek. "You're an angel."

"Thanks, Perry," Sam said as he patted Daisy on the head. "You're cool."

Perry took a mock bow, then bending down to Daisy, said, "Come on, Daisy. Let's you and I see if we can find a stall that does food for good girls, shall we?"

Daisy wagged her tail even harder.

"We'll see you guys back at the catering tent when you're done." Perry turned and walked away from them, towards the stalls.

"He's very good, isn't he?" Lady Beatrice shouted above the clapping forty minutes later as Finn presented his final dish to his fans.

Simon nodded. "Yes. And his fusion style is something quite new in fine dining. He's going to go far, that's for sure. Rumour has it Seb will move him to *Nonnina* now to take on Luca's old job of executive chef there."

That was quick! Luca had only been dead a day, and already, Seb had a plan to replace him.

"So he'll be working with Ryan then?" Lady Beatrice asked.

The noise died down as the audience filed out of the marquee.

Simon lowered his voice. "Ryan is likely to get moved to Finn's old job as head chef at *The Flyer*."

So they've both benefitted from Luca's death with substantial promotions?

As the last person left and the door closed, Finn came back onto the stage and beckoned them over. "Sam, did you enjoy the show?" he asked the grinning boy as Sam rushed onto the stage.

"It was awesome!"

Finn picked up a fork and handed it to him. "Want to try some?"

"Oh, yeah!" Sam followed Finn to the counter, where Finn's sous chef joined them and began answering Sam's questions. Members of the production team appeared on the stage, keen to taste Finn's food too.

Finn slipped away from the throng of hungry staff and joined Lady Beatrice and Simon.

"Great show, Finn," Simon said, patting the chef on the back.

"Thanks for your support, Simon. And Lady Rossex, good to see you. I think you have a budding chef on your hands in that young boyo of yours," he said, grinning.

"Indeed. And it's very kind of you to give him so much of your time. He's over the moon getting to meet and talk with you and Ryan and the other chefs. I know how busy you are, having to pick up the slack since Luca took ill. So thank you, I really appreciate it."

"Aye," Finn sighed. "It's been a mad few days, that's for sure. But you know, you just have to crack on and get it done. Us chefs are used to firefighting."

"Do you have any thoughts about what might have happened to Luca, Finn?" Simon asked.

Finn shrugged his shoulders. "The production lads say that he must have gone out foraging on Monday morning before his rehearsal and picked death caps by mistake. But I don't buy it. Luca hated foraging and was always making an excuse to get out of it."

Really? That's not what Seb said. Or what Luca's brother told the press.

"Really? I'd heard he'd loved foraging," Lady Beatrice said.

Finn shook his head. "Nah. Just ask Ryan. They've lots of foraged herbs and stuff on their menu at *Nonnina,* and Luca used to send the chefs from Ryan's team to get them."

Lady Beatrice caught Simon's eye, and he raised an eyebrow.

Sam came running over to join them. "That was amazing, chef, thanks. Your sous chef has sent me the recipe. I'm going to try it out at our food club at school."

"Ah, you're welcome, pal. Send us a picture, will you?"

Sam nodded, beaming. Patting him on the back, Finn smiled at Simon and Lady Beatrice, then headed back to the counter where he joined his sous chef in clearing up.

His gaze glued to his phone, Sam walked ahead of them as they made their way back to the catering tent.

Lady Beatrice turned to Simon. "So why did Seb say that Luca loved foraging if it's not true?"

"I don't think Seb knows it's not true."

She frowned. "What do you mean?"

"Well, it's not unusual for someone like Luca, whose restaurant promotes foraged ingredients to, let's say, encourage people to think that he's an at-one-with-nature type, even if he isn't."

"So Seb wouldn't know?"

"Probably not. It's not something Luca would want the public or his boss to find out."

"So you think Finn's right, and it's unlikely that Luca went foraging in the grounds of Fenn House?"

Simon sighed. "It would seem so, but I think I'd like to check with Ryan before we jump to any conclusions."

"Because you know, if they're right and Luca didn't forage for the mushrooms, then someone else did."

Simon grimaced. "And that someone accidentally killed Luca Mazza."

27

LATER IN THE AFTERNOON, SUNDAY
4 OCTOBER

Lady Beatrice shifted the sunglasses up her nose with her thumb as she balanced the large *Too Sweet to Share* box in her hands and pushed open the catering tent door with her back. Quickly moving out of the way of the door as it closed, she scanned the room until she spotted Perry, Simon, Sam, and Daisy on the other side. She hurried towards the table, smiling at her son as he saw her approaching and waved.

"Be careful," she warned Simon as he reached out to take the box from her hands. "It's so full" —she gave Perry a look — "that you need to hold the bottom to stop the box from collapsing."

Simon grinned as he helped her lay it down on the table.

Licking his lips, Perry leaned forward as Lady Beatrice flipped her sunglasses onto the top of her head and opened the lid. He gasped. "Wow! That must be almost one of everything they have."

Lady Beatrice nodded as she sat down. Removing her glasses, she pulled the black wig off, breathing a sigh of relief. She released her own hair from its clip with one hand and itched the back of her head with the other. *Ahhh, that feels better.* She smiled at Perry. "Indeed. It's actually one of everything they had left on the stall."

Sam, his eyes wide, was competing with Perry to see who could get their head closest to the box to peer in. "Can we have one now, Mum?"

"Darling, you've just eaten some of Finn's food, and before that, you had lunch. I don't think you really need more food right now, do you?"

Sam's face dropped as he pulled away from the box of delights, and he bent down to pat Daisy.

Simon leaned over and closed the lid. "We've all eaten a lot today. Why don't we put these away until later?"

"But—" Perry started, then catching Simon's eye, he stopped and, pouting slightly, said, "Oh, all right."

Sam's phone rang, and he straightened up, grabbing his phone from the table. "It's Archie, Mum. Can I take it?"

Lady Beatrice nodded. "But take it outside, please, darling, and don't go beyond the cordoned off area."

Sam nodded. "Hey Archie, just give me a minute. I need to go outside." Sam jumped up and headed to the front entrance, his phone glued to his ear.

"Archie's his best friend," she told Simon and Perry.

"Is he the one Sam went to stay with in Italy during the summer?" Simon asked.

"Yes. His parents have a villa at Lake Como. Anyway, now that Sam's busy for a few minutes, can we talk about the information we've gathered so far?"

"Did you talk to Finn?" Perry asked.

"Yes," Simon told his partner. "The most interesting thing he told us was that Luca hated foraging and used to delegate it to the other chefs at *Nonnina*."

"Which is in direct conflict with what Seb told us. He said Luca loved to forage, although he was new to it," Lady Beatrice added. "Seb also told us that Luca had seemed distracted and had been a little sloppy recently. That might be something to do with Marta, who I think may have been closer to Luca than mere work colleagues. At her request, Seb moved her to another of his restaurants a few months ago, but before that, maybe she was having an affair with Luca?"

"It's possible. We probably need to talk to her again," Simon said.

"Can someone else do that, please? I seem to have a knack for making people cry," Lady Beatrice said. Simon and Perry grinned. "It's not funny! Remember our last case? Everyone I talked to ended up in tears."

"It's because you have empathy," Simon pointed out. "And that's a good thing. It's why they talk to you in the first place."

Well, I wish they would just talk and not sob!

"Ryan confirmed to me he prepped the mushrooms, and he's confident that, even though it looked like some of them had been foraged, none were death caps. He also said he missed the rehearsal because he and Finn had to pick up a fish order. The producers had brought the show forward," Simon continued.

Lady Beatrice frowned. "Don't you think that's odd? Surely they would need Ryan there as Luca's sous chef for the rehearsal. So why did they go ahead without him?"

Simon shrugged. "That first rehearsal is as much about timing as anything else. The producers need to know that you can get your dishes out within the allocated time. So, really, in this case, I don't think Ryan was essential as far as they were concerned."

"So do we know who acted as sous chef?" Perry asked. Simon shook his head. "Well, I think we need to find out. After all, if the mushrooms that killed Luca were the ones he tasted during the show, then why didn't his sous chef also fall ill?"

Simon nodded. "Yes, good point. I also want to talk to Ryan again. If Luca didn't forage for the mushrooms that killed him, then who did?"

"Talk of the devil. Isn't that Ryan just walking in?" Perry nodded his head in the direction of the entrance.

Simon waved at the chef. Ryan smiled and walked towards them.

"I've just seen young Sam outside," Ryan said as he approached the table. "He saw me and loudly whispered into his phone, 'He's just gone past me'. I've no idea what that was about." He raised his eyebrows, a wide grin spreading across his face.

He has such an incredible smile. Lady Beatrice started. *Did Perry just squeak?* She looked over at Perry, who was gazing at Ryan. She cleared her throat, and two crimson spots appeared on her friend's cheeks as he returned her look.

"He's completely star-struck," Simon said, laughing.

A smile tugged at a corner of Lady Beatrice's mouth. *Sam or Perry?*

"Actually, we were hoping to bump into you before your show. Can you just elaborate on where you got the mush-rooms from that you prepped for Luca's demonstration?"

Ryan frowned and tilted his head to one side. "Er, okay. I got them from the fridge. Is that what you mean?"

Simon nodded. "And where had they come from before that?"

"We had two large deliveries from our suppliers on the Sunday. All the produce was sourced locally — the veg, dairy, and meat. Then Finn and I went to get the fish from East Sonton on Monday."

"So the mushrooms that were delivered on Sunday were

the ones you used on Monday morning?" Lady Beatrice asked.

Ryan nodded, then crossed his arms. "Am I in trouble or something?"

"No, not at all. We're just trying to work out when the death caps got into the mushroom supply," Lady Beatrice reassured him.

Could Ryan have added the poisonous mushrooms? He hadn't been there for the demo, but he'd been prepping the vegetables before he'd left. She observed the man's slightly aggressive stance. Was he hiding something from them?

Ryan shifted his weight. "Well, as I said to Simon before, I think there may have been a few added as some looked a little dirtier than the others, but it was a mixed mushroom delivery, so it's hard to be sure."

"Could death caps have come from the supplier by mistake?" Simon asked.

Ryan uncrossed his arms and shook his head. "No. We have the one delivery for everyone to use. We kept them in the main fridge, and all the sous chefs helped themselves to what they wanted." He raised his hands up to the ceiling and shrugged. "So if there'd been any in there, then everyone would've been poisoned."

He's got a good point. The death caps must have been added after Ryan had taken the mushrooms from the general stock.

"So you took what you needed on Monday morning and then prepped them?" Simon's eyes were bright as he studied Ryan intently.

Ryan frowned, then nodded. "Yes. I prepped them and then took them to the fridge in tent three where the rehearsal was going to be."

"So at that stage, you're confident there were no poisonous ones in there?"

"Very," he replied firmly.

Lady Beatrice butted in, saying, "Sorry, Ryan, but how can you be so sure? Couldn't there have just been a few on the top that only you picked up, and that's why everyone else was fine?"

Ryan hesitated, then quickly scanned the room. After, he leaned in and said in a low voice, "I know for sure because I had some on toast for my breakfast while I was finishing my prep." He rubbed his hands together. "But please don't tell anyone. It's a bit of a no-no to eat the produce before the show." He looked down and shuffled his feet.

So someone must have added the death caps after Ryan had transferred them over to the fridge in tent three, ready for the demo.

Simon interrupted her thoughts. "Don't worry, we won't say anything. Just one last question, Ryan, if you don't mind. We've heard conflicting reports about Luca's foraging skills and whether he enjoyed it or not. What's your view?"

Ryan smiled slowly, his perfect white teeth standing out against his dark skin. Lady Beatrice could have sworn she heard Perry sigh. He shook his head slowly. "Luca hated foraging, man." He shrugged. "But it was important for his image that the public saw him to be keen. So occasionally, especially if the television cameras were on, he would pretend to be really into it and go out for a few hours to collect herbs and plants and stuff. But it was a different matter when the cameras were off. On a day-to-day basis, he left it to me and my team." His grin widened. "And I'll be honest, I'm not a great fan either, so I delegate it down too."

Simon smiled. "Thanks, Ryan. We're looking forward to your show later."

"Cool. Hang around after it's done and sample the food if you have time." He left them and weaved his way towards the food counter.

Perry jumped up. "Do we want more drinks?"

Simon glanced at his watch. "Sure, we've got time. Tea for me, please."

"Coffee for me, please. Oh, and can you get Sam an orange juice?"

"No problem." Perry smiled.

Lady Beatrice watched him dart between the tables and chairs and stop at the end of the queue, just behind Ryan, who was giving his order. Lady Beatrice smiled. *So that's why he was so keen to get more drinks.*

She shifted her gaze from the serving counter to the main door. *Where's Sam?* She knew he and Archie could talk for England given the chance. *I'll give him a short while longer, then I'll get him.* As she was about to look away, a large man wearing chinos and a tweed jacket entered the marquee.

"Isn't that Luca's agent?" Lady Beatrice asked Simon, gesturing towards the pasty-looking man making his way to the far corner of the tent.

Simon nodded. "Yes. That's Ambrose Weir." He frowned. "I wonder what he's still doing here."

They watched Ambrose as he pulled out a chair and sat down. Fishing in his jacket pocket, he removed a mobile phone and quickly became engrossed with it.

A movement by the door caught their attention, and Finn Gilligan strode in. He scanned the room, then seeing them, he waved and headed over.

"I've just seen your son outside chattering away on his phone, Lady Rossex. I hope he enjoyed the show earlier."

"Yes, he loved it. In fact, he's on the phone bringing his best friend up to date," she replied, smiling.

"It's great to see someone of that age so interested in food," Finn said, returning her smile.

"Quick question, Finn. Did you use the mushrooms from the main fridge on Monday for either of your rehearsals?" Simon asked.

Finn nodded. "Sure. I went and got what I needed from the main fridge so I could prep for Seb's show and later for mine."

"And they looked okay to you?"

Finn shrugged. "Aye. It was just an enormous pile of mixed mushrooms. I prepared them in the main kitchen, then took them to tent two where our demos were and put them in the fridge there."

Simon nodded. "And did you taste them later, during either of the demos?"

The young chef nodded again. "Both my and Seb's dishes had mushrooms in them. As I told the police this morning, the mushrooms I had were absolutely fine. In fact, I used them up the next day." He laughed. "I'd so many left over, I changed my dish to incorporate them on the Tuesday. I swear they multiplied over night!" Still chuckling, he looked away and scanned the room. Then, after pausing when his gaze reached the corner, he turned back to them. "Sorry, but I need to go. Catch you later."

Lady Beatrice smiled in return as Finn walked away.

"That's interesting," Simon said, his gaze following the chef. "He's going to meet Ambrose. I wonder what that's about."

"Maybe Ambrose is looking for a new client now that he's lost Luca?"

"Backstage gossip has it that Luca was about to sack Ambrose, anyway," Simon told her.

Lady Beatrice raised an eyebrow. "Really? So maybe

Ambrose had heard the rumour and has been courting Finn as a replacement?"

"Yes, maybe. Finn is very talented, but he's not done much television work. He'd be a great catch for Ambrose."

Lady Beatrice nodded. Is that why Ambrose was still hanging around the show? Glancing over Simon's shoulder, she saw Perry heading their way and stood up. "Perry's just coming with our drinks. Would you two take Sam and Daisy for a wander around the show? I'd like to find Marta if I can."

28

STILL AFTERNOON, SUNDAY 4 OCTOBER

"Oh, can we go to the stall that sells those things that chop herbs really finely that we didn't have time to go to earlier?" Sam Wilshire asked Simon Lattimore while he bounced from one foot to another just by the side of the public entrance to the festival.

Wearing a blue baseball cap turned back to front so the peak was behind his head and pushing a pair of round brown-framed glasses up his nose, Sam looked much younger than his thirteen years, Perry Juke thought.

Nodding, Simon caught Perry's eye and winked. "Come on then," he said to Sam as he placed his hands on the boy's shoulders and steered him around to his side.

Perry grinned back at his partner. *He's* really enjoying this.

Not only did his partner love exploring all the cooking gadgets on display and taste testing all the samples available at the various stands, but Perry could also guess how much more he was enjoying it with Sam, who shared his passion for food and cooking.

"Come on, Daisy," Perry said, gently tugging the sitting

terrier's lead. Daisy jumped up and trotted by his side as they followed Simon and Sam through the arched gateway.

Eventually stopping by a stand displaying a range of time-saving kitchen gadgets, Perry watched as Sam and Simon started examining them. Perry, whose kitchen skills were limited to picking out a suitable bottle of wine and occasionally chopping up onions (Simon only had to look at an onion, and his eyes started streaming), began feeling restless after only a few minutes of waiting for them to finish.

Two stalls down, a colourful front was advertising *The best fruit gins in the country*, and Perry found himself drawn to the vibrant array of bottles set out on the counter. Inching towards it, Daisy at his heels, he saw that each bottle was adorned with a label showing a picture of a fruit or fruits. In front of each one was a stack of small plastic cups and some open tonic cans. A sign hung from the front of the stall — *Free tasting. Come and try our delicious gins*.

Maybe I should try some to take home? He could imagine a nice gin and tonic would be a good way to start off an evening. He stopped in front of the booth and read the labels.

"Would you like to try one, sir?" A plump man appeared from behind a curtain and stopped in front of him on the other side of the counter. "Do you like cherries?" Perry nodded and the man immediately grabbed a bottle with the red fruit on the front and poured a measure into one of the plastic cups, topped it up with tonic, and handed it to him. Inhaling the smell of the fruit, Perry took a sip.

As the thick fruity liquid slid down his throat, he closed his eyes and made an involuntary sound of pleasure. Mmmm. *Oh my giddy aunt. That's delicious.* He opened his eyes and grinned at the man.

"Wow. That really does taste of cherries." He placed the half empty sample cup on the table in front of him as he said,

"I'll have a bottle of that, please." Taking his wallet from the back pocket of his Dsquared2 slim-fit jeans, he handed the man his card.

Having taken payment, the seller handed it back, along with a bag containing his gin just as Sam came running up.

"Simon's just bought a herb chopper. It's so fast it's unbelievable. What are you doing, Perry?" He pushed his fake glasses up his nose and looked at the plastic cup on the counter.

"Just trying some fruit gin. It's great." Perry lifted the still half full tumbler. "Smell this…" He held the dark-red liquid just under Sam's nose. "What's that, do you think?"

Sam leaned in and all but stuck his nose into the top of the glass.

"Stop!" Simon appeared by Perry's side and whipped the cup from his hand. "You can't give Sam gin; he's too young. I'd better have that." Simon threw the remains of the gin down the back of his throat. "Mmmm, that's superb. Did you buy some?"

Perry, startled by the sudden action, nodded in response, then frowned. *Did he think I was going to let Sam drink that?*

"I wasn't going—" Perry began, but Simon cut him off.

"Come on, Sam. Let's get you away from the alcohol before Perry gets you drunk."

What? The warmth of the alcohol at the back of his throat turned to ice as he took in what Simon had said. *I wouldn't get Sam drunk!* Did Simon really think he was that irresponsible that he'd feed a thirteen-year-old gin? A shudder went down his spine. Was that what Simon really thought of him?

A confused Sam looked from Simon to Perry and back. "I wasn't going to—" he started, but Simon cut him off with a grin.

"We need to make a move if you want to visit the ice-cream tent before we watch our last demo." And putting an arm around Sam's shoulders, Simon moved forward. Turning back to Perry, whose legs felt so weak he didn't know if he could move, Simon laughed. "Come on, Patsy, let's move."

Fifteen minutes later, sitting on the bench of a picnic table in front of a red and white domed tent, Sam was crunching his way through the waffle cone containing what was left of his buttered pecan ice-cream. "I think this could be my new favourite flavour."

"No. I'm sorry, but my caramel balsamic swirl beats yours hands down," Simon said, licking a small pink plastic shovel before thrusting it back into the cup and scooping up another spoonful.

Sam grinned and shook his head. "What about yours, Perry? How's the coffee and donuts ice-cream?"

Perry slowly smiled at Sam. "You'll never know!" he said as he popped the end of the cone into his mouth and made an exaggerated lip-smacking sound. Sam and Simon burst out laughing. Perry felt light-hearted. He loved it when he made Sam laugh.

"What now, Sam? Shall we head over to the demo tents and see Seb's last show?"

Sam looked away and shrugged.

Simon, a frown furrowing his brow, caught Perry's eye. Perry raised an eyebrow at him. *I don't know either.*

"Don't you want to see Seb's show?" Perry asked Sam.

Still not looking at them, Sam mumbled. "I'd rather see Ryan's."

Perry put his hand up to his mouth to suppress a smile. *So would I!*

Simon, taking out a brochure from his back pocket and unfolding it, laid it out on the tabletop and studied the schedule. He then glanced at his watch and said, "Well, if we hurry, we can catch Ryan's show, but we won't have time to get back to see Seb's. Are you okay with that?"

Sam looked up and nodded. "If that's all right with you?"

"Yes, we don't mind, do we, Perry?"

No, not at all! Perry nodded. "That's fine by me."

"Let's go then. We've only got fifteen minutes before it starts." Simon gathered their rubbish and put it in the bin next to them while Perry bent down to look at Daisy.

"What are we going to do about Daisy? They won't let her in the demo tents, remember?"

Simon nodded, then winked at Perry. "I have an idea," he said, taking Daisy's lead from Perry's hand. "You take Sam to tent one, and I'll meet you there. Come on, Daisy."

Perry got up and, watching Simon disappear around the back of the ice-cream tent, turned to Sam. "Come on then, Sam. We don't want to miss the beginning."

Sam jumped up, and they made their way towards the white tents in the distance.

Shall I say anything about his reluctance to see Seb's show? Although not confident in his ability to handle the emotions of a thirteen-year-old boy, Perry felt he owed it to Bea to attempt to understand Sam's hesitance to go. What would Simon do? Simon would be subtle. *Right, Perry, you can do subtle.*

"Don't you like Seb then, Sam?"

Sam turned wide-eyed towards Perry and stared.

Oh no, wait, I can fix this. "It's okay if you don't, you know. Just because your mum is friendly with him, it doesn't mean that…" He trailed off when he saw Sam's cheeks turned red.

The young boy shrugged and looked down at the floor. "He's all right," he mumbled, and taking his phone from his pocket, he started scrolling through his messages.

Well, that's not very convincing. The muscles in his shoulders tightened. There had to be more to this. And he would get to the bottom of it. He opened his mouth but closed it again sharply when he heard running footsteps behind him, and a second later, a hand rested on his shoulder.

"All sorted," Simon said as he smiled at Perry.

Thank goodness! The tension left his body. Simon could deal with this now.

"Daisy is safe and sound with Fitzwilliam and Spicer."

Oh my giddy aunt. "Are you kidding? Bea will kill us!"

Simon grinned. "It's fine. Don't worry, I'll get Daisy when we're done here. Bea needn't see them."

Perry frowned. "Why them anyway?"

Simon shrugged. "I saw them going into the catering tent just as we were sitting down with our ice-creams. So I ran her over there and asked them if they'd be kind enough to take Daisy while we watch the show. They were having a late lunch break and agreed straight away. You know how those two love Daisy and vice versa."

Perry shook his head. *Bea best not find out.* She would hate to have to say thank you to Fitzwilliam for looking after her dog.

"Hey, Sam," Simon said as he moved sideways to walk next to Sam and patted him on the shoulder. "So why Ryan's show rather than Seb's?"

Sam looked up from his phone, then returned it to his pocket. "Ryan's a bit more friendly, *and* he told me I could try whatever he cooks after the show."

Aw, so it's not that he doesn't like Seb; he just prefers Ryan. Perry let out a sigh of relief and chuckled to himself. He felt the same way too.

"Oh, okay," Simon said, removing his hand from the boy's shoulder.

Perry was surprised when Sam continued to talk.

"And," Lady Beatrice's son said, looking up into Simon's face. "Daisy doesn't like him."

Oh my giddy aunt!

Lady Beatrice stared down at her Doc Martin wedged sandals as she sauntered back towards the huge white catering marquee. Her conversation with Marta had thankfully involved fewer tears than she'd feared it would, and she was grateful that the chef had been willing to talk to her again. However, Marta's revelation that she'd been foraging on the Sunday night had taken Lady Beatrice by surprise. Dropping it casually in the conversation, Marta had seemed unaware of the position she'd put herself in. And even when she'd confirmed to Lady Beatrice that Luca disliked foraging and therefore, she couldn't have imagined that he'd been out to collect mushrooms, still the penny hadn't seemed to drop with her she was holding herself up for the position of accidental poisoner.

Of course, when Lady Beatrice had asked her if she could have picked any death caps by mistake, Marta had been very firm that it wasn't possible. She'd explained she was an experienced forager and familiar with death caps. She'd insisted she wouldn't have made an error like that.

She'd seemed genuine to Lady Beatrice. *I believe her.*

Marta had also pointed out she'd not seen any in the area she'd been in, which Lady Beatrice had found interesting. If they were only in specific areas, then where had they come from? Lady Beatrice had been even more concerned when Marta had admitted she'd not told the police about her foraging activities the night before Luca had taken ill because they hadn't asked her.

Should I tell them? She stopped and let out a slow breath. She didn't want to get Marta in trouble. But Simon had been very clear about their responsibility to share anything new they'd discovered with the police. It was clearly important information.

She started walking again, her destination only a short distance ahead of her. Did Marta's explanation that she'd added the foraged mushrooms to the ones delivered by the supplier that had already been in the main fridge explain why Ryan and Finn had mentioned that some of theirs had been muddy? If that was true, then the fact that no one else had taken ill would support Marta's assertion that there had been no death caps in the batch she'd added.

It was only when Lady Beatrice had tried to get Marta to open up about her relationship with Luca that she'd felt the young chef hadn't been so straight with her. After admitting that she and Luca had fallen out in the past, she'd said they'd started to talk again recently. She'd insisted their disagreement had become water under the bridge. But then she'd clammed up, made her excuses, and left.

There's a lot more to it than that. Lady Beatrice was sure of it.

Approaching the doors of the canvass structure, she shifted her bag to the other side of her body and pushed open the door. As she entered, a bark greeted her, and recognising Daisy's dulcet tones, she scanned the room, expecting to see Perry, Simon, and Sam.

She stopped dead. Her jaw dropped open. *What on earth is that man doing with my dog?*

29

NOT LONG AFTER, SUNDAY 4 OCTOBER

"Ah, Lady Rossex." Detective Sergeant Tina Spicer rose from her chair in the far corner of the catering tent and walked towards Lady Beatrice, smiling. "Have you come for Daisy?"

Lady Beatrice, her thoughts still fuzzy, smiled awkwardly back. Looking over the blonde DS's shoulder to the table, she caught Detective Chief Inspector Richard Fitzwilliam's eye.

Is something wrong? She couldn't tell from the look he was giving her. *Why is Daisy not with the others?* Turning her attention back to Spicer, she said. "Er, yes, I think so."

Spicer continued to smile as they walked towards the table together.

Daisy, her tail wagging madly, came bounding over, her lead dragging behind her.

Lady Beatrice crouched down to greet her little dog. "What are you doing here, Daisy?"

Fitzwilliam rose as they arrived. "Lady Rossex." He nodded his head. "You seem surprised to see Daisy with us. Maybe Mr Lattimore didn't have time to tell you he'd asked us to watch her while he took your son to see a demonstration? They don't allow dogs in, apparently."

Ah... Lady Beatrice let out a long breath. "So nothing's wrong then?"

Spicer, who had reached down to grab her coffee cup off the table, shook her head as she took a sip. "No, not at all. We were about to leave to go back to our office and take Daisy with us. But now you're here…"

"Yes, thank you. I'll take her. It was very kind of you to watch her for us." She looked down to where Daisy had been by her feet, only to find the terrier had returned to sitting by Fitzwilliam's side.

Why couldn't Daisy be like this with Seb? *Really, Daisy, your judgment is completely off!*

Fitzwilliam leaned down and patted Daisy on the head. "She's no trouble. In fact, I was rather hoping she might lead us to some clues in this case." A smile tugged at the corners of Fitzwilliam's mouth as he looked up into Lady Beatrice's eyes.

Did he just make a joke, or is he having a dig?

Fitzwilliam had been more than ready to dismiss her, Perry's, and Simon's efforts in previous investigations as merely 'useful' but was happy to acknowledge Daisy's contribution in finding clues? Returning his gaze, she couldn't see anything in his brown eyes to show if he was teasing her or making a point.

A throaty growl from Daisy broke their eye contact. Lady Beatrice spun around to look towards the entrance.

Sebastiano Marchetti stood in the doorway, scanning the room, his head moving from side to side. Even from this distance, Lady Beatrice could see his Adam's apple jerking up and down. *Oh no, what's wrong now?*

He spotted her, and she waved. With a grim look on his face, he wove his way over towards them.

Daisy, who was still rumbling away, now let out a

warning bark.

"Daisy, stop it!" Lady Beatrice snapped at her.

"Well, we're off," Fitzwilliam announced as he leaned down and patted an agitated Daisy on the head.

"Thank you for having Daisy," Lady Beatrice said as Spicer moved past her, and the woman smiled in return.

As Fitzwilliam straightened up, Lady Beatrice shifted over slightly to give him room to get past.

A shiver went up her spine when he reached level with her and stopped. *What's he doing?*

Leaning towards her, his breath tickling her ear, he whispered, "You know they say dogs are an excellent judge of character, don't you?"

A wave of heat invaded her body as he slipped past, chuckling.

Rooted to the spot, she watched the two police officers head left, then snake right towards the exit.

"*Bella*!" Seb's cry pulled her attention to her right as he rushed towards her.

Sinking into the nearest chair, she took a deep breath and exhaled slowly. *What on earth just happened?*

Daisy growled again as Seb arrived at the table.

"What *is* wrong with that dog?" He reached out towards Daisy, but she bared her teeth at him. He backed off, and pulling out the chair opposite Lady Beatrice, he sat down with a huff. "You really shouldn't have her in here if she's like this, *bella*. She might hurt someone."

What, Daisy? Lady Beatrice looked down at the little white dog sitting by her side, her tail sweeping the floor, then looked up and glared back at Seb. "Daisy would never hurt any—"

"I don't know why they even allow dogs somewhere

people are eating," he continued, shaking his head. "It's unhygienic, if you ask me."

Well, no one did! Feeling the hair on the back of her head stiffen, she clenched her jaw as she waited to see if she could get a word in edgeways.

"So where were you for my last show? I was expecting to see you and Sam there, but..." He lifted his hands by his sides and shrugged his shoulders.

Rats! She'd been so wrapped up in talking to Marta, she'd completely forgotten about Seb's show. She frowned. *Hold on, wasn't that where Sam, Simon, and Perry were?*

Seb reached out and grabbed her hand before she had time to react. "I'm disappointed you weren't there, *bella.*" His blue eyes were wide and a little bloodshot.

Her face softened. *Poor Seb. He's had a rotten few days.* She smiled and patted the hand holding hers. "Look, I'm sorry. I got involved in something else, and the time just disappeared. How did it go?"

He pulled his hand away and leaned back in his chair. "It was good." He lifted his chin. "The audience gave me a standing ovation."

She smiled again. "You deserve it. You've worked so hard to make this festival a success."

He leaned forward. "I wish you'd been there to see it."

She leaned back. He should let it go now. *I've said sorry.*

"What did the police want?"

She frowned. The police?

"I saw you talking to that tall policeman you don't like when I came in. What did he want?"

To warn me off you!

As Fitzwilliam's parting comment came to mind, her throat constricted. *How dare he suggest Daisy didn't like Seb because he was a bad person!* Just because Daisy, for some inexplicable reason, adored Fitzwilliam, that didn't make her an expert judge of character. Indeed, it was just the opposite.

Lady Beatrice took a calming breath and shrugged. "Oh, nothing. They were in here having a coffee and—"

"But I saw him say something to you as he left. Was it about me?"

Startled, she stared at Seb. Had Fitzwilliam said something to him already? "Why do you think that?"

"Well, he's made it very clear he doesn't like me. When they interviewed me early this morning, he was very rude. He asked me if I went foraging before the show. Like I had time!" He huffed and threw his arms into the air.

Lady Beatrice's heart sank. So Fitzwilliam was gunning for Seb and trying to blame him for Luca's death? She hadn't wanted to believe Fitzwilliam would go down that route, but clearly, he had. They must hurry and find out what had really happened so they could prove to Fitzwilliam that Seb had nothing to do with Luca's accident.

Seb lunged at her again and grabbed her hand. Under the table, Daisy gave a low growl.

"Come and have dinner with me tonight at the hotel, *tesoro*. And maybe you could stay? We can make plans to go away next week. I need you, *bella*."

Pressure! A quiver in her stomach, Lady Beatrice shifted in her seat. She wanted to be supportive. But…

She shook her head from side to side. "I'm sorry, Seb. But it's Sam's last night at home, and we're having dinner with my parents and their guests."

"What about after?"

She shook her head. "The press will have a field day if I come over late at night."

His cheek twitched as he dropped her hand. "It's always about the press with you. What about me, heh?" He crossed his arms over his chest and scowled, his lip curling over his teeth and making him look like an angry beaver.

You're like dealing with a child sometimes! She sighed, feeling her energy levels drop. She didn't think she could do this much longer... "Look, Seb. It's been a difficult time for you, and you are understandably feeling very emotional. Maybe we should take a break until this has blown over and—"

Seb jumped out of his seat, his arms flying. "You think I'm a murderer too, don't you?"

Her heart racing, she stared up at the man on the other side of the table, his face pinched and his hands clenched into fists by his sides. *Who said anything about murder?* "Of course I don't!"

Conscious that the noise level in the tent had dramatically dropped, she looked around as people hastily averted their eyes.

"Now please sit down. Everyone is staring."

He threw himself back into the chair and flung his arms onto the table with a thud. "That policeman of yours has poisoned you against me, hasn't he?" he hissed, his voice low and his eyes narrowed.

Talk about overdramatic!

She reminded herself that he wasn't English and therefore hadn't been born with that stoic, stiff upper lip she was used to. Maybe she should stop trying to be polite and instead be brutally honest with him?

She caught his eye and held his gaze. "He's not *my* policeman, and you're being ridiculous. Listen to me, Seb. I don't think for one minute that you had anything to do with Luca's death."

He looked away, and raising his hand, he pushed it through his short brown spiky hair. He shrugged. "Then why, *bella*?" He studied her face, his eyes blinking rapidly and his voice monotone and flat.

Her stomach dropped. *Now what do I say?* She wasn't sure that brutal honesty was for her. "It's nothing to do with Luca's accident, Seb. I just need a break. It's all been happening too fast, you and I. It feels too soon for me. I need some time to catch my breath."

She reached over to take his hand, but he snatched it away. She sighed. "I'm sorry, Seb. Please, just give me some time."

They sat in silence for a few minutes. Seb slumped in his seat, staring at his hands resting on his knees. Lady Beatrice darted glances at him, worried he was about to explode. Finally, he rose, his face flushed as he stared at the floor.

"I'm going now, *bella*," he mumbled as he pushed his chair backwards and sloped off towards the door.

Hers weren't the only pair of eyes that followed him as he slowly weaved his way around the tables and chairs before tugging at the door handle and disappearing into the bright afternoon.

Lady Beatrice put her elbows on the table and, raising her hands to her forehead, she exhaled long and hard. *I hope I've done the right thing.*

30

LATE-AFTERNOON, SUNDAY 4 OCTOBER

"So Mrs Talaska-Cowley, we're specifically interested in your movements on Monday, the twenty-eighth of September. Were you staying at The King's Hotel the night before?"

The petite woman sitting across from Fitzwilliam in the old security office nodded. Her long straight hair fell into her eyes, and she brushed it away from her face, then tucked it behind her ears.

Fitzwilliam, his hands resting on the desktop, continued, "And did you have breakfast at the hotel before you went to the show site the next morning?"

Marta shook her head, then looked down at her hands clasped in her lap.

This is going to be painful. Fitzwilliam struggled not to sigh out loud. Spicer had told him off for doing that. Apparently, it made interviewees think they were being difficult. *Well, if the cap fits...* "So you went straight to the site from the hotel?"

She nodded.

"And what time was that?"

The young woman shrugged. "I don't know. I was in the car with Ryan and Finn. Maybe they will know?"

Spicer busily scribbled away next to him. He'd have to look at the other two chefs' statements to check, but he was fairly sure they'd said they'd arrived just before eight in the morning.

"So what did you do when you got on-site?"

Marta shifted in her chair and sat on her hands. Her green baggy t-shirt hung loosely off her hunched shoulders and a long loose plait ran down the length of one thin arm. Fitzwilliam thought she looked like a beautiful pixie perched on a stone.

"I prepped in the main kitchen for the show later that day and then took all the produce to tent one where the demo was going to be held and got everything ready to go."

"And was anyone with you during this time?"

"Ryan and Finn were prepping in the main kitchen with me. There was no one else in tent one."

"Did you prep mushrooms?"

She nodded.

"And where did you get them from?"

"From the fridge in the main kitchen. We all shared them." She kept her eyes on the floor.

Is she just shy, or is she hiding something? Fitzwilliam cleared his throat and took a sip of lukewarm coffee. "And what did you do when you finished your food prep?"

Marta gazed at him with wide green eyes, then hung her head.

She looked young and vulnerable. Hardly old enough to be married. For a moment, Fitzwilliam felt uncomfortable pushing her for information. But he had a job to do…

"Mrs Talaska-Cowley? Can you answer the question, please?"

Still looking at the floor, she shook her head, this time allowing her long brown bangs to fall and cover her face.

Is she refusing to answer the question? He turned to Spicer and raised an eyebrow. Maybe his DS would have more luck.

Spicer nodded at him. "Marta?"

The woman removed one hand from under her leg and parted the curtain of hair to peek out at Spicer.

"Marta, we really need you to tell us where you were. It's important we can account for everyone's movements so we can piece together what happened to Luca. Do you understand?"

Marta nodded at Spicer, then leaning forward, she took a sip of water, her full red lips standing out against the white of the plastic.

"I went to meet someone." She returned the cup to the table with shaky fingers.

"Who did you go to meet?" Spicer asked in a soft tone.

Marta sighed. "Luca."

"Well, that was useful," Tina Spicer said as she closed the door behind Marta. "Now we know for definite that Luca didn't forage for mushrooms himself on Monday morning."

She walked back to the table in the corner of the room and, grabbing her notebook and mug, made her way to the cluster of desks in the middle where Fitzwilliam had already seated himself.

"If we believe her," Fitzwilliam said, opening his laptop.

"Why wouldn't we, sir?" Spicer took the seat opposite him.

"There was something about her manner that makes me think she knows more than she's letting on."

Ugh. Just listen to me! What would Lady Beatrice say if she heard him talking about him 'feeling' Marta wasn't telling them everything she knew? A smile tugged at the side of his mouth as he recalled the argument he'd had with her about a woman's intuition during their first case together. He'd dismissed her instinct that the case had been connected with a certain event in the past, given there had been no evidence to support her theory. She'd rubbed his face in it when it had turned out she'd been right. Of course, in that instance, it had been just a lucky guess on her part. Whereas it was years of experience that currently led him to believe that Marta was holding something back. Two completely different things.

"Sir?" Spicer looked up at him from her laptop and frowned. "Did you hear me?"

"Er, no, sorry. What did you say?"

"I said that we now also know who acted as sous chef for Luca."

"Ah, yes, our slippery friend, Mr Marchetti. We'll need to talk to him again. I wonder why he didn't tell us he'd stepped in for Ryan Hawley when they'd brought forward the rehearsal?"

Spicer tilted her head to one side, a grin on her face. "Probably because we didn't ask him?"

"Umm." Fitzwilliam rose, and grabbing his almost empty cup, he moved to the coffee pot sitting on a hot plate on the counter along the wall and filled it up. Sebastiano Marchetti! *I think we'll do some background checks on Mr Marchetti.* Pleased to have an excuse to see what dirt he could pick up on the man, he returned to his desk.

"And what are you smiling about, sir?"

Am I? Fitzwilliam cleared his face. "So the famous Chef Seb adds some death cap mushrooms to Luca's demonstration dish during the rehearsal so that…"

"So what, sir? I can't think of a motive, can you?"

"Jealous of the younger man stealing his fans?"

"It's hardly compelling, sir."

Fitzwilliam sighed. *If only it was him…*

"And anyway," Spicer continued, "apart from having no motive and no evidence, that would make this a murder case, not an accidental death. However, we *can* talk to Mr Marchetti and find out if he ate any of the mushroom dish during the show. That will help us establish if something poisoned Luca before, during, or after the demonstration."

Fitzwilliam nodded. That would have to do for now.

"Mum! Mum! Ryan says he'll come to my school and give the food club a master class!" Sam cried, his cap and glasses swinging from his hand as he came hurtling across the fenced-in grassed area in front of the catering tent towards Lady Beatrice and Daisy.

Catching her son in her arms, Lady Beatrice returned his hug. Then gently pushing him away from her, she took the cap and glasses from his hand. "That sounds wonderful, darling. Now we have about thirty minutes left if you want to explore the stalls for the last time."

Sam nodded.

"Fine, well then, you need this on." She placed the cap on his head and pulled it down so it was secure. "And these." She pushed the glasses onto his nose. "And I need this." She removed her black wig from her bag, and after securing her own hair with a clip, she popped it onto her head. "Does it look straight?"

Sam nodded.

"Right, well then, we're ready."

As Simon and Perry caught up with them, Simon stared at Daisy, frowning. "Where did you get her from?" he asked as Perry put his hand up to his mouth to disguise a grin.

"Funny old thing," she said, giving Simon a sarcastic smile. "I found her with my least favourite person in the world. Any idea how that happened?"

Looking rather sheepish, Simon shrugged. "Sorry, Bea. It seemed like a good idea at the time."

"Indeed." Pulling the pair of oversized sunglasses out of her bag, she slid them onto the bridge of her nose. "Shall we go then?"

They walked in the direction of the security gate separating the backstage area from the public showground. Sam, who had grabbed Daisy's lead from his mother, was running ahead of them, out of earshot, so Lady Beatrice filled Simon and Perry in on what Marta had told her.

"And she's not told the police?" Simon asked.

Lady Beatrice shook her head, the thick black hair touching the side of her cheek. She pushed it out of the way. *Last afternoon of this pesky wig.* Thank goodness for that.

"So did you tell Fitzwilliam and Spicer when you collected Daisy?"

Rats! What with Seb's arrival and Fitzwilliam's strange departing gesture, it had completely skipped her mind. "No. We got interrupted by Seb arriving not long after me, and I clean forgot."

"Bea!" Simon's voice was deep and insistent.

"Yes, I know. I'll tell them as soon as we're done here."

Perry grasped her arm and tugged her towards him. "So

Seb turned up, did he? Did Fitzwilliam arrest him on the spot?" he asked, grinning.

"Oh, ha ha. No. They didn't speak. Seb wasn't in the best of moods as I missed his show." She turned to her other side to look at Simon. "And so did you. What happened?"

Simon leaned back and gave Perry a look behind her back.

What are they up to? "Simon?"

"Er, well, we gave Sam the choice, and he wanted to see Ryan's show instead."

Really?

Perry jumped in. "Ryan had promised him he could try the food afterwards, which we did, and it was amazing. I think that was the lure for him."

"Indeed."

31

SHORTLY AFTER, SUNDAY 4 OCTOBER

Ma: *Darling, is it true you and Seb have had a big falling out backstage at the show? xx*

Bea: *How do you know that? xx*

Ma: *Press rumours, Bea. So it is true? Do you want to counteract it? xx*

Lady Beatrice frowned as she stared at her phone screen. *What shall I do?* This was the perfect opportunity to use her mother's influence with *The Society Page* to fashion her own version of her relationship with Seb. Should she use this advantage to play it down?

Bea: *I'll ring you in five minutes. xx*

32

STILL LATE AFTERNOON, SUNDAY 4 OCTOBER

The Society Page online article:

Is Lady Beatrice and Chef Seb's Romance on the Wane?

The relationship between Lady Beatrice (36), the Countess of Rossex, and television fan's favourite, Sebastiano Marchetti (38), is rumoured to be in trouble by the popular press today. The much talked about romance, which started in mid-August when the author and celebrity chef Simon Lattimore introduced them, is reported to be in ruins after the couple were seen having a heated argument backstage at The Fenn House Food and Wine Festival in Fenshire earlier today. The result of which was the famous chef storming off and leaving the countess in tears.

There has been no official comment from either party's representatives, but a source close to Lady Beatrice tells us that the seriousness of the relationship between the couple has been wildly exaggerated and described them as merely 'casually dating'. They also dismissed the claim that the couple had argued backstage at the show, instead stating that all those involved in the event were upset at the death of their friend, Luca Mazza, announced yesterday. The source went on to dismiss recent claims made by The Daily Post *that Sebastiano is about to propose to the countess as 'pure fantasy'.*

Closing the browser on her phone, Lady Beatrice let out a deep breath and sighed. Would the world believe this played down version of her and Seb's relationship? It was her mother's premise that years of building *The Society Page* up to be the authority on the royal family by dropping in titbits of information only someone close to them would have access to, had resulted in *TSP* being accepted as 'in the know', and the popular press took notice. *We'll have to see if she's right...*

How would Seb react? She'd told him she needed a break to help soften the blow, but she knew now, without a doubt, that she wanted to end the relationship. *I'll have to tell him the truth.*

She flicked the volume control to silent in case Seb rang and shoved the mobile phone into her bag. She'd tackle him later if she had to. Right now, she needed to deal with another unpleasant task — talking to Fitzwilliam.

Exiting the showground, she walked ten metres to the black wrought-iron gate leading to the gardens and punched in the security code. Whipping off her wig and sunglasses, she stuffed them into her bag. Unclipping her hair, she then smoothed it down and smiled up into the surveillance camera. The sound of a *click* told her security had verified her, and pushing the gate, she held it open to let Daisy through first. As the door shut behind her, she bent down and unclipped Daisy's lead. With the small white dog bounding ahead, she headed towards the old security building visible in the distance.

Ten minutes later, standing outside the only door that was ajar in the rundown block, she heard a rumble of voices coming from inside. Her heart thudded. Was Fitzwilliam going to pursue his theory that Seb was in someway connected to Luca's death? If so, it would make another confrontation between them inevitable. *Please just let me get in and out quickly without saying something I'll regret.* She swallowed and, lifting her chin, gingerly pushed the door open and shouted, "Hello?"

Daisy, less polite than her mistress, tried to push her body through the gap. "Daisy!" Lady Beatrice hissed, but it was too late, and with a thud, the door flew open, and the terrier went charging into the room.

"Hey, Daisy." DS Tina Spicer looked up from greeting the little dog as Lady Beatrice walked into the room. "Hello, my lady," she said, smiling and straightening up.

"Hello, sergeant." She turned, her eyes following Daisy as she scampered to Fitzwilliam, who was leaning against a desk in the middle of the room. She caught his eye. "Chief inspector."

He nodded, then bent down to fuss Daisy.

Turning back to face Spicer, Lady Beatrice continued, "Sorry to disturb you, but I have some information that you may not be aware of. I thought it best to pop in and share it with you before I leave."

Spicer nodded and moved towards a round table with four chairs scattered around it. "Please take a seat, my lady," she said, gesturing towards the table as she grabbed her notebook from the desk and followed her across the room. "Sir," she called. Straightening up, Fitzwilliam strode over, Daisy at his heels.

"So Lady Rossex. What do you have for us?" he asked as he pulled out a chair and sat down opposite her.

"Have you spoken to Marta yet?"

Fitzwilliam leaned back in his chair and crossed his long legs. "Yes, we've spoken to Mrs Talaska-Cowley. Why?"

"Did she tell you she went foraging on Sunday evening and picked up mushrooms, which she then added to the ones delivered from the supplier that were kept in the main fridge?"

It was clear to Lady Beatrice from Spicer's furious scribbling and Fitzwilliam's rapid unfurling of his legs that Marta hadn't.

"And she told you that herself, did she?" Fitzwilliam asked, leaning forward and placing his hands on the table.

She nodded. "We were talking about foraging, and she dropped it in the conversation. I don't think she quite understood the relevance of what she was saying."

Fitzwilliam brought his hand up to his chin and raised an eyebrow. "Which is?"

Is this a test, or does he not see that Marta is the prime suspect for accidentally killing Luca?

She bit the inside of her cheek. Should she say more or just leave them with the information? They could re-interview Marta and find out for themselves. *I'll probably wish I hadn't, but...*

"Well, if she's the only one admitting to foraging, then she must now be the prime suspect for collecting the poisoned mushrooms that Luca eventually ate." She shrugged. "Admittedly, she told me she didn't pick up any death caps. In fact, she said she didn't even see any in the area where she was. But it seems like too much of a coincidence to me…" Fitzwilliam's brown eyes fixed on her. Heat crawled up her neck. She looked away. *Why is he staring at me?* Had she got it wrong? Had someone else admitted to the police that they, too, had been foraging?

"And what's your theory about how, once added to the general pile of mushrooms that everyone had access to, they ended up only in Luca's dish?"

She sighed. *Of course, that's the crux of the matter.*

"Maybe it was only the odd one that randomly got picked up amongst all the others by Ryan, Luca's sous chef?" Even to her own ears, it sounded a weak theory.

Fitzwilliam shook his head. "Mr Hawley told us he cooked and tasted the mushrooms he'd prepped before he took them to the demo tent."

Yes, of course! She remembered now. Ryan had confessed to Simon that he'd had some on toast for breakfast that morning. Screwing up her face, she sighed. "None of it makes sense then, does it?"

Tilting his head to one side, Fitzwilliam smirked. "I don't agree, your ladyship. There are two other scenarios that fit. Either Luca Mazza added them himself just before the demonstration started or—"

"But everyone agrees Luca hated foraging," Lady Beatrice broke in.

"Or," Fitzwilliam continued as he leaned back and crossed his legs, "someone else added them to his dish before or during his demo."

What? She swallowed down the sour taste that had evaded her mouth. Surely he's not suggesting that someone deliberately added the mushrooms to kill Luca? That would be murder!

Fitzwilliam was still talking. "Someone maybe like his sous chef?"

Ryan? But he was... "Ryan was collecting fish with Finn and missed the demo."

"Yes, so someone had to fill in for him..." Fitzwilliam looked like the cat who'd got the cream.

Her stomach rolled. *Oh, no...* She, Perry, and Simon hadn't found out yet who'd stepped in for Ryan when the producers had pulled the show forward. From the look on Fitzwilliam's face, she could guess who it was. She flinched as he continued.

"... and that person was none other than your reported soon-to-be ex-boyfriend."

Her eyes widened as she stared at him. His lips curled up into a smile. *Is he mad?* Why is he pursuing this ridiculous line of inquiry? He might not like Seb, but this was crazy.

She hurtled up from her chair, causing Daisy to jump up and stand by her side, looking up at her mistress as if questioning what they were going to do now. "You seem determined to prove Seb is involved in Luca's death, chief inspector, but that's just laughable. Why would he, or anyone else, want Luca dead? Why are you even considering that this was anything other than an accident when you've no evidence to prove otherwise?"

Fitzwilliam uncrossed his legs and slowly stood. "And how do you know that, Lady Rossex?"

There was a reduced timbre in his voice that made her start. *Does he know something we don't?* "Well, er..."

"Because you may not be aware that we've just found out that Mr Mazza's laptop has disappeared from his hotel room. Now that's rather suspicious, don't you think, Lady Rossex, if, as you say, Luca Mazza's death was an accident?"

Rats! She drew in a good slug of air through her nose. Why would someone take Luca's laptop?

Fitzwilliam shifted his weight. "What *I* don't understand

is why you're defending Mr Marchetti. I understand from the papers that you two have fallen out. So surely now you can take off your rose-coloured glasses and see that he's a credible suspect with the means and the opportunity."

She gasped. *How dare he comment on my love life again!* The man was obsessed. He was the one wearing whatever the opposite of rose-tinted glasses was when it came to Seb! He'd been gunning for him from day one. But he didn't know Seb like she did. *I knew I shouldn't have got into this with him.* She took a calming breath, but it didn't seem to do much to quell her desire to scream. *Get a grip, Bea. Be dignified. Be the bigger person.*

"Don't believe everything you read in the papers, chief inspector. Sebastiano Marchetti is no killer, and I will prove it to you." She stormed towards the door. "Come on, Daisy," she shouted as she shot through the door and charged down the gravelled path.

33

EARLY EVENING, SUNDAY 4 OCTOBER

"You have a face like thunder, darling. Is everything all right?" Her Royal Highness Princess Helen, the Duchess of Arnwall, whispered as she leaned over the dining table and addressed her daughter. "It's not the *TSP* report, is it? I thought you wanted to underplay the seriousness of your relationship with the chef?"

The chef? Lady Beatrice had been under no illusion about her mother's approval of her budding romance. Not long after she'd got back from her trip with Seb to Mauritius, her mother had begun making her feelings clear.

"But who is his family, darling? Do you know anything about them?" Princess Helen had asked the day after she'd returned.

"Why does it matter, Ma?" Lady Beatrice had asked, deflecting the question.

The truth was Seb had said very little about his family to her. He'd briefly mentioned his mother had never worked, raising him and his older brother while his father had been busy with his business. But when she'd asked more questions about them, he'd clammed up. On another occasion, she'd asked him if he saw them often, and he'd replied that they weren't around anymore. She'd assumed he'd meant they were dead, but she hadn't pried any more given he'd clearly been uncomfortable talking about it.

Why is everyone so set against Seb? Her mother, Fitzwilliam, Daisy. Even her son.

She looked across the Rose Dining Room at Sam, his brown hair falling over his face as he listened intently to her father sitting next to him. *He looks so much like James when he does that.* Sam's admission on their way home to Francis Court earlier, that he was glad she wasn't romantically involved with Chef Seb anymore, had made her want to stop the car and jump out. *How does my thirteen-year-old son know what is being reported in the papers about my love life?*

Following a mild interrogation, it had turned out that his best friend Archie kept his finger on the pulse of gossip about the family (he was *TSP's* number one fan according to Sam) and had texted him the link to the most recent report five minutes after they'd published it. When she'd moved her focus from how Sam knew to why he'd felt that way, her son had admitted he'd thought Seb hadn't been friendly and had reminded her that Daisy didn't like him. "And Daisy normally likes everyone," he'd pointed out. Sam's take, unlike Fitzwilliam's unreasonable bias and her mother's snobbish prejudice, had been honest and had given her the most pause for thought. *But even if Seb is not the one for me, that doesn't make him a murderer!*

"Bea?" her mother hissed.

"I'm fine, Ma. It's just been a tiring day. And thank you, the *TSP* report was a helpful counterbalance." Her mother nodded and, with a brief smile, turned to the man on her left.

Lady Beatrice jerked as the woman sitting on her other side grabbed her arm. Looking down at the bony fingers gripping her, she was surprised at the strength with which the wrinkled hand of her maternal grandmother's cousin held on to her.

"I've not talked to you properly, my dear," the older woman said, her eyes a mass of creases as she smiled up at her. "It's been a while since I was last at Francis Court visiting your grandmother. I can't believe how much Sam has grown." She patted Lady Beatrice's arm. "And isn't he handsome?"

Lady Jane Vickers chuckled, a rich throaty sound, and Lady Beatrice couldn't help but smile at the woman, who at eighty-five still looked so elegant, her thinning grey hair piled high on top of her head.

"Well, *I* think so. But then I'm a little biased."

"Of course you are, my dear. That's a mother's job." Her liver-spotted hand still rested on Lady Beatrice's forearm, and she squeezed it. "And doesn't he look like his father? That must be a great comfort to you."

Was it? Lady Beatrice still found it hard to think about her late husband James without a mixture of emotions washing over her. Only twenty-four years old when he'd died, he would be forever young. His boyish good looks were the last physical memory she had of him, and yes, Sam was definitely his father's son to look at. But it was the emotional memories that she still struggled with. Trying to reconcile her kind and devoted husband with the man who had written that letter to her the day before he'd died, telling her he was leaving to be with Gill Sterling, the estate manager's wife…

"And he was such a lovely man." Lady Vickers's voice broke into her thoughts. "So thoughtful too. I'll never forget what he said to me when he handed me that cash donation on the day he died. 'Lady Jane,' he said, taking my hand, 'Please accept this to help your donkeys in Cyprus. I know they mean the world to you, and without your help, they would have such an awful life'.'' The old lady sighed. "So kind of him…" Her blue eyes filled up with tears, and she retrieved a lace handkerchief from the sleeve of her cobalt blue evening dress and dabbed at her eyes.

Lady Beatrice smiled. James had always had a soft spot for animals, and it was typical of him to… *Hold on.* "Did you say he gave you a cash donation on the day he died, Lady Vickers?"

"Yes, my dear. He slipped me an envelope as we finished up our committee meeting on that Tuesday. He was there representing your mother, if you remember. I opened it later when I got home, and there was ten thousand pounds inside!" She smiled and shook her head. "So kind…"

Lady Beatrice nodded, and hastily picking up her wine-glass, she took a sip, her mind a jumble of thoughts she couldn't quite control. *Ten thousand pounds cash… Gill depositing the same amount in cash into her bank just before the accident… the committee meeting in London the day he died… but if he didn't give that money to Gill Sterling, then…?* As the warmth of the red wine moved down her throat, she was grateful that Lady Vickers had turned to talk to the person on her other side, giving Lady Beatrice time to think.

She let her thoughts drift back to April when she'd discovered that James had taken the money out of his bank account a week before he'd died. So when Fitzwilliam had confirmed that Gill had had a substantial cash deposit made into her account around the same time, it had all fitted together, and they'd agreed that it had most likely come from James. *But now…* She frowned. If James had given that money to Lady Jane Vickers for her donkey rescue charity in Cyprus, then where had the cash come from that Gill had had in her bank account when she'd died? If James hadn't given it to her, then who had? *Should I tell Fitzwilliam?* As part of the original team who had investigated James's accident almost fifteen years ago, he'd been interested in her theory about what had happened between her husband and Gill Sterling, the woman who'd died in the car accident with him.

Would Fitzwilliam want to know about this fresh development? Did it change anything? She needed time to think...

34

LATER THAT EVENING, SUNDAY 4 OCTOBER

"Bea?"

Lady Beatrice looked up and realised Perry and Simon, sitting opposite her around the large wooden table in their kitchen, were looking at her expectantly.

"You were going to tell us how you got on with Fitzwilliam. Though by the look on your face, it didn't go very well," Perry said, picking up his wineglass and taking a sip from it.

Concentrate, Bea! Her mind had been turning over what she'd found out about James's donation earlier at dinner, and she was still unsure about whether it was significant or not. *Leave it for now, Bea.* She needed to focus on the current investigation, not on something that had happened all those years ago. Seb's reputation was on the line. He needed their help.

"Indeed. Sorry, I was miles away. So I told Fitzwilliam and Spicer about Marta's foraging, and they weren't aware of it. So hopefully that was helpful." She sighed. "But then it all took an unexpected turn."

Simon and Perry leaned closer as she took a sip of wine.

"And?" Perry huffed.

"And... Luca's laptop has gone missing from his hotel room, and now they're not so sure Luca's death was an accident."

Perry gasped and covered his mouth with his hand while Simon leaned back and rubbed his beard.

"Interesting," Simon said. "I assume they think someone has stolen it?"

Lady Beatrice shrugged. "That was the implication. Fitzwilliam didn't elaborate, and I didn't hang around to ask any more questions."

If only I kept my cool, I could've probably found out a lot more details. Heat concentrating on her cheeks, she took another sip of wine.

Perry frowned and tilted his head to one side. "So what did you do?"

"What do you mean?"

"Oh, come on, Bea. The look on your face says that you had another confrontation with Fitzwilliam."

She sighed and put down her wineglass. "He's just so judgemental! It turns out Seb was sous chef for Luca during the rehearsals, so now Fitzwilliam thinks *he* could've added the mushrooms to the dish. He had the audacity to imply Seb killed Luca! He's mad." Her heart rate rose as she remembered Fitzwilliam's comment about her wearing rose-tinted glasses.

"And?" Perry stared at her, his mouth slightly open.

"And..." She picked up her glass and took a fortifying slug of Merlot. "I might have told him that Seb wasn't a killer and I would prove it."

She looked down at the table as she carefully lowered her glass. *Did I go too far this time?* How were they going to prove anything when they had so little to go on? She raised her eyes and studied the two men in front of her. *Will they even help me?* After all, she'd been the one who had made the bold statement that she would prove it. Maybe this time they'd tell her no, that she was on her own. Could she blame them if they did?

After a few seconds, Simon reached for his phone and started typing. When he finished, he looked up. "Okay. So I've sent Steve a text asking him if they have any more info about the laptop. Perry, get a piece of paper. Let's write down everyone who could be a suspect."

Lady Beatrice's heart felt lighter. Of course, she should have known that Perry and Simon would help her. *I'm so lucky to have their unquestioning support.* She swallowed the lump that had risen in her throat.

As Perry jumped up from the table and headed towards a bureau in the far corner of the open-plan kitchen diner, Simon looked directly at her and smiled. "I think we should treat this as a murder investigation and see where that takes us. Okay?"

She smiled back and nodded. "Thank you."

He raised his glass to her and took a sip as Perry returned, notepad and pen in hand.

"Right," Simon said. "We need everyone who was around on the Monday that Luca ate the mushrooms. Let's start with Ryan, Finn, and Marta."

Perry scribbled down the names, then said, "We also need to add Fay, Luca's girlfriend. She was there, wasn't she?"

Simon nodded.

"Oh, and there's Ambrose Weir, Luca's agent," Lady Beatrice said.

"Talking of agents, Mal Cassan was also around and his PA Klara Damas," Simon told Perry, who wrote their names on the list. "Is that everyone?"

Lady Beatrice tapped her fingers on the table. "Um… oh yes. What about the production staff?"

"When I spoke to Steve yesterday, he told me all the production staff had been accounted for on Sunday and Monday. I think we can rule them out."

Perry turned, a grin spreading over his face. "So you talked to Steve about this yesterday, did you? So much for the 'let's leave it to the police and get on with our busy lives'."

Simon smiled sheepishly. "Well, I like to know what's going on…"

Lady Beatrice laughed. "Well then, that's everyone."

The smile on Perry's face disappeared. "Er, no," he said quietly.

Lady Beatrice frowned, mentally going through the list. Yes, that was everyone.

Perry scratched his neck and mumbled, "We haven't added Seb."

He can't be serious! Surely, Perry didn't think Seb had killed Luca…

35

FIRST THING, MONDAY 5 OCTOBER

Pulling open the large glass door of The Breakfast Room, Lady Beatrice followed Daisy into the warm restaurant. The smell of bacon and fresh bread enveloped them as they headed towards the table Perry had taken over at the end of the bank of large windows. The low sun beaming through the glass heated the room nicely, and Lady Beatrice removed her jacket, placing it over the back of a chair as she greeted Perry and sat down.

Perry peeked up from the edge of the large wooden table where he'd been stroking an excited Daisy, smiled, and pushed a large black coffee towards her. "I assumed you didn't want food?"

She shook her head. "It's too early for me; although that bacon smells delicious," she said, glancing at the half-eaten bacon roll in front of him.

"Well, hands off. It's mine. And I mean you too, Daisy," he said, addressing the little white dog, who was now leaning against his leg gazing up at his plate, her eyes full of hope.

Lady Beatrice laughed, and they chatted about their plans for the day. Perry wanted to return to Fenn House as he was expecting deliveries of fabric and paint for the next two sitting rooms, while Lady Beatrice agreed to stay at Francis Court and chase a video Mrs Kettley, the head housekeeper at Drew Castle, had promised them, showing the first two rooms they needed to design ahead of starting the project in the new year.

"I'll join you at Fenn House as soon as I've received it."

"Fine, then do you want to take this?" Perry asked, taking a white mobile phone from his pocket —their office mobile— and sliding it across the table. "I thought I'd better have it handy in case Mrs Kettley rings."

"Of course." She pocketed the phone, then lifted her cup to drain the last of her coffee as she looked at her watch. Almost eight-thirty. "In fact, this has saved me a trip to the office. I'll ring from my apartment. It's turned so cold today, I need to change into something warmer."

Lady Beatrice rose and signalled for Daisy to follow as she headed off in the other direction, towards the back entrance of the restaurant. This exit would lead her through a corridor and via The Salon into the Painted Hall and across to the staircase that gave her access to her apartment on the second floor. Approaching the door, she stopped as someone pushed it open from the other side. An attractive woman in her mid-forties emerged from behind the large wooden door.

"Ellie, what a nice surprise. I haven't seen you for ages." Lady Beatrice smiled at Francis Court's catering manager.

"Hello, your ladyship. Hello, Daisy." Ellie Gunn bent down and fussed Daisy, an enormous smile cracking her freckled face as Daisy attempted to lick her. "How are you getting on up at Fenn House, Lady Rossex?" she asked, standing up and pushing her dark-blonde fringe away from her eyes.

"Good, thank you. We've only four more rooms to do, and we'll have finished there."

"I read a visiting chef died there a few days ago. Mushroom poisoning or something. Is that right?"

"Indeed. A very sad business."

"Well, you have to be careful with mushrooms around here." Ellie shifted her weight to one side and placed one hand on her curvy hip. "Pete says the death caps in this area are everywhere right now, and if you don't know what you're doing, it's very easy to pick them up by mistake."

Lady Beatrice nodded. She had a soft spot for Pete Cowley, the ex-military head gardener at Francis Court, ever since she'd been involved in investigating the murder of Alex Sterling, the estate's manager, earlier on in the year. Pete was also the rumoured new love interest of Ellie's. Rumoured by Perry, that was.

Lady Beatrice liked Ellie. She'd been instrumental in helping her untangle some of the mystery surrounding Alex's wife's presence in her husband's car fourteen years ago. Ellie had been Alex's mistress before his wife had died, and she'd been with him the night he'd got the call to say Gill had been killed.

I hope the rumour that she and Pete are together now is true.

"Indeed. The police seem to think that's what happened," Lady Beatrice replied. They both started when they heard "Vogue" by Madonna playing faintly somewhere close by. Lady Beatrice looked around, as did Ellie, as they tried to figure out where the sound was coming from.

"Is it your mobile, my lady?" Ellie asked.

Lady Beatrice shook her head, glancing down at the phone she clutched in her hand.

"It seems to be coming from you somewhere..." Ellie pointed at her.

The office phone!

Lady Beatrice laughed and pulled it out of her pocket just as the noise stopped. "I completely forgot Perry gave me the office phone!" She looked at the screen. A missed call from *Mrs K HH Drew Castle*. A message popped up — there was a voicemail.

"Perry normally carries it around with him when we're off-site," she explained to Ellie. "As you can see, I get confused with more than one phone to keep track of. To be honest, I've always thought if you had multiple phones, you were up to no good."

Ellie laughed. "Like in television shows or movies? It's a burner phone because someone is selling drugs or black-mailing someone!"

Lady Beatrice nodded, grinning. "Or having an affair."

The smile on Ellie's face disappeared, and she frowned. *Bea, you dufus!* Ellie had been having an affair with Alex Sterling. *Have I touched a nerve?*

"Did you know that Gill Sterling had two phones?" Ellie said. "Alex was convinced she was having an affair."

Lady Beatrice's grin disappeared as her stomach flipped. Was that how Gill had communicated with James? She frowned. She didn't remember anyone saying at the time of the investigation that they'd found a second phone. Would Fitzwilliam know? Her stomach dropped. *Oh no!* Had he found the phone and read the messages? Her mouth dry, she cleared her throat as she shook her head.

"She denied it to him, of course," Ellie continued. "She said it was an Irish phone so she could talk to her mother. I don't think he believed her." She suddenly gasped and raised her hand to her mouth. "I'm so sorry, Lady Rossex. That was insensitive of me."

Of course, not just Ellie, but everyone assumed that Gill Sterling had been having an affair with her husband, their explanation as to why she'd been in the car with him when they'd both died. But it had all happened more than fourteen years ago. Would the speculation ever go away? Would the mention of her husband and his death ever not floor her like this? *Will I ever get used to this?*

Lady Beatrice shrugged. "There's no need to apologise, Ellie. It's all water under the bridge now." She smiled at Ellie, who looked up from staring at the floor and met her gaze, then returned the smile.

"Vogue" started up again, and this time, Lady Beatrice grabbed the phone immediately. It was the same number. "I'm really sorry, Ellie. I need to take this call."

Ellie Gunn smiled. "Of course, my lady. It was good to see you again." She turned and walked across the room. Watching her leave, Lady Beatrice pressed the call accept button.

36

EARLY MORNING, MONDAY 5 OCTOBER

Seb: *I'm sorry about my behaviour yesterday. Can we meet? I'm at Fenn House helping organise the equipment returns. Are you here? xx*

Bea: *Not at the moment, but I will be soon.*

Seb: *Can we have coffee? The catering tent is still open. xx*

Bea: *Yes. See you there in thirty minutes.*

"Now, Daisy." Lady Beatrice crouched down outside the entrance to the catering tent and addressed her little westie. "I need you to be nice to Seb, please."

Daisy, sitting on the ground, her tail wagging, tilted her head to one side.

"No growling or barking, all right?" She patted the little dog on the head as she gave her a treat. Then standing, Lady Beatrice took a deep breath and pulled the door open. Scanning the inside of the marquee, she spied Seb sitting in the far corner at a table for four, nursing a cup of coffee while staring at his phone. *Come on, Bea, you can do this.*

Seb turned and smiled as he saw her, then waved. She smiled back, and tugging on Daisy's lead, she weaved her way to him.

"*Bella*!" Seb stood up as she approached and held out his hands. As she was about to reach out, a low grumble came from Daisy.

Really, Daisy? Just this once, can't you pretend to like him?

Lady Beatrice moved around the table to avoid the little dog getting too close, and Seb sighed, letting his arms drop by his sides.

Lady Beatrice took the seat opposite him and, taking her jacket off, gave him an apologetic smile as she sat down. "Sorry, but Daisy—"

"Why did you bring her?" Seb muttered across the table to her. "You know how I feel about having dogs around where food is served."

Her hackles rising, she inhaled deeply through her nose and silently let her breath out. *If he carries on like this, he'll make it easier for me to end things.*

Seb pushed a takeaway cup towards her and smiled. "I got you a black coffee."

"Thank you." She took hold of the cup and lifted it to her mouth as they sat in silence.

This is awkward. She felt like they were strangers meeting on a blind date. "Um, so how are you doing?"

Seb huffed. "The police still insist that we all stay here

while they complete their investigation. I wish they would speed it up. My chefs have jobs to get back to, and I'm due to attend an industry awards dinner on Thursday evening. It's just so... inconsiderate of them. And they don't seem to be very clear about what they want from us. Last night, they asked me if I sampled the mushrooms during Luca's demonstration. How am I supposed to remember if I did or not? It was a week ago! Have they any idea how many dishes I've cooked since then?" He sighed heavily and grabbed his cup.

"Well, it's a murder investigation now. I imagine they need everyone close by in case they want to talk to anyone."

Seb gasped as his fingers let go of the cup in his hand, and it dropped onto the table. For a few seconds, it tottered on its base, swaying from side to side.

Lady Beatrice instinctively reached out and grabbed it, the hot cup warming her hand as she lifted it slightly off the table and set it down again.

Seb, meanwhile, appeared to be in a trance. His eyes were glazed over, and his mouth was slightly open. "Murder?" he mumbled as his eyes refocused, and he examined her face. Then he shook his head. "No, no, no," he said more forcefully. "You must have got it wrong. They didn't mention murder to me last night. It was an accident."

"It seems Luca's laptop has gone missing from his room and—"

"What's that got to do with anything?" Seb cried.

"They think it's suspicious. Can you think of any reason why someone would steal Luca's laptop?"

Seb shook his head. "I didn't even know he had one with him."

"Can you think of why someone would want to kill Luca?"

"Of course not. Everyone loved Luca. It's..." He trailed

off, then frowned. "Why are you still asking all these questions, *bella?* You're not the police."

"No, but I'm trying to—"

He held his hand up. "Luca's death was an accident. Let's
talk about something else."

If he cuts me off one more time, I'll... Swallowing her
words, she took a sip of her coffee and composed herself.
This was it. Now was the right time to tell him they were
over.

"I wasn't happy about what the press were reporting
yesterday, *bella*," he continued. He gave a dry laugh. "It said
our relationship is in trouble. Then *TSP* said a source close to
you said we were only casually dating. Tell me that's not true.
I know you said you wanted to slow things down a bit, but
we're still good, aren't we? You're still my little *bella*..." A
slow smile split his face, his white teeth contrasting against
his tanned skin. His blue eyes sparkled as he held her gaze.

Oh no, don't give me that look.

Her heartbeat quickened. He's so good-looking. She
broke away from his gaze and looked at the cup in her hand.
"Well, actually—"

"Because I think all we need is some more time alone
together. Like a holiday. We can put this business behind us
and look to the future. Our future."

He did it again! Her resolve hardened. "Seb! Please listen
to me and don't cut me off!" She raised her voice, and he
stared at her as if seeing her properly for the first time since
she'd arrived.

He closed his mouth. There was silence for a few
seconds, then she noticed his gaze had shifted to somewhere
over her shoulder. A smile spread across his face, and as she
turned around, two young women wearing T-shirts that all the
catering staff wore, stopped by the side of their table. One

hugged a copy of a hardback book to her chest and clutched a pen, while the other clasped a mobile phone.

"OMG, Chef Seb. Can we get a selfie?" the tall blonde asked, reaching out to touch his arm.

"And will you sign my copy of your cookbook?" her shorter darker friend added, sliding in close, her back to Lady Beatrice.

Is he really going to do this now?

He gave them a charming grin that took over his entire face. "Of course, ladies."

Obviously he is! And was it her imagination or had his voice got deeper and smoother?

Still smiling, he reached out and took the book and pen from the woman. "Who shall I make it out to?"

She giggled and gave him her name.

Watching him turn on his charm, it occurred to her that, as a famous chef and someone frequently in the public eye, he, like her, had a facade he hid behind much of the time. *Shouldn't that mean we understand each other better?* Until recently, she'd not seen much beyond that front. He'd been as charming with her as he was with these two fans right now. Attentive. Smiling. As if he wanted nothing more than to make her happy. It had been a heady combination for those first few weeks. Of course, she'd seen glimpses of the ambitious and purposeful chef underneath. After all, no one became as successful as him without a bucketful of talent and a razor-sharp focus. She'd even admired him for that drive and determination.

But since Luca's illness and subsequent death, that wall had come down, and she'd seen the other side of Seb. The childish, possessive, self-centred behaviour that led him to be rude to others and constantly shut them (and her) down.

She stifled a sigh. *Am I being too hard on him?* Should

she give him another chance?

Once Seb finished, he handed the now signed cookbook back. "Shall we do that photo now, ladies?"

They nodded, sniggering. Then standing on either side, they leaned down to crouch beside him so they could all fit in the photo.

As they stood up and said thank you, he pointed to himself and Lady Beatrice and said, "Do you want one with us as well?"

What? Lady Beatrice froze. *Surely he's joking?*

But he appeared to be serious. She glared at him. *How dare he offer me up like some bonus prize?*

She turned to the two women and shook her head. "Sorry, ladies, but now's not a good time."

They shrugged, and tittering to each other, they waved at Seb as they mooched off.

That's it! "What on earth—"

"Why did you do that? I—"

They stopped and stared at each other.

Daisy, who had been quietly snoozing under the table, began to grumble as she move to a sitting position, and Lady Beatrice patted her on the head to reassure her.

Suddenly, Seb's shoulders slumped, and he let out a deep sigh. "They're my fans, *bella*. Without them, I would be nothing."

"I get that, Seb. But I'm not here to be paraded around to increase your public visibility. I'm sorry, but it seems clear to me now that this won't work."

His blue eyes widened, and he spluttered, "You're going to end our relationship because I offered a photo of us with two of my fans?"

She shook her head. "Of course not. I just don't think we're suited. You love the attention, Seb. You're happy in the spotlight. It's not for me. I do it when it's required. When it's my duty. But in my private life, I want to be left alone."

"So that's it? That's what you want, is it?" Seb pouted.

"I'd like to stay friends, Seb. I like you; I really do. You're funny, talented, and smart. But we want a different type of life."

"But surely we can work it out?" His eyes gazed into hers, wide and pleading. He reached out to take her hand, but she moved her arms off the table.

She looked away as she shook her head. "I'm sorry."

"Can we at least have dinner tonight and talk about it?"

She looked up and studied his handsome face, hoping to feel something other than relief, but she didn't. "There's really nothing more to say, Seb."

He leaned back in his chair and slowly shook his head. There was silence between them, only broken when his phone vibrated. He picked it up from the table and rapidly typed a reply to the message he'd received.

"I need to find Klara, Mal's PA, to sign some papers."

She nodded. "I should be with Perry. We have deliveries coming in."

Their gazes met, and for a few moments, it felt to her as if time stood still. Then he nodded.

"Okay, *bella*. I understand. So let's be just friends for the moment. But please don't give up on us completely. You need time, so I'll give you time. Maybe once this is all over, you will see what a good team we make. I will hold on to some hope."

You can hold on all you want. She was sure she'd made the right decision. There was no point rubbing it in, though.

She smiled, and rising from her chair, she grabbed her jacket from the back and tucked her arms into it. Daisy stood, looking up at her mistress.

"I'll walk you out," Seb told her, rising. She nodded, and they slowly made their way to the door.

Five minutes later, when they stepped out of the tent, she was blinded by flashing lights.

Click, click, click.

"Lady Beatrice, this way!"

"Chef Seb, over here!"

Click, click, click.

Lady Beatrice's mind raced almost as fast as her heart was as she raised her hand to screen herself from the cameras.

What are they doing here? How did they get into an area that was off-limits to the public?

"Security!" Seb shouted as he took her arm and steered her left, away from the crowd jostling each other. Holding on tightly to Daisy's lead, she peeped under her arm and saw four security men rushing across the grass towards them.

Click, click, click.

"My lady, Chef Seb, over here!"

"Is it true you're about to propose, Seb?"

Click, click, click.

She heard rather than saw the kerfuffle as the security team arrived. When she looked up, they had already formed a barrier between her and the handful of press, blocking their view. She let Seb guide her away towards the nearest tent, and she breathed a vast sigh of relief when they were finally out of view. She immediately bent down and scooped up Daisy. "Are you okay, sweetheart?" she asked the little terrier in her arms. She laughed as Daisy licked her nose.

"Are you all right, *bella*?" Seb's voice was full of concern.

She gently put Daisy back on the floor and looked up at him, smiling. "Yes, I'm fine." Shuffling forward slightly, she peeped around the tent canopy to where they'd just come from. The security team was escorting the last few paparazzi to the exit of the grass enclosure. She sighed. Maybe security had become lax since the public were no longer on-site? Had those two women told the press she and Seb were in the catering tent before coming over and then waited around for her and him to come out? If she'd left on her own... *Thank goodness Seb was with me.*

"Thank you for rescuing us," she said as she turned around to face him.

He bowed slightly. "It was my pleasure." He held his arm out. "I'll walk with you to—"

Placing her hand on his arm, she shook her head. "There's no need. They've all gone now. I'm going to stay here and make a call. You go on, and thanks again."

He hesitated, his gaze searching her face. Returning his stare, she removed her hand and nodded.

Be resolute, Bea. Don't let his handsome face deter you.

He reached out to grab her hand. Daisy gave a low growl, and he dropped his arm by his side, giving a deep sigh.

She held his gaze. *Please, just go.*

Slowly shaking his head, Seb turned and trudged off.

Lady Beatrice let out her breath, then grabbing her mobile from the back pocket of her jeans, she found her mother's number.

Bea: *Are you free, Ma? The press somehow got on-site and have pictures of Seb and I. Need to do some damage limitation via* TSP *please. xx*

Ma: *Of course, darling. I'll ring you now. xx*

37

STILL MORNING, MONDAY 5 OCTOBER

Strolling across the gravel path on her way to Fenn House, Lady Beatrice let Daisy overtake her as she passed a bed chock-full of agapanthus growing in tufts with large white, pink, blue, and purple flowers on display. She was relieved to be away from the show area and in the safety of the grounds of her uncle's stately home. Her legs were still wobbly after her encounter with the press as she turned the corner at a low border of bedding plants. Their purple, red, and yellow flowers provided a welcome splash of colour, breaking up the evergreen bushes lining the path to the main house. Heading along the path, her mind churned over the phone conversation she'd just had with her mother.

"Well, darling, I don't think our rather veiled attempt to play down your relationship with the chef worked as well as we'd hoped. If they are still asking questions about a possible proposal, then I think it's time we are more direct and to the point."

"But, Ma, I don't want to upset Seb. He took it quite badly, and it feels like I'd be rubbing it in."

"Are things over between you?" her mother had asked bluntly.

"Yes, Ma."

The princess had let out a short *humph*. "And have you told him?"

"Yes, Ma."

"Good. So now that's done, it's time to move on."

HRH Princess Helen had not bothered to disguise her disapproval of her daughter's new relationship, but she'd never explained why. "Why do you dislike him so much?"

"I only met him a few times, darling, and he was very charming, so I didn't dislike him as such. I just didn't think he was right for you."

I may as well ask… "Why not?"

Her mother had sighed. "It's hard to be specific, Bea. You just didn't seem comfortable around him. Also, he didn't have much of a sense of humour, I noticed. When your father teased him about how Italian cooks use too much lemon, he took it seriously and pointed out why lemon is so important in cooking. It was just your father being your father. I'm never comfortable around people who cannot laugh at themselves. It shows a level of self-absorption that's unhealthy."

About to open her mouth to defend her ex-beau and point out that her father's sense of humour was very dry and not everyone got it, she'd hesitated, recalling an incident when she, Perry, and Simon had got the giggles during dinner one evening.

Perry had placed an order that afternoon with a company whose sales rep's name was Christopher Bacon.

"Wouldn't it be perfect if his middle name was Peter?" Perry had said. "And then he'd be Chris P Bacon."

The three of them had fallen about with laughter, but Seb had remained unmoved. At the time, she'd thought maybe the joke had got lost in translation with him, and so later, when they had been alone, she'd attempted to explain to him why it had been funny.

"Chris P Bacon," she'd said. "Like crispy bacon."

He'd given a dry smile. "Yes, *bella*, I understood the joke. I just don't see why it's so funny."

She'd crossed her arms. "It was just a bit of fun, Seb."

"You and Perry are always laughing and having fun." He'd air quoted 'having fun'. "I think you would get more work done if you didn't laugh so much."

She'd been mildly shocked. Yes, she and Perry had a laugh, but they also worked very hard. That's why she enjoyed her job so much. *Maybe Mother is right...*

"And," her mother had continued, "Daisy doesn't like him, and you know what they say about animals being good judges of character."

So everyone keeps telling me!

"Okay, Ma, I agree that maybe when the initial attraction waned, we weren't such a good match. But even so, I don't want to kick the man when he's down and to publicly dump him seems—"

"Beatrice Rose." Her mother had interrupted. She only used her daughter's full name when she was deadly serious. "If things are over between the two of you, then there's no point pussyfooting around. The press are ruthless, darling, and if you leave them in any doubt, then they will continue to badger you both relentlessly."

And of course, as always, her mother had been right. Shutting it down completely was the only way to get the press to drop it. *Seb will not be happy about it, but it's the best thing for both of us.*

The sound of Daisy's paws speeding up on the gravel drew her attention, and she looked up to see her little dog bounding towards a petite woman with straight blonde hair walking towards them.

Lady Beatrice hadn't seen Fay Mayer since Luca's death, and she felt a little on edge as the woman approached. *What do I say?* Fay stopped in front of Daisy and crouched down to pat the dog's head as Lady Beatrice caught up with them.

"Hello, Fay. I'm so sorry about Luca. How are you?"

The woman raised her oval-shaped face towards her and gave a wry smile. "I'm bearing up, thank you." She brushed down the bottom of her jeans and straightened up.

When Lady Beatrice looked closer at Fay's heavily made-up eyes, it wasn't hard to see the black puffy shadows beneath them. Knowing the heartache of losing a partner so young, Lady Beatrice smiled at the woman. "I know it's not much help right now, but it will get easier in time."

The woman nodded, then sighed. "I've been looking at the video I shot of Luca's rehearsal repeatedly, trying to make sense of what happened." She shook her head. "It was all so normal, just another show. No sign that it would be life changing for all of us."

There's a recording of the demo? *That will be useful.*

"Indeed." Lady Beatrice nodded. "We never know when something will come out of the blue and throw us off course."

Fay's brown eyes stared into hers, and she bit the bottom of her small pink lips. "You think you have it all under control and then…" She shrugged and looked down at the floor.

"I know this may sound like an odd request, Fay, but is there any chance I can get a copy of the video you took of the rehearsal?"

The woman's head jerked around, and she frowned. "Can I ask why?"

"Indeed. The police have it in their heads that Seb might be involved in Luca's death and—"

"That's silly," Fay jumped in. "Seb wouldn't accidentally pick death caps. He's an experienced forager, much more than Luca was."

"I know, and I'm trying to prove that to them. Watching the rehearsal again might help me."

"Well, then yes, of course." She held out her mobile phone. "Type in an email address, and I'll send it to you."

Lady Beatrice typed in the office email and handed it back. "While I've got you, is it true that Luca was about to fire Ambrose Weir as his agent?"

Fay nodded. "In fact, he attempted to do it on Sunday night."

Really? That might move Ambrose up to the top of their suspect list. "How did Ambrose take it?"

"To be honest, I don't think he really believed him. He told Luca that if he sacked him as his agent, then Luca would be walking away from the big deal that Ambrose was negotiating on his behalf with Mal, and the production company would find an alternative chef to host with Seb. His parting comment to Luca was that he should reflect carefully on what he wanted, and they would talk the next morning."

"And did they?"

Fay shook her head. "I don't think so. We didn't see Ambrose at breakfast at the hotel on the Monday morning, and what with the demo getting brought forward, there wasn't much time. Whether they caught up later on, I don't know. If so, Luca didn't mention it."

"Do you think Luca would have changed his mind about leaving Ambrose?"

Shrugging, she said, "Luca could be impulsive sometimes. Maybe the threat of losing the television job with Seb was enough to make him reconsider." She glanced at her watch. "I'm really sorry, your ladyship, but I have an appointment with the police, and I don't want to be late."

"Indeed. Well, I hope it goes well and thank you again for letting me have a copy of the rehearsal recording."

Watching Fay scurry off towards the old security block in the distance, Lady Beatrice continued walking to the main house. *So does that give Ambrose a motive to kill Luca? She shook her head. Surely a dead client isn't worth anything to an agent?* She'd have to check with Simon, who knew more about how these things worked than she did.

———

"Thank you for coming, Miss Mayer. I'm DS Spicer and this is DCI Fitzwilliam. I know this is a difficult time for you, so we'll try to be brief."

Detective Chief Inspector Richard Fitzwilliam stared out of the murky window of the cramped office in the old security block, happy to leave the pleasantries to his sergeant. He disliked this part of the job, the interviewing of suspects. No one told you everything. You needed to prise it out of them. *And it's painful.* People hid secrets. Sometimes they did it to protect others. Sometimes they thought what they knew wasn't relevant or important. They lied or omitted information for their own reasons, and often it took more than one interview to drag it out of them. And sometimes you never found out what they knew…

Turning away from the wall, he moved towards where Fay Mayer sat opposite Spicer around the rickety round table they'd inherited with the room. Fitzwilliam, preferring to perch on something rather than sit, moved over to the desk closest to them and leaned back, folding his arms across his chest.

I wonder what Miss Mayer knows but won't tell us today?

He cleared his throat. "Yes, thank you for agreeing to talk to us again, Miss Mayer. Can I start by asking you if you knew that Luca Mazza had a laptop with him?"

Fay nodded. "He took it everywhere he went."

"And when was the last time you saw it?"

Fay frowned. "Er, Thursday morning, I think. Luca was feeling much better, and after breakfast, he said he was going to look through his recipes one more time before the demo."

"And you haven't seen it since?"

She blushed and looked down at her hands. "Er, no."

She's hiding something already. Let me guess... "Were you sharing a room at the hotel with Mr Mazza, Miss Mayer?"

Fay's eyes opened wide, and she stared at him for a few seconds, then she hung her head. "No," she muttered. Lifting her chin, she said, "I had editor deadlines to meet, and Luca gets... I mean got... quite strung up when he was doing anything live with an audience. We thought it best to have separate rooms so as not to disturb each other."

Fitzwilliam uncrossed his arms and lifted his hand to rub his chin. Of course, they'd already found out about the separate rooms from the information the hotel had given them. *But there's more to this. I'm sure of it.* He'd come back to it later. "So can you now take us through your movements on the Monday Mr Mazza took ill, please?"

The woman coughed, and Spicer poured her a cup of water from the jug in the middle of the table. With shaky hands, Fay Mayer picked up the half-full plastic cup and raised it to her lips. Returning it to the table a few seconds later, she clasped her hands together and laid them in her lap.

"Er, well, Luca and I had breakfast together at the hotel that morning. Luca left with Seb and one of the producers just before nine to get on-site early, but I stayed behind to pack as I was leaving to go back to London later that evening."

"So what time did you arrive on-site, Miss Mayer?"

She took another sip of water. "Just before ten, I think."

"And then what did you do?"

"Um, I had a quick look around the site and grabbed a coffee at one of the stands. I got a message from Luca to say that his rehearsal was being brought forward, so I went to watch it."

"Did anyone see you?"

She shrugged. "I don't know. Maybe the people at the coffee stall might remember me?"

Fitzwilliam nodded. "Can you give us the name of it then, please?" Fay Mayer turned to Spicer and gave her the details. "And did you notice anything unusual during Luca's demonstration?" Fitzwilliam continued.

She shook her head.

Come on, give me something to work with! He suppressed a huff and instead placed a hand over his mouth and coughed.

"Was he nervous, excited, distracted? Any different from normal?" Spicer pressed.

Thank you, Tina...

Fay shook her head again. "He seemed his usual self. Luca is... I mean, was... a showman. He came alive when he had an audience in front of him, so the rehearsal was a bit flat, but no different to others I've watched. He was more concerned about getting the timing right than anything else."

Tina Spicer stopped scribbling and asked, "And did he taste the food as he was cooking it?"

"Yes. Luca took his cooking seriously. He treated anything he cooked as if he was serving it in his restaurant."

Fitzwilliam shifted his weight, stretching out one leg in front of him. "Sebastiano Marchetti acted as his sous chef, didn't he?" Fay nodded. "Did he taste the food?"

She shrugged. "I wasn't watching Seb, sorry."

I bet he didn't... I wish I could prove it though... "And what did you do after the rehearsal?"

"I left to return to the hotel. I had a virtual meeting to attend."

"And Luca, what did he do?"

She hesitated, then shrugged. "I think he was meeting up with one of the other chefs."

"Do you know which one?"

Fay blinked rapidly, then looked away and shook her head.

Now why don't I believe you? He glanced at Spicer and raised an eyebrow. She nodded and made a note.

Spicer looked up from her notebook. "And did Luca say what he'd been doing that morning before the show?"

Fay shook her head. "We talked about how the demo had gone. He thought he needed to shave some time off the cooking section so he could interact more with the crowd. He was going to talk to Ryan about it later."

Fitzwilliam's brain just had time to register a brief smile that had flashed across her face, before it was gone. *There's something not right here. But what?* Before he could stop himself, Fitzwilliam puffed out a long breath. *Blast!* He tried to cover it up by raising his hand to his mouth and yawning, but if the look on Spicer's face was anything to go by, it clearly hadn't helped.

Spicer cleared her throat, and Fay Mayer's attention shifted from him and back to the sergeant, who flicked back a few pages in her notebook. "In your previous statement to

Fenshire CID, you said that Luca hadn't mentioned to you that he'd been foraging while he was here. Is that correct?"

Fay nodded. "Luca wasn't a big fan of foraging, although he did it when he had to. You know, if Seb asked him to or if he was filming. But most of the time, he delegated it if he could."

"Thank you. Can you remember what time Luca returned to the hotel on that Monday?"

"It was about six, I guess. I was in a meeting when he got back, so he went to his room to have a shower. Then we went to dinner in the restaurant." She paused and swallowed before grabbing the water in front of her and taking a sip. "Sorry," she said to Spicer. "It's just so strange to think that he'd already been poisoned by that stage. He didn't seem any different."

"Did he say what he'd been doing all afternoon, Miss Mayer?" Fitzwilliam asked.

She shook her head.

Really? There's something wrong here. His instincts and experience told him that Fay was hiding something about her and Luca's relationship, and he was determined to get to the bottom of it. "How long were you and Mr Mazza together, Miss Mayer?"

Spicer's shoulders tensed. She was always telling him he was too forward. *I should probably let her handle this.* But he was growing impatient. *I haven't got time for this pussy-footing around.* It was a murder enquiry, and this woman was a prime suspect.

"About a year."

"And you're considered a power couple in the food world, I understand?"

She nodded. Spicer stared at him, frowning. *Don't worry. This is going somewhere.*

"And how would you describe your relationship with Mr Mazza?"

Fay Mayer winced, and as she glanced at him, he held her gaze. *Come on, tell me the truth. You know you want to…*

"Em, we were good friends," she stuttered.

"So you weren't in love then?"

Bright pink spots appeared on Fay's cheeks, and she looked down at the floor. "Luca and I had an arrangement," she muttered.

Ah. Now we're getting somewhere. "And what exactly does that mean, Miss Mayer?"

Her shoulders slumped, and she let out a deep sigh. "It means we were both seeing other people, but as far as the press and public were concerned, we were still together. We didn't want to make things difficult for the organisers of the show…" She trailed off as she pulled herself up straight in her chair.

Well, that wasn't what I expected.

"And how long had you and Mr Mazza been in this arrangement?"

"For a few months now. Look, we've always been great friends first and foremost. It just turned out that we didn't love each other, not in that way. But our relationship was good for both of our careers and there was so much advance publicity about the show and us both being involved in it together that we decided we would keep it quiet until after it was over. I still cared about him…" Pools of tears had formed in the bottom of her brown eyes and threatened to spill down her face at any moment.

Fitzwilliam shifted and looked over at Spicer. *Help!*

"Yes, of course, Miss Mayer. We understand." Spicer leaned over and topped up the empty cup in front of Fay. Fay gave her a watery smile and took a large gulp.

"Did anyone else know about this arrangement? I mean that you and Luca were no longer together romantically?" Spicer asked in a gentle voice.

Fay shook her head. "Only the other two people involved."

"And they are?" Fitzwilliam barked, no longer able to hold it in.

She swallowed loudly as a crimson tide climbed her neck. "Ryan Hawley and Marta Talaska-Cowley."

38

MID-MORNING, MONDAY 5 OCTOBER

The Society Page online article:

BREAKING NEWS Lady Beatrice and Chef Seb Call it a Day on Their Romance

A source close to Lady Beatrice (36), the Countess of Rossex, has confirmed that the reported relationship between her and Sebastiano Marchetti (38), known to his army of fans as Chef Seb, is over for good. Despite pictures that surfaced earlier this morning of the couple together at Fenn House in Fenshire, the source reiterated that their 'so called romance' was never as serious as the popular press made out, and the two remain firm friends.

Lady Beatrice has been offering her support to the chef following the death of his colleague and friend, Luca Mazza, who tragically died two days ago.

Lady Beatrice stared out of the large window, three panes high, watching the grey clouds roll across the sky, threatening rain. Not that it would matter so much now. The last of the stalls was being packed up over at the show area, the owners surely relieved that they'd survived the whole four days of the festival without their customers getting wet. She had no intention of going back that way anytime soon. Her encounter with the press had seen to that.

Hearing a gentle snore coming from behind her, she turned away from the window and saw, across the bedroom, Daisy curled up next to Lady Beatrice's jacket on the bare four-poster bed, her furry body rising and falling as she slumbered. Lady Beatrice sighed. *Oh, Daisy!* She knew she should wake her up and move her off the furniture, but the little dog looked so peaceful, she didn't have the heart to disturb her. *Where's Perry anyway?* She looked beyond the bed towards the soon-to-be sitting area where Perry perched on a plastic covered two-seater sofa, staring at a fabric brochure. Except, Perry wasn't turning the pages or indeed even moving his head. He was the stillest she'd ever seen him.

"Perry?" she called softly as she walked across the room, the sound of her footsteps bouncing off the rug-free wooden floorboards and up into the high ceilings where they echoed back down into the room.

"Eh?" Perry looked up at her with dazed eyes, as if she'd woken him up way too early in the morning and his brain had yet to start functioning.

"Are you all right? You look like you've been struck by the *immobulus* charm."

He wrinkled his brow, his blue eyes staring into hers, a look of confusion on his face.

"You know, like in *Harry Potter*?"

Nothing.

"They use it to stop something dead in its tracks?"

Why am I doing this? "Never mind. You looked frozen in time is what I'm trying to say. Is everything okay?"

"Simon thinks I'm irresponsible and would make a dreadful father!" he blurted out.

What? She hurried to the sofa and flopped down next to him, feeling herself slide slightly as she landed on the polythene. "Why? What did you do?" she asked, crossing her legs and resting her hands in her lap.

"I didn't *do* anything. It was what he thought I was going to do that's the problem."

"Indeed. So what did he think you were going to do?"

Perry huffed, lifting his fingers up to his temple and rubbing it. "He thought I was going to give Sam a glass of neat gin! How can he think I would do something like that?"

What? "When was this?" The covering made a crackling sound as she moved around, and she placed her hands on either side of her on the couch.

"Yesterday, when we were wandering around the stalls. I was at the fruit gins counter, and Sam asked what I was doing. I held up half a cup for him to smell. It was cherry flavour and smelt lovely. And suddenly, Simon grabbed it out of my hand and told me off for trying to get Sam drunk."

Lady Beatrice tried to suppress a smile tugging at the corners of her mouth.

"I tried to explain, but he didn't give me a chance." Perry stuck his bottom lip out.

"But I thought you didn't want children, anyway. So what's the issue?"

Perry looked down and scuffed his feet on the floor. "I don't. But what if Simon does?" He turned to face her. "You've seen how good he is with Sam. It makes him so happy. He'd be a great dad."

She reached over and placed her hand on his arm. "Maybe. But that doesn't mean he wants to be one."

Perry covered her hand with his and sighed. "He let slip a couple of years ago that one reason he got married was to, and I quote, 'settle down and have a family'."

She squeezed his hand. "But that's just a phrase, Perry. You need to talk to him about it."

Pulling his hand away, he turned to face her, his eyes wide. "And what happens if he says yes, he wants children?"

"Then you'll talk about it. Come on, Perry. You and Simon are a team. You'll figure it out."

They will, won't they? Her stomach felt rock hard all of a sudden. *Of course they will.*

Perry pressed his lips together, then looked away. "I guess so," he mumbled. His phone beeped. Picking it up, he read the message. "Simon's editorial meeting has finished. He asks, are we going back to Francis Court and if so, shall we meet for coffee and discuss the case?"

The case! She'd been so wrapped up in the thing with Seb and then Perry's worries, she'd forgotten about reporting back to them on her conversation with Fay. She jumped up, making Daisy wake with a start. "Yes, come on. I could do with a coffee anyway."

"Thank you, Nicky." Simon smiled at the Breakfast Room server as she deposited their coffees and a plate of goodies on the table in front of them.

"Chef Hutton says these need eating up." She pointed to the pile of miniature pastries, macaroons, and biscuits in front of them. "He's been practicing for an afternoon tea event the princess is hosting tomorrow afternoon, and he has these left over." She looked around the empty restaurant. "As you're the only ones in here, it falls to you."

"Well, we'll do our best," Perry said as he picked up one of the treats and popped it into his mouth. "Oh my giddy aunt, that is delicious."

"And this is for Daisy." Nicky placed a plate of strips of carrot and chunks of cucumber in front of Lady Beatrice, then bent down to pat the little dog on the head.

"Thank you," Lady Beatrice said to Nicky's retreating back as she picked up a piece of cucumber and gave it to Daisy.

Simon distributed their drinks and, turning to Lady Beatrice, said, "So how are you holding up, Bea? All the papers seem to have picked up on the *TSP* report about you and Seb being over."

Perry picked up his latte and took a sip. "We got papped arriving at the main gates. It was crazy," he told Simon, his eyes shining bright.

"I'm doing fine. It was me who instigated the report via Ma anyway, so I was prepared for the fuss. But are you okay about it, Simon? I know he's your friend, and I don't want to make things awkward between the two of you."

"All that matters is that you're all right," he said, picking up his cappuccino. "Seb's a great guy and no doubt our paths will cross again, but now the show is over, my agent has made it very clear to me I've got to concentrate on my writing." He raised his eyebrows and grinned.

"I'm hoping Seb and I can remain friends." Raising a large black coffee to her lips, she took a sip. "But either way, I still want to prove he had nothing to do with Luca's death."

Simon and Perry nodded in agreement, and she told them about her conversation with Fay.

"Has a copy of the video arrived yet?" she asked Perry.

He scrolled through the emails on the office mobile and shook his head.

"Okay. We'll give her a little longer, and if it's still not arrived, I'll chase her up. I really think it will be worth a look at. Did CID Steve have anything to add about the laptop theft?"

"Only that they know it disappeared sometime between Thursday when they took Luca to hospital and Friday mid-morning. I've also spoken to Roisin. They didn't find any fingerprints in Luca's room other than the maid's. Which is odd as Luca's should have been in there too. They have therefore concluded that whoever took the laptop must have wiped the room clean of prints."

"So they're sure someone stole it?" Perry asked.

Simon nodded. "And therefore, their theory that someone deliberately poisoned Luca seems to make more sense now."

"But surely, Luca's death and the stolen laptop could be unrelated?" Perry said. "Someone might have simply taken it when they realised he was in the hospital."

"Yes, you're right, it's possible." Simon agreed. "But the police don't like coincidences. They think the two incidents are linked. I don't know if they know something we don't. Steve can only tell me so much. But for now, it makes sense for us to update our list of suspects and look at means, motive, and opportunity. That will at least help us focus on who to talk to next." He retrieved a piece of paper from his jacket pocket, and unfolding it, he laid it out in front of them. "This is the list you wrote, Perry."

"So who's first?" Lady Beatrice asked, putting down her coffee and feeding Daisy a piece of carrot.

Perry leaned over. "Ryan Hawley."

"Well, we know he had an opportunity. He could have

easily added death caps to the prepped mushrooms at any time, and we only have his word that he ate some for breakfast. He also had means—he forages and could have gone off either the night before or that morning to collect them," Simon said.

"What about a motive?" Lady Beatrice asked. "Didn't you say he'll be stepping into Finn's old job as head chef at *The Flyer*? Is that a big enough incentive, do you think?"

Simon shrugged. "It's a significant promotion, but I don't know if he would kill for it."

"I imagine Finn is similar in terms of opportunity and motive. He could have gone foraging at any time too, and they prepped together in the same kitchen before going to their respective tents," Perry said as he looked at the next name on the list. "But what about means? Could he have got death caps into Luca's mushrooms without Ryan being aware of it?"

"It seems unlikely, but I don't think we can rule it out," Simon said as he placed his finger on the paper. "Marta is next. We know she went foraging on Sunday, so she's up there with means, and again, like the others, she was in the kitchen while they were prepping, so she may have had an opportunity as well. And we know she had a relationship of sorts with Luca." He shook his head. "But I've spent a lot of time with her over the last week, and I just don't believe she could kill someone."

Lady Beatrice nodded. *I like her too.* "I want to talk to her again and see if I can get a better understanding of her and Luca's relationship."

"Okay. So let's consider Fay next. She seems devoted to Luca, so I can't imagine a motive. She was around on Sunday night and Monday morning, so she had an opportunity, although I think someone would have seen her if she was hanging around the kitchens. Does she know anything about poisonous mushrooms, do you think?"

"She's a food critic, so she knows about food," Perry added.

Lady Beatrice frowned. "I know this might sound a bit odd, but something she said to me earlier is bugging me. I just can't work out why."

Perry leaned in. "What did she say?"

"She was talking about watching the video of the rehearsal, and she said she'd no idea it would be 'life-changing for us all'."

"And?" Perry grabbed a miniature cinnamon bun. "Is that it?" he asked, popping it into his mouth.

"Yes, sorry. I don't know why, but something about that made me think it was odd."

Simon frowned. "I think it's the word 'all'. If she just meant her and Luca, she would have stopped at the word 'us'. So who else was she referring to?"

Perry wiped something sticky from the side of his mouth. "I think you're both overthinking it. She probably meant his family or Seb and the other chefs. It doesn't sound strange to me."

Lady Beatrice shrugged. "Indeed. I'd still like to talk to her again though."

Simon looked back down at the list. "So now we have Ambrose Weir to consider. We have confirmation that Luca tried to fire him on Sunday night, but we're not sure if he followed through with it. And why was Ambrose still here Monday morning? Was it so he could kill Luca for depriving him of future earnings?"

Perry shook his head. "I think it's more likely he hoped Luca would change his mind. It seems to me, from what Fay said, that Luca had more to lose from ending their relationship than Ambrose did."

Lady Beatrice took another sip of coffee. Hadn't Seb told her and Simon that it was him, not Luca, that the television producers wanted? "Ambrose and Mal would probably have just given the producers of the television show another option, and Luca would have lost out," she suggested.

Simon nodded. "And we know Ambrose has been talking to Finn. That could've been his backup plan. I think one of us needs to talk to him and find out if Luca got back to him on Monday. Plus, we know nothing about his means and opportunity."

Lady Beatrice and Perry nodded.

"And finally, we have Mal Cassan and his PA Klara." Simon shrugged. "I don't know if either of them had a motive to want Luca dead. I can't think of anything, can you?"

Perry frowned. "Didn't Mal tell us that Luca was being difficult about the terms of the television show he and Seb were being offered and it might jeopardise the negotiations?"

Simon's eyes widened. "Yes. Well remembered. I suppose that could be a motive."

"And what about Klara?" Perry asked.

"I know nothing about her, to be honest," Simon replied. "We need to speak with her."

"So that just leaves Seb," Lady Beatrice said, looking up from the paper.

Simon and Perry darted a glance in her direction.

"It's okay," she said. "He's on the list for a reason. We know he had means. He's an experienced forager, so would know death caps and what they can do. He was also around the kitchens all morning, *and* he was Luca's last-minute replacement as sous chef. So he had the opportunity. But no motive that I know of. Luca was a close friend of his. I can't believe he would want to hurt him."

Simon nodded. "Well, let's park Seb for the moment. After all, he's the reason we're investigating this murder. So, Bea, you're going to talk to Marta and Fay. I'll try to contact Mal and meet up with him today. I might be able to catch Ambrose too. Perry, do you think you could turn your charm on Klara? And that just leaves Finn and Ryan." He looked at Perry.

Perry shook his head. "I don't think Finn likes me. How about I talk to Ryan instead?" He looked innocently at Simon, but his leg bounced under the table opposite her. *Cheeky!*

Simon smirked. "Okay, lover boy. You take Ryan, and I'll talk to Finn."

Perry blushed, then reaching over the table, he plucked the last pastry from the plate and popped it into his mouth. "Off to Fenn House again we go," he said through a mouthful of mini croissant.

39

LATE MORNING, MONDAY 5 OCTOBER

"Thanks for agreeing to meet with me, Marta." Lady Beatrice smiled at the young woman sitting opposite her in the all-glass Garden Cafe on the Fenn House estate. "And sorry for the whole disguise thing." She indicated the black wig and large blue-framed clear glasses (sunglasses were no longer appropriate since the recent change in weather) she was sporting. "It's the only safe way I can be out in public at the moment."

Marta nodded, her long dark brown hair falling over one side of her face. "Yes, I can imagine," she said, tucking it behind her ear. "The press is camped out at the hotel at the moment. Poor Seb is being hounded by them." She stopped and raised her hand to her mouth. "I'm so sorry," she said, removing it slowly. "It must be awful for you too. Are you okay?"

Lady Beatrice nodded. "Yes. I'm fine." *I really am.* "It's sad that we weren't able to make it work, but we're still friends. The press will get bored soon enough and move on to the next big thing."

It was funny how it was bothering her much less than it

would have done six months ago. Back then, the kind of press attention she was receiving now would have had her locked away in her room, praying for the swarm of paparazzi to leave Francis Court and find someone else to torture. But now, even though she'd had to drive through a hoard of them when she'd left Francis Court earlier and another smaller but still determined group when she'd entered the Fenn House estate only a short while ago, here she was (admittedly in disguise) in a (not very busy) public place and she was (just about) fine with it. *I've made progress!* Maybe her mother was right. Having some say over what was being said about her made her feel more in control and less at their mercy. *Who am I fooling?* Of course her mother was right. She always was!

"So you wanted to ask me a few questions?" Marta asked, picking up a beautifully decorated Burleigh pottery teapot and pouring tea into a delicate China cup in front of her.

The Garden Cafe was too smart and expensive to attract the everyday tourist. It was mainly used by local ladies who lunched and those treating themselves or their friends to a special afternoon tea, prepared by the renowned pastry chefs who worked at Fenn House. Lady Beatrice, who had been fortunate enough to taste their amazing delights when she'd been to tea with her aunt and uncle, could see why people were prepared to make the effort to travel to Fenshire and pay the seemingly extortionate prices to sample the same food as the king and queen.

"Yes." Lady Beatrice pushed the plate of exquisitely presented home-made biscuits towards Marta. "Please help yourself. Um, yes. Forgive my curiosity, but when we spoke yesterday afternoon, I felt you weren't being completely honest with me about your relationship with Luca." She held up her hand before Marta answered. "I know it's none of my business. But I just want you to know that I'm trying to help. The police are treating Luca's death as deliberate rather than accidental, so information that wasn't so important before could now be vital to protect the innocent and help find his killer."

Marta gave a sharp intake of breath and stared at Lady Beatrice, her large green eyes wide open. *Have I laid it on too thick?* As Lady Beatrice met her gaze, Marta's eyes filled up with tears. *Oh no, please don't cry.* Then Marta took a deep breath, appearing to get hold of her emotions. *Come on, Marta. Talk to me…*

Marta smiled sadly at Lady Beatrice. "You're right. I didn't tell you the complete truth. But now…" She shrugged. "I think I have no choice. It's a serious matter."

Lady Beatrice nodded encouragingly, and Marta continued, "Luca and I were best friends and lovers until about a year ago. My husband is very kind, but he's much older than me. He understands I want to be with someone my own age, so he indulges me as long as I am —how do you say— discreet? But we have a deal — whatever happens, I will remain his wife and not leave him."

She picked up her teacup and took a sip before putting it down again. "Luca wanted more, but I couldn't give him what he wanted." Shaking her head, she sighed. "It was a difficult decision, but we finally agreed he needed to move on. When he met Fay, I was happy for him. But it was hard for us to work together every day, so I asked Seb to move me to another of his restaurants."

She shrugged. "Everyone thought Luca and I had fallen out, and we were happy for people to believe that." She looked down at her hands clasped together on the table. "It was hard, and we missed each other. But being with Fay brought a lot of good press for both of them, so even though they realised after a while that they weren't in love, they stayed together for the sake of their careers."

Oh my gosh. Lady Beatrice frowned. Fay had played the devoted girlfriend so well...

"Don't misunderstand me, my lady. They made a good couple, and they really cared about each other. But it wasn't enough. About two months ago, Fay met someone else. She and Luca agreed they would officially stay together until after the show as all the advance publicity had been done and they didn't want the show to be overshadowed by their relationship. Seb had worked so hard to get it up and running and to include us all. We felt we owed it to him."

"We?"

Marta nodded. "Luca and I got back together not long after Fay had told him about her new love interest."

"And did she know about the two of you?"

Marta nodded. "And so did Ryan, her new man."

Ryan? Not Ryan...

"Yes, Ryan Hawley."

Lady Beatrice gasped, and grabbing her teacup, she took a gulp of Earl Grey. *How complicated!*

Marta slumped in her seat as if someone had suddenly drained her of all energy. She looked up at Lady Beatrice, her eyes brimming with unshed tears. "Today is the day that Fay and Luca were going to announce their relationship was over. Then, after a few weeks, she was going to be spotted with Ryan."

"And you and Luca?"

She rubbed under her eyes and sniffed. "He accepted I wouldn't leave my husband, but nonetheless, we loved each other. We were going to carry on and try to make it work."

Her eyes itching, Lady Beatrice reached out and took Marta's hand in hers. "Marta, I'm so sorry for your loss."

Marta met her gaze and gave her a weak smile. "Thank you. I know you have known loss too. It is kind of you to think of me."

They sat silently for a few minutes, then Marta took away her hand and refilled her cup. After taking a sip, she said solemnly, "I would like to know how Luca died."

Lady Beatrice nodded. "Indeed. I will do everything I can to help you. So is there anything more you can tell me?"

Marta put her cup down and leaned forward. "Well, I know Luca didn't go foraging on Monday morning as I was with him from when he finished his prep to when he received the message from Seb about the producers bringing his rehearsal forward."

That's useful to know.

"What about his laptop? Did you know he had one with him?"

Marta nodded. "Yes. It was in his room. It was me who told the police it was missing."

"And when did you notice it had disappeared?"

"He was using it while he was ill. He said he was writing his life story." She shrugged. "Anyway, it was there on Thursday morning for sure. I popped in to see him before I left for the show, and he was going to meet Fay for breakfast. They were in separate rooms at the hotel. He was using it then. I went to his room to pick up some things for him on Friday morning before I went to the hospital, and it wasn't where he'd left it. But I was in such a panic, I didn't really register it at the time. But later, I went back. I wanted his room to be tidy as his family were arriving, and that's when I couldn't find it."

Lady Beatrice picked up her cup. So Luca's laptop had disappeared while he'd been in the hospital. She took a sip of tea. Had someone been worried that with Luca not around, someone else (Fay? Marta?) would have access to it? Or, had they known that Luca wasn't going to survive and needed to dispose of whatever was on it that was incriminating before the police searched Luca's room? She put down her cup. She would talk to Perry and Simon about it when they caught up with each other at lunchtime.

40

A SHORT WHILE LATER, MONDAY 5 OCTOBER

Lady Beatrice hugged her jacket around her as she walked away from the Garden Cafe and headed towards Fenn House. She shivered. The threat of rain had subsided, but it had left a damp feeling in the air. Turning a corner, she recognised Fay Mayer walking towards her.

"Hello, Fay." Lady Beatrice stopped in front of the blonde woman and smiled. "How did it go with the police?"

"Okay, I think." Fay Mayer looked around their feet. "Where's your little dog?"

Lady Beatrice laughed. "I've just been to the Garden Cafe up by the visitors' centre. It's much too smart to let Daisy loose in there."

Fay grinned. "Yes, I've heard it's very posh. Ry... er, a friend has promised to take me there for their famous afternoon tea if we get stuck here much longer."

"Ryan? Is that Ryan Hawley who is going to take you?" Lady Beatrice held her breath. *Will she admit it to me now, or will I have to prise it out of her?*

Fay tilted her head to one side, her gaze holding Lady

Beatrice's. Lady Beatrice let her breath out silently through her nose and gave Fay a tentative smile.

"You know then?" Fay asked.

Lady Beatrice nodded. "Sorry."

"Marta or Ryan?"

"Marta. We've just had tea together, and she opened up to me."

Fay shrugged. "Well, I've already told the police, so I suppose it was only a matter of time before it came out. At least it means they've knocked me off their list of suspects. Ryan and I were together Monday morning until he got called off to collect the fish with Finn."

"And does that clear Ryan too?"

Fay frowned. "I don't know. The police didn't say. But Ryan and Luca were friends."

"There was no jealousy between the two of them over you?"

Fay smiled. "Luca was in love with Marta. In fact, I think he never really stopped loving her. When we met, he tried so hard to move on, but his heart wasn't really in it. And when I realised I wasn't falling in love with him either, we moved forward on a business-like basis. As a food industry 'power couple'"—she air quoted 'power couple'—"we worked well together and both benefitted. It was only when I fell for Ryan that we agreed to end things." She shifted her weight and put a hand on one of her slender hips. "To be honest, I think Luca was relieved. It gave him an excuse to get back in touch with Marta and persuade her to take him back." She shook her head. "So you see, Ryan would have no desire to hurt Luca on my behalf. He already had me. Did you know he ate some of the mushrooms for breakfast just before he came to see me? So whoever added the death caps must have done it after that."

Looks like both Fay and Ryan are in the clear then. Then she recalled something Marta had said about Luca writing while he'd been ill. "Were you aware Luca was writing his life story on his laptop?"

Fay frowned. "I'm not sure. I know Ambrose said something to him about maybe doing an autobiography, but at the time, Luca said he wasn't interested. He did collect a lot of recipes and write them down." She grinned. "He had a document on his laptop which he called 'idea brillante' and at all times of the day and night, when he was seized with a good idea, he would add to it." Suddenly, the smile slipped from her face and was replaced with a grave expression. Tears welled up in her brown eyes.

Please don't start crying on me! "Are you all right, Fay?" Lady Beatrice whispered.

Fay swallowed twice, then nodded. "Sorry, it reminded me of when Luca was in hospital on that first day. He was so restless and drifting in and out of consciousness. He kept saying Marta's name and grabbing my hand. I felt so bad, but Marta couldn't come too often as the press were camped outside, and she was worried…"

She took a deep breath, then continued, "Anyway, there was this one time Luca suddenly jumped up and cried Seb's name. Seb wasn't there. He'd gone to get us both a coffee. So I explained to him Seb had gone but would be back soon, and he looked like he was going to settle down quietly, but then he grabbed my hand and started rambling about secret things and how he'd written it all down. Then he told me I must tell someone. Then he said Seb's name again, and just before he lost consciousness, he shouted a random string of words to me — calamari, lobster, perch, ricotta, peas, and then he asked for a coffee."

A coffee? *That's so Italian.*

"Well, at least that's what I thought he said. But thinking about it, he probably said *cosa* not *costa*, and that's Italian for 'what', so I guess that makes more sense." She shook her head slowly. "Anyway, it was all very strange."

"Indeed, I can imagine. So do you have any idea what he was trying to tell you?"

Fay gave a short laugh. "None. But when I told Seb later, he seemed to think it was a recipe given the word for recipe in Italian is *ricetta*, and that sounds a lot like ricotta to me. He thought Luca was trying to tell me about an important recipe he wanted Seb to have."

"Did you tell the police, Fay?"

"No." The woman shook her head. "To be honest, I forgot all about it until now. Luca was just rambling. I agree with Seb. It was probably just a secret recipe or something. My Scottish grandmother swore she wasn't giving up her ginger shortbread recipe." She sighed. "That is... I mean, it was just like Luca to be thinking about recipes when he was dying." She gave a little huff and straightened up, looking at her watch as she did. "I'm really sorry, my lady, but I'm supposed to be meeting with Luca's family back at the hotel."

Lady Beatrice nodded. "Indeed. You need to go then. Oh, just a quick reminder that you were going to send us a copy of the rehearsal video."

"Yes, of course. I'll do that as soon as I get back to the hotel."

41

LUNCHTIME, MONDAY 5 OCTOBER

Perry looked down at his watch. "I wonder where Simon is. Hopefully, he's had more luck talking to the people on his list than I did on mine. No one seems to know where Klara is, and Ryan went back to the hotel." He unwrapped the foil from his lunch and, placing it on the top of the cardboard-covered side table in front of them, he took a bite.

"I suppose now the festival is over, they are less likely to be on-site."

Perry nodded as Daisy opened her eyes and, slowly standing up, performed a downward dog stretch. Just as she finished, Simon walked through the door of the Blue Room and headed towards them.

He stopped to bend down and greet the little dog. "Sorry I'm late. I found Ambrose and then, just as we were finishing our chat, Finn joined us. So I thought I'd kill two birds with one stone."

He grabbed a plastic folded chair and, opening it, sat down next to Perry. "This room is immense." He stared up at the high ceiling and gave a low whistle as he took in the enormous four-poster bed over the other side.

"Yes, it used to be one of the private family suites," Perry told him as he handed him a sandwich and a packet of crisps. "We've still a lot to do in here, but it will look amazing when we've finished."

"I have no doubt," Simon replied, taking his food.

Lady Beatrice handed him a takeaway coffee cup. "We're going full on opulence."

Simon nodded as he took a sip of his cappuccino. "So how did you get on, Bea?"

"I managed to speak to Marta and Fay."

"Anything new?"

"Indeed. Marta admitted that she and Luca had a relationship that ended about a year ago. Shortly after that, he met Fay. That's when Marta asked Seb to be moved to another restaurant. But get this… he and Marta got back together recently after Fay and Luca decided the romantic side of their relationship was over. "

Perry, who had had been taking a gulp of his latte, jerked and planted his plastic cup down. "What?"

"There's more… Fay knew about it and was fine because she'd met someone else too!"

Perry, who was now wiping his chin with a napkin, stopped, his eyes wide.

"And you'll never guess who she's fallen for…" *I'm sorry, Perry, you're not going to like this.* "It's Ryan Hawley."

Simon's eyebrows shot up while Perry cried, "What?" then covered his mouth as he started to cough.

"I know. I was shocked too. There she's been, playing the devoted girlfriend glued to her dying boyfriend's bedside, when all along, she's been in love with someone else."

"So did Luca know about Fay and Ryan?" Simon asked.

Lady Beatrice nodded. "Indeed. They all know about each

other and were fine with it, apparently. Fay and Luca had decided to keep it quiet from the press until after the festival was over so as not to overshadow it."

"Well, that's interesting information," Simon said, lifting his hand to stroke his short beard. "But what impact does it have on our suspect list?"

"So Marta told me she was with Luca on Monday morning from after they'd finished up in the kitchens doing their prep until he got the call to say his rehearsal had been brought forward."

"So he definitely didn't go foraging then?" Simon said.

"Indeed. As I said, I also spoke to Fay. She confirmed what Marta had told me about their rather complicated relationships and then said that she was with Ryan from when he'd completed his prep up until he got pulled away to go with Finn to collect the fish."

"So if Ryan confirms that, then Fay and Ryan have alibis?" Perry said in a rather hoarse voice.

"Indeed. And if we believe Marta, then that's her off the list too."

"And do you believe her?" Simon asked Lady Beatrice.

She nodded. "I think she really loved Luca and wouldn't have wanted him dead."

Perry put what remained of his brie and cranberry panini down, frowning. "So does Marta's husband also know about this?"

Lady Beatrice swallowed a mouthful of tuna mayonnaise sandwich as she shook her head. "Not specifically, but from what she told me, he tolerates her affairs as long as she promises not to leave him. He's quite a lot older than her apparently."

"So could he be a suspect?" Perry asked.

I didn't think about that.

"That's a good shout." Simon turned and nodded at Perry. "Maybe he's less understanding than she thinks. Do the police know about this love quintet?"

Lady Beatrice tilted her head to one side. "They know about Fay and Ryan, but I don't know if they know about the others."

"I wonder if Marta's husband has an alibi?" Simon said. "Anyway, well done, Bea. That's good stuff and certainly narrows our list down further. And—" He took the last mouthful of his cheese and ham roll, then took a sip of his coffee. "I can reduce it even further…"

Perry, who had been sneakily (*or so he thinks!*) feeding cheese to Daisy, shot up and said, "Don't tell me you managed to get alibis for some of our suspects too? I haven't even been able to find Klara or Ryan yet to talk to." He frowned. "Ryan has an alibi now, though, doesn't he? So I suppose I won't have an excuse… I mean, need to talk to him now."

Simon winked at Lady Beatrice and turned to Perry, smiling. "It would still be good to get what Fay told us confirmed."

Perry blushed as he nodded. "Okay."

"But, yes, anyway, I have managed to get two more alibis — Ambrose Weir and Finn Gilligan."

They were together?

"They were together!" Simon proclaimed triumphantly.

"Really?" Perry murmured, pursing his lips. "Don't tell me Ambrose was doing the dirty with Finn behind Luca's back?"

Simon grinned. "If you mean was Ambrose signing Finn up so he could represent him, then yes, he was."

"What about Luca?" Lady Beatrice asked. "Was Ambrose planning on dropping him or representing them both?"

"Good question. Ambrose was a bit cagey about that. He admitted that Luca had spoken to him on Sunday evening, but in his version, Luca had only threatened to fire him. He said he'd pointed out to Luca why it would be a bad idea and told him to think about it. He met with Finn on Monday morning after he'd finished in the kitchen, and they were together until Finn got called away to pick up the fish with Ryan. According to Ambrose, his meeting with Finn was pre-planned, and it had been his intention to sign him up regardless of whether Luca stayed with him or not."

"And did Luca and Ambrose talk on Monday?" Perry asked.

Simon shook his head. "No. Ambrose said he'd expected to catch up with Luca later as he intended to go and watch his rehearsal, but after Finn got called away, Ambrose met with Mal Cassan about the television show they were in talks over. He said that by the time they'd finished, he'd found out that the producers had brought the rehearsal forward and he'd missed it. He said he'd looked for Luca, but he'd already disappeared off-site at that point."

So Mal met with Ambrose? "I suppose that means we also know Mal was in the vicinity that morning if he met with Ambrose. That gives him opportunity."

Simon nodded at her while Perry tilted his head to one side. "So I guess we'll never know if Luca would have gone ahead and fired Ambrose or not?"

"No. But I don't think it matters to the case. Signing up Finn would have more than made up for losing Luca as a client if the worst had happened. And anyway, Ambrose was with Finn at the critical time, and Finn confirmed that when he turned up just as I was leaving. So that's both of them off our list."

"So now we know that Luca wasn't alone at any time that

morning. Can we assume that someone added the mushrooms to the stock in tent one before the show?" Lady Beatrice asked.

Simon nodded. "And we know where all except three of our suspects were that morning, so we can rule them out."

"So our three remaining suspects being Mal, Klara, and Marta's husband," Lady Beatrice said. Perry turned to Simon, and she thought she saw Simon shake his head slightly. *What's that about?* Before she had time to consider it further, there was an unfamiliar *ping* and Daisy gave a short woof.

"I think that's the office mobile," Perry said as he retrieved it from the pocket of the coat hanging on the back of his chair. "It's an email from Fay Mayer."

"That must be the video of the rehearsal," Lady Beatrice said, leaning forward to try and see the screen.

Perry nodded. "It is, but the screen on this isn't as nice as a laptop's. Let's watch it in the office."

42

EARLY AFTERNOON, MONDAY 5 OCTOBER

"Well?" Lady Beatrice leaned back and looked at Perry and Simon standing to her right. "What do you think?"

"I think that's forty minutes of my life I'll never get back," Perry said, huffing as he straightened up from the desk in his office in Francis Court. He sighed and stretched out his neck.

"Perry!" Simon turned and stared at his partner.

"Well, I'm sorry, love. But you know I need at least one glass of wine to watch *you* cook, and I love *you*. Watching someone else on a small wobbly screen with bad sound quality and people shouting out time checks every five minutes — I'd need a whole bottle to get through that again!" He shrugged as he moved away from the desk. Lowering himself down onto the small sofa sitting along the wall of their office, he crossed his legs.

Suppressing a smile, Lady Beatrice walked around the desk and sat down in the chair opposite. Daisy, alert to her mistress's movements, opened one eye from her bed in the corner, then sighed and closed it again. "That's not what I meant, Perry. I meant, what do you think about how Luca was during the demo?"

Perry looked down at the floor and mumbled, "*Sorry,*" while Lady Beatrice caught Simon's eye. She raised an eyebrow. "Simon?"

Simon pushed himself up from the desk and shrugged. "He looked perfectly normal to me, no sign of distress or concern. I was also watching the mushrooms the whole time, and I certainly didn't see anyone add to the pile that was there at the start of the demo or during the show."

She let out the deep breath it felt like she had been holding throughout the whole replay. *Thank goodness you agree.* She nodded. "Me neither. So that's Fitzwilliam's theory that Seb added death caps during the rehearsal blown out of the water. Do you think the police have seen this?"

"Did Fay say if she'd told them about it?"

She shook her head as she stood up. *I know he's going to say we need to tell them...*

"Then we need to tell them," Simon said, moving around the desk towards the door. "And when I say 'we', I actually mean you two, as I must get back home and do some work." He turned and grinned. "And while you're there, don't forget to tell them about Marta's husband being a possible suspect, that Luca may have been writing a book of some sort, and that he was babbling about secrets on his deathbed, possibly about a recipe. They may know it all already, but you never know. We may have uncovered something new."

"Bea, I'm really sorry, but I'm not going to be able to make dinner tonight." The voice of Frederick Astley, Earl of Tilling, sounded contrite at the other end of the phone. "Something has come up, and I've got to stay in London for the rest of this week."

Although disappointed that she wouldn't get to see her older brother as planned, Lady Beatrice was also aware that the nature of his job (not that she really knew what Fred *actually* did, just that he worked for the Foreign Office as some sort of roving ambassador) meant he frequently had to change plans at the last minute, and along with the rest of the family, she was used to it by now.

She shifted her weight, resting her hand on the black leather seat in the back of the Daimler. Daisy leaned over from Perry's lap and tried to lick it. She grinned as she looked up at Perry. He raised an eyebrow. She mouthed, "It's Fred," and he nodded.

She continued, "That's a shame. We'll have to catch up at the weekend instead."

"That would be great. So how are you doing? Is it true what I read in the papers? Are you and Seb done?" Fred, an ex-army colonel, had the military trait of getting straight to the point.

"Yes. We'll stay friends, I think, but we wanted different things from life." She was surprised at how easy it was to say it out loud now. All she felt was relief.

"Well, if you know it's not going to work, then there's no point carrying on."

Lady Beatrice frowned. There was a hint of something in his voice. *He sounds pleased!*

Although only her mother had been openly against her relationship with Seb, she suspected the rest of her family hadn't really approved of her involvement with the celebrity chef either, but she'd no idea why. "You sound relieved, Fred. Didn't you like him?" She too could be direct if she needed to be.

"I didn't dislike him, Bea. After all, I only met him that one time when we had dinner at his restaurant in London. He didn't seem your type, that's all."

What does that mean? She wasn't aware she had a type! Now she was curious to know more. "What do you mean by 'not my type'?"

Fred sighed. "He seemed a bit superficial to me. He appeared to court the spotlight, and I know that's not something you've ever sought. I did a bit of digging, and his business set-up is very complicated, which as you know, always makes me suspicious."

A small smile escaped her lips. *Suspicious* should be her brother's middle name. It must be his ex-Army intelligence Corps background. She frowned. *Hang on, did Fred just say he'd been checking up on Seb?* About to tell her brother that he should mind his own business, she paused. *Come on, Bea. You're not naive enough to think that someone you date isn't going to be checked up on by the intelligence services, which you know Fred has some sort of link to.* She let out her breath steadily and took in another. In fact, Fred's ability to find out information about people could prove useful.

"Bea, are you all right?"

Maybe she could use him to give them some background on Luca?

"Yes, sorry, Fred. Can you do me a favour? Can you see what you can find out about Luca Mazza?"

"Is he the chef that died from death cap mushroom poisoning at the Fenn House Food and Wine Festival a few days ago?"

"Indeed."

"I hear it may not have been a straightforward accident. Don't tell me you and your sidekicks are getting involved in the investigation?"

Sidekicks? She hoped Perry hadn't heard him say that. *I'm not sure Perry and Simon would like to be described that way.* She looked over at Perry, but he was looking out of the window. *Phew!*

But now that it was in her head, she couldn't help but grin. "Maybe a bit."

"I see. Can I therefore assume that Fitzwilliam from PaIRS is heading things up?"

Why would you assume that? "Yes. How did you know?"

Fred chuckled. "Just a wild guess. So what are you looking for?"

"A reason why someone wanted to kill him. So I wondered if he was in any financial difficulty or anything like that. Or maybe he had a will, and someone stands to benefit?"

"Okay, leave it with me. I'll see what I can do."

───────

Wrapping her suede jacket around herself, Lady Beatrice was glad she'd replaced her T-shirt with a long sleeve jumper before she'd left Francis Court. *How did we go from unexpectedly-hot-for-this-time of year to colder-than-your-average-October in three days?* She thrust her hands into her pockets as she hurried along the path leading to the old security block, Daisy running ahead of her.

"What's the hurry?" Perry shouted from just behind her. "I thought you hated going to see Fitzwilliam. Now you're almost running to get there!"

She stopped and turned around. "It's cold, and I think it's going to rain," she said, looking up at the ominous dark-grey clouds forming above their heads.

He reached her and raised his eyes to the sky too. "Okay,

you could be right. I'll move as fast as these shoes will allow."

They reached the door of the temporary office shared by CID and PaIRS just as the first spot of rain landed at their feet. Grabbing the handle, Lady Beatrice turned to Perry. "As well as giving them information, let's see if we can subtly find out what they know and who they suspect, shall we?" Perry nodded as they followed Daisy into the room.

"Ah, Lady Beatrice, Mr Juke. What a delight." Detective Chief Inspector Richard Fitzwilliam stood and walked around his desk to greet Daisy.

Lady Beatrice scanned the cramped, shabby room. *Where's Spicer?* The blonde sergeant was nowhere to be seen. *Blast!* It was bad enough dealing with Fitzwilliam in the first place, but having to talk to him without his DS to keep him in check was even more of a challenge. *Keep your cool, Bea.*

Fitzwilliam straightened up, then leaning back against the desk, he crossed his arms. Daisy moved to sit by his side. *I swear if she could, she'd fold her arms too!*

"So what can I do for you two?" he asked.

Lady Beatrice looked at Perry, who in turn looked back at her. She sighed. *Okay, I'll start.* "Er, are you aware that Marta Talaska-Cowley and Luca were having an affair?"

Fitzwilliam nodded. "Yes, thank you, my lady," he said in a bored voice.

"So is Marta's husband a suspect?" Perry blurted out.

Perry! What happened to subtle?

"I can't discuss that with you, Mr Juke." Fitzwilliam uncrossed his arms and pushed himself up from the edge of the desk. As he walked around to his chair, followed, of course, by Daisy, he twisted to look at Lady Beatrice. "I've a lot of work to do, your ladyship. Was that all?"

Lady Beatrice racked her brains to remember what else

they had wanted to discuss with him. Not that he looked much in a discussing mood. *Luca's autobiography!* "Luca was documenting his life story. Is that what was on the laptop, do you think, chief inspector?"

Fitzwilliam leaned back in his chair and crossed his legs, his arms resting on the sides. "Are you going to tell me something I don't know, Lady Rossex?"

Rude! And he wasn't giving anything away. Spicer normally helped with a bit of encouragement. Without her here, it looked like they were wasting their time.

Perry cleared his throat. "Did you know Luca talked to Fay while he was in hospital and semi-conscious?"

A frown quickly appeared and disappeared on Fitzwilliam's face as he uncrossed his legs and pulled his chair closer to his desk. *Ah, so he didn't know that.* She suppressed a smirk.

Fitzwilliam laid his arms on his desk and clasped his hands together. "As I said, I'm very busy. So if there's nothing else?"

He's not going to admit that we've given him new information! Her stomach clenched. *Should I call him out?* She was so tempted. *No, Bea. He knows that you know he didn't know.* That would have to suffice at the moment. She really wanted to find out if the police had narrowed their list of suspects down to three like they had, but it was clear they'd get nothing out of Fitzwilliam today. Lady Beatrice looked over at Perry, and he shrugged.

"Well, thank you for your time, chief inspector," she said with what she hoped he would spot as a hint of sarcasm. "Come on, Daisy."

As Daisy trotted over, she and Perry turned to exit. *Seb!* Had Fitzwilliam seen the rehearsal video? If so, he would surely now have to give up on his ridiculous theory that Seb had poisoned Luca. Lady Beatrice turned back and took a few steps towards his desk until she was standing in front of him.

He looked up at her and sighed. "Yes?"

"I assume you have seen the recording of Luca's rehearsal?"

He gave a sharp nod.

"So you will have clearly seen that Seb didn't add anything to the mushrooms during the demo?" She crossed her arms and gave him a smug smile.

Fitzwilliam stood up and came around the desk towards her. She stepped back as he stopped in front of her and crossed his arms too. Looking down at her, his eyes narrowed. "I'm not sure that's what I saw at all, my lady."

What? Was he going to blatantly deny it?

"But it was crystal clear to all of us," she cried as she turned to Perry for support.

"Crystal," Perry agreed.

"And just how did you get a copy of the video, my lady? You wouldn't be interfering with my investigation now, would you?"

She bristled. Fay had given her a copy. What was wrong with that? He was just saying that to avoid the issue. *Well, I won't let him...* "I don't see how you can continue to believe Seb was in anyway involved, chief inspector, when the video undeniably exonerates him."

Fitzwilliam leaned a little closer towards her.

Hold your ground, Bea. She lifted her chin and returned his gaze.

"It depends on what you saw, Lady Rossex. You saw someone not adding mushrooms. Do you know what I saw?"

So he did *see that Seb hadn't added the mushrooms!* She uncrossed her arms and, shifting her weight to one side, placed a hand on her hip. *Go on, admit it!*

"What I saw was a sous chef who didn't taste the mushroom dish he was preparing. Now that's odd, don't you think, my lady?"

Lady Beatrice's heart sank as Perry gasped behind her. *Surely Seb tasted the dish?* Fitzwilliam must be wrong. *But hold on. It was only a rehearsal.* Would someone like Seb taste a fellow chef's dish when it was just a run-through and he was merely a stand-in? She felt better. It was perfectly normal that he would have left it to Luca.

"No, chief inspector, I don't think it's *odd* at all. Seb was only helping Luca get his markers and timing right. He wasn't there to check the dish for him."

Fitzwilliam sneered. "And obviously, he wouldn't have if he already knew it contained poisonous mushrooms, would he, Lady Rossex?"

It's useless. He's obsessed with his idea. There was clearly nothing she could do to deter him from his path. *Except prove him wrong.*

With a renewed determination, she ignored him, and turning her back, she stomped across the room to join Perry and Daisy, who were still waiting for her by the open door.

"Oh, and Lady Rossex." She twisted her head around to look at Fitzwilliam as he continued, "Ask your precious ex-boyfriend what he was doing that morning before the show. I think you'll find out he doesn't have an alibi."

Ignore him. He's just trying to make me mad.

Her blood boiling, she jerked her head forward as she huffed, and thundering past Perry and Daisy, she stormed out of the room.

43

MID-AFTERNOON, MONDAY 5 OCTOBER

"Can you believe that man? He's so arrogant and smarmy about everything. Did you see how he pretended he already knew about Luca talking to Fay before he'd died?" Lady Beatrice took a deep breath. "And then he has the audacity to suggest Seb didn't taste the mushrooms because he'd already poisoned them!"

"Can you slow down, Bea?" Perry shouted from behind her, Daisy trotting by his side.

She stopped and turned, slightly out of breath, as she waited for them to catch up. Her knees suddenly felt weak as she stood, hands on hips, and watched Perry dodge a puddle as he stopped in front of her, a look of concern on his face. *What?*

"Can we just take a minute?" Perry asked as he looked around, his gaze resting on a small gazebo just over to their left. "Let's sit down." He led them to the covered seat and sat down with a puff as Daisy jumped up to join him.

"Are you all right?" Lady Beatrice asked as she sat next to Daisy.

"It's not me, Bea. It's you."

She frowned. *Me? What's wrong with me?*

She turned to look at him. His blue eyes stared back. "What is it, Perry? You're really worrying me now."

He reached across Daisy and took Lady Beatrice's hand. "Please know this comes from a place of love... er, but you're being a bit of a ninny."

How dare he! She tried to grab her hand back, but he held on to it.

"Bea, you're ignoring the fact that Seb is a credible suspect because you don't believe he killed Luca."

Of course he didn't! But did Perry now believe he did?

Perry held his free hand up in front of his face, palm out, and continued, "And neither do Simon or I." He lowered his hand at the same time as he let hers go. He shook his head. "But this isn't the way to go about it, love. You can't stick your head in the sand and refuse to listen to reasonable observations. We need to find the answers, not simply ignore the question."

He dropped her gaze, and looking down at Daisy sitting between them, he patted the small dog on the head.

Is he right? Am I blind to hearing anything that suggests Seb could be involved? She let out a deep breath and stared out at the garden before her, plants and trees twitching as water dripped off their leaves. She turned her head. "Perry?"

He swivelled to face her.

"I'm sorry. You're right. I'm being almost as unreasonable as Fitzwilliam."

Perry grinned. "But not as boorish."

She smiled and pulled a face at him.

He sighed. "If we want to prove Seb is innocent, then we need to treat him like every other suspect. So first, we need to find out what he was doing Monday morning and then see if we can prove it."

Lady Beatrice nodded, still smiling. "All right, Dixon of Dock Green, I agree. Let's re-look at Seb's means, opportunity, and motive and show how he couldn't have done it."

Fitzwilliam had accused her of wearing rose-tinted glasses when it came to Seb. Well, they were well and truly off now. *I'll show Fitzwilliam that I'm unbiased.* Which was more than could be said for him!

———

Twenty minutes later, Lady Beatrice strode across the now almost empty area where the stalls had been only hours earlier and across the grass towards the site offices. To her left, two of the four marquees had been removed and a third was half down. Scanning carefully for any lurking press, she was relieved to see only a few stall holders completing their last bits of packing up and the workmen dissembling the huge tents. Even so, she was glad she'd put her wig and glasses on and had left Daisy with Perry. *You never know with the press. They can be hiding anywhere.* As she approached the five trailers making up the temporary production suite, she hesitated. *How do I approach this?* Her tummy fluttered at the thought of seeing Seb again so soon after their breakup. And now she needed to question him about his whereabouts the morning Luca had been poisoned. She took a deep breath and climbed the stairs to the mobile office she knew Seb used. She could see the outline of someone sitting at a desk inside. *Here goes...*

The woman sitting at the desk jumped up as Lady Beatrice walked in.

What's Klara Damas doing in Seb's office?

"Lady Rossex. Can I help you?" Klara shot her an unfriendly look as she pushed her coral-coloured glasses up her nose and smoothed down her pink and white spotted A-line dress.

She looks like an ice-cream cup.

"It's Klara, isn't it?"

The middle-aged woman nodded, her piercing green eyes staring at Lady Beatrice.

I don't think she likes me.

"I'm looking for Seb. I thought this was his office?"

A pink tinge coloured the woman's makeup-free cheeks. "It is, but I'm checking some invoices for him while he's being interviewed by the police…" Her voice trailed off as if she'd said too much, and she looked away.

So he's with Fitzwilliam. *I just hope that bully isn't accusing Seb of anything.*

Klara sat down again and leaned back in her chair. Then she stuck out her chin and said, "Is it true what they say in the papers, my lady, that you and Seb are no longer a couple? I asked Chef Seb, but he was very vague about it." Her green eyes looked up at Lady Beatrice.

Oh my gosh. Lady Beatrice could tell from the woman's eyes that Perry was right. Klara had a massive crush on Seb. *Or, even worse, is it love?* Recalling how dismissive Seb had been of Klara last week in the restaurant, Lady Beatrice was flooded with sympathy for her. *Poor woman.*

"Yes. Seb and I decided that we wanted different things and now we're just friends."

Klara raised a shaking hand to her mouth, and water gathered in her eyes.

Oh no, please don't cry! She needed to distract her. "Um, so I wanted to check how he was and ask him a couple of questions about last Monday."

Klara Damas sniffed, and removing her glasses, she wiped them with a cloth she plucked from the table and then placed them back on her face. She frowned. "Isn't it the police who ask questions?"

Maybe this woman and I can be allies if I tell her the truth?

"Er, yes. But they seem to be fixated on proving Seb was involved in Luca's death, and I'm trying to prove them wrong."

Klara gasped. "No, they can't think Seb would hurt anyone." She shook her head. "He just wouldn't."

"I agree. So I really need to ask him where he was Monday morning. Then I can show them he's innocent. I don't suppose you know where he was, do you?"

Klara leaned forward and pulled a piece of paper towards her. "I think he was meeting Mal."

Bingo! That will give him an alibi. "Any idea where Mal is today?"

"He's at the hotel. He has a virtual meeting with another client."

"That's great. Thank you, Klara."

The woman smiled for the first time. It made her look much younger.

Remembering that Klara was on their rapidly decreasing list of suspects, Lady Beatrice said, "Just one last thing. Can I ask you where you were on Monday morning, please?"

The smile dropped off Klara's face and was replaced with a scowl. "I've already told the police."

Well, it had been worth a try. *So much for Simon's theory that people talk to me.* Klara seemed oblivious to her charms. *Maybe I should have brought Daisy?*

"Do you think I'm a suspect too?" Klara asked in a quiet voice.

Lady Beatrice shrugged. "I suppose that depends on what you were doing and if anyone can confirm it."

Klara's shoulders dropped, and she slumped back in her chair. "I was here for a while, then I just wandered around the show, you know, looking at the stalls and watching them being set up."

"So you weren't present for Malcolm and Ambrose's meeting?"

She shook her head. "Am I in trouble, do you think?"

"If you've told the police the truth, then you don't need to worry."

The woman looked down at the desk in front of her and said nothing.

She doesn't look like a killer.

But as Lady Beatrice left the office, she reminded herself she'd met two murderers so far this year and neither of them had looked like killers either.

44

LATE-AFTERNOON, MONDAY 5 OCTOBER

"Lady Rossex, come in." Detective Sergeant Spicer leaned her head around the door and smiled.

Rats! As soon as Lady Beatrice had reached the door of the rundown security office being used by PaIRS and had peered in to see if Seb was inside, she'd caught the sergeant's eye. Having ducked down below the window as quickly as she could, she'd hoped she could get away and try to catch up with Seb. No such luck…

Spicer stood standing at the doorway, waiting for her.

"Er, I was just passing…"

"I'm sorry I missed you earlier." Spicer shivered and crossed her arms. "Please do come in. It's freezing out here."

Although it was still light outside, it was getting cold as more dark clouds amassed above them. *What harm can it do?* Spicer was always more willing to share information than Fitzwilliam was. Maybe she could learn something new to share with Simon and Perry.

"Twice in as many hours, Lady Rossex. What a treat."

Instantly regretting her decision to follow Spicer into the room, she scowled and turned to face Fitzwilliam, who was leaning on the front of a desk, his arms crossed. About to make a scathing remark about her bad luck, she paused when she saw the grin on his face. *Is he joking?* The man was infuriating. *But when he looks at me like this, I don't know what to think.*

"Yes, for me too," she replied, giving him a wry smile, then turned to Spicer. "Did you find out if Marta's husband has an alibi?"

DS Spicer nodded and opened her mouth. A glare from Fitzwilliam stopped the sergeant from elaborating. She closed it again.

So that's another one off the list. The only person left seemed to be Klara Damas, but that made no sense. Why would she want to kill Luca?

"What do you know of Mr Marchetti's financial situation, Lady Rossex?"

Seb's finances? Only what Fred had told her — that they were 'complicated'. So what did Fitzwilliam know? She held his gaze for a few seconds. *He looks smug... and something else.* She'd not seen it in previous cases, when they'd all felt like they were getting nowhere, but this time, he seemed confident. *Triumphant. That's it.* He looked like a man who was about to announce to all and sundry who the killer was. *Oh, no, please don't say he's about to arrest Seb?*

"Seb has an alibi!" she blurted out.

Fitzwilliam raised an eyebrow at her, but said nothing. He slowly uncrossed his arms and stroked his chin. "Did you know—"

A ringing desk phone interrupted him.

He stopped while Spicer picked it up.

Did I know what?

After a few seconds, Spicer said, "Thank you," and

replaced the receiver. "They need us up at the hotel, sir." She grabbed her handbag and slung it over her shoulder

Fitzwilliam jumped up. "I'm sorry, Lady Rossex, but we have to go."

What? You can't leave me hanging like this.

But it was too late. Spicer and Fitzwilliam swept past her and disappeared out of the door.

What was happening at the hotel? Had they gone to arrest Seb? She choked back a cry. She'd let him down...

She took her phone out of her pocket and opened up a group chat window.

Bea: *Fitzwilliam and Spicer have rushed off to the hotel. I think they might have gone to arrest Seb! xx*

Simon: *I'll see what I can find out. Leave it with me x*

Perry: *We were just discussing going to the pub for an early dinner. 6:30? xx*

Bea: *See you there xx*

"So I wonder if their search found anything," Lady Beatrice said, pushing away her empty plate and picking up her gin and tonic. She was grateful that The Ship and Seal in Francis-next-the-Sea was quiet tonight and they had the dining area to themselves. Although Dylan Milton, the landlord, was great at keeping the pub press-free, it was lovely to be able to completely relax knowing there was no one around to observe them.

"Steve is off this evening, so I don't think we'll know any more until tomorrow," Simon replied, plucking a carrot off his plate and feeding it to Daisy sitting next to him on the wooden bench seat.

Lady Beatrice smiled. *Thank goodness for CID Steve.* Earlier, he'd been able to reassure Simon no one had been arrested yet and that the reason Spicer and Fitzwilliam had rushed off was because the warrant to search the rooms at the hotel had been issued.

"Are they looking for the missing laptop?" Perry asked as he wiped his mouth with a napkin.

Simon nodded. "I expect so."

Lady Beatrice sighed. "Well, let's hope so because as things stand right now, we only have one suspect—Klara, and I can't imagine what her motive to kill Luca could be."

"We still haven't confirmed that Seb and Malcolm were meeting, and if so at what time," Perry pointed out.

"And we need to check Ryan's whereabouts too," Simon added.

She took another sip of her drink. "I know. But it does feel like we're running out of options."

"Look, we always get to this point, remember?" Simon picked up his pint and took a sip.

Lady Beatrice thought back to their previous two cases. He was right. They had hit a brick wall both times, and she'd been tempted to give up.

"But," Simon continued, "we just have to stay focussed on what we know and continue to ask questions and gather information around what we don't know."

Thank goodness for Simon's past experience at Fenshire CID. He knew it was a slog, but he kept them going.

"So, Bea, you still need to talk to Seb and find out his exact movements. Perry, you need to get Mal's version of what he was up to on Monday and get Ryan's confirmation that he was with Fay. I'm going to talk to the producer to find out why the show got pulled forward. Okay?"

Lady Beatrice and Perry nodded. They had a plan.

45

LATE EVENING, MONDAY 5 OCTOBER

The Society Page online article:

BREAKING NEWS *Woman Arrested Over Luca Mazza's Death*

In the last half an hour, Fenshire CID have released a statement confirming that they have arrested a woman in connection with the death of Luca Mazza.

The celebrity chef died on Saturday at aged 38 after eating death cap mushrooms. Although originally it was assumed his death was a self-inflicted tragic accident, his family have been putting pressure on the police to investigate further, believing that the chef would not have mistakenly collected and eaten the poisonous mushrooms himself.

The arrest took place shortly after a police search of the King's Hotel in King's Town, where the production crew and the chefs involved with the Fenn House Food and Wine Show are staying. It is understood that the woman was arrested at the hotel, which is just a few miles away from Fenn House, *the Fenshire private residence of their majesties King James and Queen Olivia.*

In their statement, Fenshire police say the suspect is helping them with their inquiries and has not yet been charged.

There are no further details at this time.

46

BREAKFAST, TUESDAY 6 OCTOBER

"Marta?" Lady Beatrice cocked her head to one side, her eyes wide. "Really?"

Simon nodded. "I spoke to Steve first thing."

She slumped back into her seat and reached for her coffee. *Marta?* She would have put money on the fact that Marta loved Luca and was genuinely devastated by his death. But Simon would probably point out that people killed for love more than they did for hate.

She looked around the Breakfast Room at Francis Court while thoughts ran amok in her head. It was still early, and many staff weren't on-site yet, so the restaurant was quiet. It was Nicky's day off, and Lady Beatrice didn't know the two servers working in the room today. They bustled between the tables, clearing plates and wiping down.

Poor Marta! She always looked so young in her oversized clothes, too young to be alone in jail. Was she being looked after? Was her husband there with her? A server across the other side of the room moved to take a breakfast order from two staff members. *Is Marta getting breakfast?*

Lady Beatrice sat up straight and looked over at Simon,

who also seemed to be in a world of his own, his full English breakfast half eaten as he stared out of the window, his eyes glazed over. Perry, sitting next to him, quietly demolished his cheese and mushroom omelette.

Simon turned away from the window, and she caught his eye. "Do you get food when you're in custody?"

"Yes. They've not charged her yet, so they'll be keeping her in the custody suite at CID HQ, which is well-run. She'll be fine."

Lady Beatrice nodded. "I still can't believe it." Then a thought struck her. "Is it possible that it was an accident? We know Marta went foraging on Sunday. Could she have accidentally picked death caps, and it's all a tragic mistake?"

Simon shook his head. "That's not the way they're going. They found Luca's laptop in Marta's room. Someone deleted a bunch of files from the hard drive. They're going for a charge of murder."

Perry, putting his knife and fork down on his plate, wiped his mouth with a napkin. "But the two things could be unrelated, surely?"

Simon shrugged. "The police don't think so." He pushed his plate out of the way and picked up his coffee. "Also, it would seem Marta lied to them when she'd said where she'd been foraging on Sunday."

Lady Beatrice put down her cup. "Really? How do they know?"

"Someone saw her coming out of an area of the park where the police have established there are death caps. She had previously told them she'd been foraging in a patch further back."

"Who saw her?" Perry asked, picking up his coffee and taking a sip.

Simon glanced at Lady Beatrice and sighed. "Seb told the

police he saw her on Sunday afternoon coming out of that particular spot with a basket of mushrooms."

Seb? What was he doing there on Sunday? Hadn't he told her he'd not had time to explore the area?

Simon continued, "She admits she walked past that location but denies she came out of it."

"So it could simply be a mistake on Seb's part?" Perry said.

Simon nodded. "Possibly. The police will interview them both again today."

Perry put down his cup and fished a piece of uneaten bacon from Simon's plate, holding it under the table for Daisy. "Did CID Steve say anything else?"

"Only that they're attempting to retrieve the files from the laptop, but it could take days. They're still reviewing everything on Luca's phone as well. The only slightly strange thing is that there were no fingerprints found on the laptop, not even Marta's. She could have wiped them off, of course, but why would she?"

Lady Beatrice frowned. "That seems a bit odd. Unless, of course, she was worried they would find it? Do we know where it was in her room? Was it well hidden?"

Simon shrugged. "I don't know. I didn't ask Steve."

They sat in silence as a server approached. Perry grabbed a last piece of bacon for Daisy as she removed their used cups and plates.

"So what happens to Marta now?" Lady Beatrice asked.

"They can hold her for up to twenty-four hours before they must charge her with a crime or release her. However, as she's suspected of murder, which is considered a serious crime, they can apply for an extension to hold her for up to thirty-six hours or even sometimes ninety-six hours."

Her stomach clenched. *Poor Marta.* "Is there anything we can do?"

Simon shook his head. "Not really. We'll have to wait and see what happens."

"So I suppose that means we're done with our investigation?" Perry asked, picking up his phone.

"Yes, at least for the moment," Simon replied.

"So you don't think it's worth following up on the plan we agreed to over dinner last night?"

They both turned to her.

"Do you?" Perry asked.

Is it because I don't want to accept that Marta is guilty?

"You don't think she did it, do you?" Simon asked.

She shrugged. "We only took her off our suspect list because I believed her when she'd said she'd been with Luca on Monday morning. So yes, she could have done it. And the laptop in her room is incriminating, that's for sure. But, if I remember rightly, it was Marta who told the police about the laptop being missing in the first place. So why would she do that if she was the one who had stolen it? I think there are enough inconsistencies for there to be doubt. And…"

Perry leaned towards her. "And what, Bea?"

"I like her, and I don't think she's a killer."

Simon opened his mouth, but she put her hand up. "I know that's not how things work, Simon. But it's how I feel."

Simon smiled. "Actually, I was going to say I agree. I've got to know Marta over this last week, and I don't think she's capable of murder."

Perry clapped his hands. "Good. I like her too. So shall we carry on as planned?"

Simon and Lady Beatrice nodded.

Perry jumped up. "Great. Well, I'm off to Fenn House. Are you coming, Bea?"

She shook her head. "I need to get those draft plans off to the head housekeeper at Drew Castle and follow it up with a call. After that, I'll join you at Fenn House as I want to talk to Seb, assuming he's still on-site." She really needed to check this time. She didn't want to be chasing after him like yesterday.

"I'll come with you, Perry," Simon said, rising from his seat. "I'm hoping the police won't have let everyone go yet, although I expect they will by this afternoon. It may be our last chance to talk to any of them."

"Indeed." Lady Beatrice nodded. "Well, let's keep in touch, and I'll see you both later. Come on, Daisy."

"That's great, Mrs Kettley. I'll leave it in your capable hands, and I'll look forward to getting your feedback later this week." Lady Beatrice cut the call and placed her mobile on the desk in front of her.

"I'm so excited about going to Drew Castle in the new year, Daisy," she told her little dog, who was sitting on the office floor beside her. "And you're going to have such a good time running over the heath and chasing rabbits. It might even snow."

Daisy sat up and tilted her head to one side, her tail wagging. Lady Beatrice bent down and patted the wiry head of her small terrier.

"Just the two of us, Daisy. Well, apart from Perry. And maybe Simon if we can persuade him to come too."

Daisy licked her mistress's hand, then sank down on the wooden floor and closed her eyes.

Leaning back in her leather chair, Lady Beatrice took a deep breath, and her muscles relaxed. She closed her eyes, picturing the old castle in the highlands of Scotland surrounded by cliffs and heather. *I can't wait to get up there.* She sighed and opened her eyes. But first, they needed to complete the project at Fenn House and hand it over. Now that the show was done with, they should be able to speed up and have the rooms completed in the next two weeks. Then she would have a well-earned break with Sam at half-term. Maybe they could go somewhere hot and sunny. She smiled. *That would be lovely...*

A sudden beeping wrenched her out of her daydream, and she looked down to see a text message had flashed up on her phone screen.

Ma: *Darling, have you read what the popular press is reporting today? xx*

Bea: *No. Is it something to do with a woman being arrested for Luca's murder? xx*

Ma: *No, darling. It's an interview Seb gave to The Daily Post. You're not going to like it. If you're still at FC, come to me and we'll decide how to respond. xx*

Bea: *On my way. xx*

Ma: *All right, darling. Will get a bucket of coffee ready. You'll need it. xx*

How dare he! Lady Beatrice stormed down the corridor leading from her parents' apartment on the second floor and yanked open the door at the end, entering the balcony surrounding the stairwell. *Wedding bells on the horizon!* How could he be that delusional?

Charging down the opulently carpeted flight of stairs, followed by Daisy, she paused when she reached the first floor and debated whether to go to her own apartment or to carry on. *I need time to think...* Her racing heart slowed slightly as Daisy passed her and headed off to the door leading to her rooms. *Looks like Daisy has made the decision for me.* Following the little dog at a slower pace than before, she opened the door to allow Daisy to lead her down the corridor and onward to her apartment.

Unlocking the door, she let Daisy in first. Watching Daisy head for her water bowl, Lady Beatrice moved to the butler's pantry and grabbed a bottle of water from the fridge. Nursing it in her hands, she enjoyed the slight jolt the coldness gave her. She took a deep breath, and walking into her sitting room, she headed for the teal two-seater sofa opposite the window and plonked herself down, letting the plush velvet hug her in a warm embrace.

What am I going to do? She shifted her weight to one side and took her mobile phone out of the back pocket of her jeans. *I need to talk to Seb and find out what the heck he's up to.* She tapped the screen and *The Daily Post* article shone brightly up at her: "Chef Seb Reveals All."

Reading the headline and seeing the picture of him smiling so smugly made her jaw clench. What had possessed him to agree to an interview with such a paper? She swiped up and cleared it from her screen, wishing she could swipe her mind clear of the ridiculous things the article had included. *Did he really tell them he hoped we would get married?* They'd known each other for just over a month! But as her mother had pointed out, he'd said it had been love at first sight for him. *Rubbish!* The only person Seb loved that much was himself.

She wanted to scream. It was all just so embarrassing. The final straw for her had been his mention of Sam and how much he'd been looking forward to meeting him and teaching him to cook. *The arrogance of the man!*

Well, she'd like to see how confident he was when she asked him to make a statement retracting the article. She opened her text messages and typed.

Bea: *We need to talk.*

Seb: *Sorry. I guess you've seen the article in The Daily Post? It was weeks ago, and I swear I didn't say half the things they are attributing to me. Trust me, bella.*

No! I'm never making that mistake again.

Her hackles rose when she recalled her mother telling her that her sources in the newspaper world had reported that Seb had tipped off the paparazzi to their whereabouts during their holiday in Mauritius and yesterday when they'd left the catering tent. *How could he have done that to me?* And he'd been so considerate after that encounter—asking her if she was all right, offering to walk her back. And all along, it had been because of him that she'd had to go through it in the first place! *What a manipulating shark he is...*

. . .

Bea: *Where are you?*

Seb: *Packing up at the hotel, then I'll be at Fenn House at the production offices. Shall we meet at the Garden Room restaurant for lunch?*

Really? She shook her head slowly in disbelief. *He wants to meet me in a public place?* She smiled wryly to herself. Either he feared what she'd do to him (*and so he should!*) and hoped she would behave better if she was on show, or he really was that desperate for the publicity.

Bea: *No. I'll come and find you at Fenn House.*

She pressed send and threw the phone down beside her on the couch. Then springing up, she walked around the low coffee table and the other sofa opposite, moving to the large window to gaze out.

Grey clouds moved across the sky as, looking beyond where the drive split in two, she focused on the trees to the left of the long drive. There were no deer to be seen this morning. Feeling disappointed (she found observing the deer to be a calming activity), she looked down at the grand seventeenth-century water feature in the middle of the courtyard called the Cascade. As she watched the water flow from the set of fountains on the top and down the two sets of twenty-two stone steps to the bottom, her shoulders relaxed and her back softened. She took a deep breath. *You need to be dignified and calm when you talk to him, Bea.* She knew there was no point in losing her temper. She couldn't trust him not to sell his story to the press. They would love to hear about her having a very un-royal meltdown.

Turning away from the serene scene in front of her, she collected her phone and padded across the room. When she reached the hall, she shouted for Daisy to join her. She heard a *thump* as Daisy jumped off the bed, and a few seconds later, her little white dog trotted out of the bedroom and into the hall. Stopping in front of Lady Beatrice, her tail wagging, she waited patiently for her mistress's command.

"Come on, Daisy. This will be the last time you'll have to see him ever again. I promise."

47

MID-MORNING, TUESDAY 6 OCTOBER

Click, click, click.

"Are you and Chef Seb getting married, my lady?"

"Are you back together, Lady Beatrice?"

The shouting was audible inside the car as the Daimler inched forward through the crowd of press surrounding the main entrance of Francis Court.

Lady Beatrice shielded her eyes from the flashes as she slid further down the black leather seat in the back.

Shhhuuuu. The glass panel dividing the front and the back of the Daimler slid open.

"I'm sorry, your ladyship. I was going to take us through the tradesmen's exit, but it's just as bad there according to security." Ward, her driver, shook his head. "The police seem to be having trouble with the press today. I'll get us through here as soon as I can."

"Indeed. Thank you, Ward," Lady Beatrice mumbled as she pushed herself into a corner and peeked out of the window.

Click, click, click.

"Are you moving to London to live with Chef Seb?"

"This way, my lady!"

Where did they all come from? It wasn't unusual for a small contingent of press to be outside the main gates at her home, but she'd not seen this number since the day she had returned from her holiday with Seb in September.

"The problem is they've broken through the barrier, my lady." Ward enjoyed commenting on these press encounters. Lady Beatrice suspected he saw it as part of his job to keep her fully informed. "Ah, here we go, my lady. We'll be out of here in a jiffy now."

Shhhuuuu. The internal glass panel glided back up, and the car pushed forward.

Click, click, click.

Lady Beatrice jumped as a thud banged against the side of the car and a face loomed up against the glass. "Lady Beatrice, over here!"

She shifted herself into the middle seat and breathed a sigh of relief when the car gathered speed.

Click, click, click.

The sounds were fainter now, making her heartbeat seem louder. She put her hand to her chest. *And breathe...*

The last few shouts faded away as Ward turned left. Lady Beatrice looked behind her and sneaked a quick look at the pile of press falling over themselves to follow, knowing that it was futile now she was on the road and speeding up. *This is all Seb's fault!* A fresh surge of anger enveloped her.

Taking another calming breath, she picked up her phone and opened the group chat.

Bea: *I'm on my way to FH, but I'm going to be a tad later meeting you than planned. You may have seen the press reports? I'm off to have it out with Seb first! See you both later. xx*

"Oh my giddy aunt!" Perry Juke lifted one hand to his forehead while using the other to thrust his phone into Simon Lattimore's face. "Have you seen this?"

Simon swiped his partner's arm away. "No, Perry. I'm driving, remember."

"Sorry," Perry replied sheepishly.

Simon's voice softened. "Read me what is says."

"Well, it's an interview Seb did with *The Daily Post*. It's everywhere online. Hold on, I'll skim read it for you. So, okay. There's a short bit about his expansion plans, blah, blah, oh, and here we go. He talks about him and Bea."

"Oh dear, she won't like that," Simon commented as he turned onto the road leading to the tradesmen's entrance at Fenn House.

"He says it was love at first sight for him. Aw, that's sweet."

"Perry!"

"Sorry. Hold on. There's some stuff about their holiday and how romantic it was. Then a bit about the Fenn House show, blah, blah. Oh, okay, here's the money shot. He says he hopes there will be wedding bells for him and Bea in the future. Now that *is* cheeky."

"Poor Bea. She'll be furious."

"Well, I guess it explains the message she just sent. Will she be all right, do you think?"

Simon nodded as he pulled the car up to the security barrier. "She'll be fine. It's Seb who should be worried." He held his hand up to the man on duty as they were waved through.

Perry's phone beeped. "Hold on, that might be Bea." He opened his messages. "No, it's Fred, Bea's brother."

Simon accelerated his BMW through the gates. "Fred? What does he want?"

"Hold on, I'm just opening it. It's bound to be something James Bond like. Maybe it will be in code?"

Simon chuckled. "Make sure it doesn't self-destruct after you read it."

Perry grinned. "Okay, so he says he's tried ringing Bea, but she's not answering. He has some info for us. Oh, this is interesting. Luca was sound and solvent financially when he died. His money goes to his next of kin, who are his parents. But Seb's business empire is heavily in debt and has some significant investment bonds due to be repaid next month, whatever that means."

"It means people who have lent money to Seb's business are due to have it paid back soon."

Perry shrugged. "Anyway, he says Seb's business has been running at a loss for the last two years." He turned to Simon. "I wonder if Seb got paid for that interview?"

"Possibly," Simon said as he pulled into a parking area at the back of Fenn House. "Can you tell Fred thanks and we'll let Bea know?"

Perry nodded and began to type.

Simon Lattimore walked along the path, having left Perry on his way to the main house, his feet crunching on the gravel as he headed towards the old security block in the distance. Dodging a large bush bursting with late blooming red roses encroaching on the walkway, he turned the corner. His legs felt heavy, and he moved his head from side to side to relieve the tension in his neck. He passed the low privet hedge separating this path from a thin stream, its banks covered with hostas, their leaves dying back. Glancing at the water gently running parallel to him, he sighed. So it had been Seb who'd instigated the rehearsal to be brought forward. Of course, that wasn't actually what the show's producer had told him just now on the phone. She'd told him Seb had approached her with concerns that they wouldn't fit everything in, and it had been she who'd suggested they bring the rehearsals forward. But Simon was ex-CID, and he had seen how easy it was to manipulate someone into thinking something was their idea. Watching the dust kicked up from his feet puff into the air, he frowned.

But does it mean anything?

He still wasn't sure. Seb could've had other reasons for why he'd wanted the show brought forward. *It doesn't make him a murderer.* But Simon recognised a pattern was emerging.

Seb's a schemer. A puppet master for his own gain.

And now Simon feared Seb had been exploiting their friendship to get close to Bea. And even worse, he'd been using Bea to gain the public seal of approval to get his investors off his back. After all, who would bankrupt someone about to marry into the royal family? It was Machiavellian behaviour, to be sure.

But did he kill Luca?

As he sidestepped a large puddle, Simon still couldn't think of a good reason why he would. In fact, it seemed as if Seb needed Luca and Luca's success to protect him from losing his business. Turning another corner, he sensed a presence before him, and as he looked up, he stopped short of knocking the woman over by grabbing her arms.

"Sorry, I wasn't looking where I was going," he said as he steadied them both. Dropping his arms, he smiled up into a face dominated by a large pair of green glasses.

She must have them in every colour to match her outfits. Today, Klara Damas was wearing a long-sleeved bright-green shift dress. She looked like a square of lawn.

"Mr Lattimore! Sorry, it was my fault. I was miles away." She ran her fingers through her short brown bob and cleared her throat.

"Are you okay, Miss Damas?" he asked.

She gave him a shy smile. "Please call me Klara. I was looking for the police, but there doesn't seem to be anyone in the office. I have some information that I should tell them. Well, at least I think I should. I don't really know what to do now. Maybe I should just leave it?" She clasped her hands together in front of her and shrugged.

"Is it anything I can help you with, Klara? I used to be a policeman. I can advise you if you're unsure?"

She sighed. "Oh, that would be so helpful, Mr Lattimore. You see, I don't know if it's important or not."

Simon nodded. "And please call me Simon, Klara. So what is it you think may be useful to the police?"

"Well, I read in the papers the police have arrested someone for Luca's murder. A woman. Well, you know how everyone talks… and no one has seen Marta since yesterday when the police were at the hotel searching our rooms. So I wondered if it's Marta they've taken. Anyway, the police have been questioning us all about where we were on Monday morning, and the talk has been that someone added the poisonous mushrooms after the chefs had prepped but before the demo." She took a deep breath and continued,

"But, you see, I saw Marta on Monday morning. She was with Luca, so how could she have doctored the mushrooms? I thought it might be important."

Simon nodded and opened his mouth to speak, but she carried on.

"But when I mentioned it to Seb because I thought he'd have seen Marta and Luca too, he wouldn't confirm whether it was Marta they've arrested."

Her eyes filled with tears. "He said the police have it all in hand and I should mind my own business." She swallowed noisily and sniffed. "He was quite rude, you know." She hung her head and wiped her face with her hand.

"Well, I think you should tell the police, Klara."

She raised her head and gazed at him.

He smiled. "Before, Marta's alibi wasn't confirmed, but now you're an important witness."

A smile slowly spread across her face. A big toothy smile that lit it up.

She's really quite pretty when she's not so glum.

But then she frowned. "I don't want to get in trouble with Seb. He's our most important client, you know."

Simon smiled softly. "Well, I know the officers who are investigating this case. Would you like me to run it past them and ask them to call you?"

She nodded, still smiling. "That would be lovely. Thank you."

She moved past him and carried on in the opposite direction.

Simon, took a step away, then paused and turned back. "Klara, wait!" he shouted, moving towards her. "Did you say you told Seb because he may have seen them too?"

She nodded, letting out a heavy breath. "But of course! Seb would have already told the police. That must've been

why he said I didn't need to say anything to them as well."
She stood up straight and smiled.

I'm not so sure. "What makes you sure Seb saw them,
Klara?"

"Well, because he was heading towards the tent where the
rehearsal was happening. He must have passed them as they
left."

But how? "Wasn't he with your boss Malcolm?"

"He was earlier. After that, he went to get something from
his car. That's where he was coming from."

"Sorry, Klara, I'm a bit confused. Can you take me
through what you saw and when that morning?"

"Sorry, it's me. I'm all over the place." She ran her
fingers through her hair. "So when I arrived on-site, I went
straight to the offices as I'd promised Seb I would help with
some invoices. I was engrossed in what I was doing, then
suddenly I heard a *clunk*, and looking out of the window, I
saw Seb getting something out of his car. I got up, ready to
greet him, but he didn't come into the office. When I looked
out of the door, he was heading towards the marquees. Just on
the other side, Marta and Luca were laughing together and
coming my way." She stopped and frowned, then shook her
head.

"What is it, Klara?"

"I've just realised I'm an idiot! Seb wouldn't have seen
them, as they were on the *other side* of the tents to him."

"And what time was this? Do you remember?"

She tilted her head to one side. "It was about half an hour
before the rehearsal. I remember not long after, the producer
came in looking for Seb. She said they were going to start,
and they needed him as he was going to act as Luca's sous
chef. I told her he was already there, and she left." Red rose
up her neck and seeped into her cheeks.

What's she hiding? "So what did you do then?"

She bit her lip. "I told the police I had a wander around the stalls and watched them setting up."

But? "And what did you really do?"

She fidgeted with the sleeve of her dress. "I watched the demo," she mumbled. She looked up and held his gaze. "I know I wasn't supposed to go backstage. But Mal was with Ambrose, and I was bored of pushing paper around in here. And I wanted to watch Seb… I mean, Luca do his show." She looked away. "Will I be in trouble with the police?"

Simon shook his head. "No, Klara, you just need to make sure you tell them everything you've just told me, and it will be fine."

She sighed and smiled at him. She looked at her watch. "Sorry, I really need to get back to the offices and help pack up. Thank you for your help, Simon. I feel much better now."

Simon watched her leave as he picked up his phone. *I'd better tell Fitzwilliam.*

48

SLIGHTLY LATER IN THE MORNING, TUESDAY 6 OCTOBER

The Society Page online article:

Sources Close to Lady Beatrice Deny That Marriage to Chef Seb Was Ever on The Cards

A source, described as a close family friend, has disputed claims made in this morning's press that Lady Beatrice (36), the Countess of Rossex, and Sebastiano Marchetti (38) were ever planning on getting married. 'Poppycock!' was how they responded to the claims being made by The Daily Post, *explaining that the countess and the chef had only been in the early stages of getting to know each other when they'd ended their budding romance a few days ago. The source cited 'not wanting the same things from life' as the reason for the split. 'There was never any talk of them getting married,' the source revealed. They claimed the interview had taken place before their relationship ended and charged Chef Seb with being 'delusional' if he thought that Lady Beatrice would marry someone she had only known for a short time. Sebastiano's PR agency has so far refused to comment.*

Meanwhile, the police are still holding a woman in connection with the death of Luca Mazza, the television chef who died on Saturday after eating poisonous mushrooms. The police have still not charged the woman, and it is not known if they have applied for an extension to hold her beyond the regular twenty-four hours.

———

"Daisy, what *are* you doing?" Lady Beatrice cried as she rushed towards the little terrier who was on her hind legs sniffing the open back passenger door of the blue car parked next to the mobile production offices. As she drew closer, she slowed down, her stomach dropping. She recognised the Mercedes. *So Seb is here.* The boot of the car was open too and inside were bags that looked to her like Seb's luggage. *Was he leaving already?*

The walk from where Ward had dropped her to the offices had calmed her down. The anger that had spurred her on earlier this morning had depleted and been replaced with a nervous energy brought on by the thought of a confrontation with Seb. *I just need to ask him to make a statement retracting the article.* She was relieved she'd caught him before he left and hoped it would be that simple.

She sighed and looked around. *Where's Daisy now?* Walking towards the car, she saw a white furry tail peeping out of the footwell of the back seat. "Daisy!" The tail began wagging. *Cheeky!* "Get out of there!"

"What's she doing in my car?" A shout came from behind Lady Beatrice. As she swung around, Seb marched towards her, his face like thunder.

Lady Beatrice's hackles rose. *How dare you be angry with*

my dog when you've just plastered me all over the papers! "Daisy, come here!" she hissed.

"Get her out of there!" Seb was almost upon them.

Daisy, who had turned around, peeped out of the open door.

What's she got in her mouth? Lady Beatrice took a step forward just as Daisy jumped down, her prize still firmly in her jaws, and ran towards her mistress.

"*Daisy!*" Seb shouted.

Even from a distance, she saw Seb's face was a reddish purple. He drew closer, and she spotted a raised vein by the side of his tanned temple. She'd never seen him this angry.

"Daisy, drop!" Lady Beatrice commanded, and Daisy stopped, sat, and dropped a small brown hessian sack at her feet. Bending down, intending to retrieve it, Lady Beatrice was almost knocked off balance when Seb swept in from her right and grabbed it before she had a chance.

"That's mine," Seb barked as he snatched it up in his hand and rose. "What on earth was she doing in my car, Bea?"

He stood in front of her, his hands on his hips, a reddish hue still covering his face. Lady Beatrice's heart raced. A *rushing* sound pumped in her ears. She recoiled and took a step backwards. "Sorry, she was just exploring. No harm done."

He huffed. "You need to get control of that dog."

Stay calm, Bea. He's angry. Now is not the time to fight fire with fire. She needed to let him cool off first.

He stared at her for a few seconds, his blue eyes slightly glazed over.

Please let it go.

He dropped his gaze, and moving over to the back of his car, he slammed the boot closed. "You'd best come into the office."

Simon: *Have found out some new info, Bea. Can you come and find us before you read the riot act to Seb, please? x*

Perry walked into the first floor sitting room he and Bea had yet to finish and handed Simon a steaming mug of tea. Picking up the coffee he'd been halfway through when Simon had burst in earlier to tell him what he'd learned that morning, he leaned back against the back of a sideboard still covered in cardboard and strapping tape. He looked at his partner and tilted his head to one side. "So you think Seb could be a killer, but you're not sure. He could simply be a manipulative megalomaniac who is using Bea as cover to keep his creditors off his back?"

"Pretty much." Simon took a sip of his tea. Then, placing it on the top of a side table covered in thick polythene, he joined Perry by the sideboard. Resting his weight on the furniture, he crossed his arms. "So what do we do now?"

Perry frowned and returned his mug to the countertop. It was unlike Simon to ask *him* what they should do. "Tell the police?"

Simon sniffed. "Yes. We should do that. But I mean what do we do about Bea?"

"Let's see how she is when she arrives. In the meantime, we can go through our other suspects and work out if what you've found out changes anything. That might also help us assess just how likely it is that Seb killed Luca."

Simon leaned to his side and nudged Perry's shoulder. "Check you out, Columbo."

Perry turned and raised his hand to his heart. "Columbo?

Really? I don't think a dirty old Mac and a cigar is my style, do you?"

Simon threw his head back and laughed. Perry noticed his partner's shoulders relax. *That's better!*

"Right." Uncrossing his arms and raising one hand in front of him, Simon flicked up his thumb. "First, is Klara. She says she was alone in her office and saw Seb from the window. She stayed there for a while after that, spoke to the producer, and then watched the show."

Perry nodded. "Okay, so we should be able to get collaboration from the producer that they spoke, and someone must've seen her in the wings while the demo was on. She may even be in the video that Fay took."

"Good idea. I wonder if she would've had time to add the death caps between speaking to the producer and watching the show? We'll need to look at the exact timings. But what we don't have at this stage is a motive. Why would Klara want to kill Luca?"

Perry shook his head. "I've got nothing."

"All right, so two" —Simon extended his index finger out — "is Malcolm. We know he was with Seb earlier and with Ambrose during the rehearsal, but what did he do in between? Was there time for him to add poisonous mushrooms to the ones ready to use for the demo?"

Perry shrugged. "I guess so. But again, what about motive? We know he wasn't happy with Luca's diva demands regarding the television show, but we also know they were unlikely to impact Seb and therefore Malcolm, as it was Seb the show producers wanted more than Luca."

"Agreed. So next at number three" —Simon raised his middle finger— "is Marta. The police think she's guilty. She went foraging on Sunday, but she may have returned Monday early and got the death caps—"

"Oh, or Sunday's foraging was a recce to establish where they were?" Perry added.

"That would make sense if Seb spied her in an area where death caps were."

"But wait," Perry said, picking up his mug. "Klara confirmed she watched Marta with Luca leaving the marquees on Monday morning, so would she have had time?"

Simon stretched his head to one side and puckered up his lips. "Only if she went into their tent before that, possibly on her way to the one she was working in. I certainly think it's possible."

"And if she was worried Luca was going to reveal their affair to her husband, then she also has a motive." Perry took a sip of his coffee.

"Yes, but why would she think Luca would do that? They'd been together before, and he'd kept it under wraps. So what was different this time?"

Perry put his cup down and clapped his hands together. "I've got it! What if it was to do with the autobiography? She took his laptop, after all. Was she worried that something he was going to reveal in that would upset and embarrass her husband?"

"Good point. That seems like the most credible suggestion we've got at the moment." Simon lifted his ring finger. "And finally, there's Seb. We know he was with Malcolm earlier on Monday, but then Klara clocked him before the show on his way to the demo tent. So we know he had an opportunity to deposit death caps in with the mushrooms already prepped just before they started the rehearsal. Regarding means, he was out and about Sunday because he said he'd seen Marta. He could've collected them then or earlier on Monday before he met up with Malcolm."

Perry straightened up and moved around to face Simon.

"So he had the opportunity too. And you think he manipulated the demo rehearsal to be brought forward while Ryan and Finn were collecting fish so he could act as Luca's sous chef?" Then he frowned. "But why would he need to be there if he'd already added the mushrooms? Wouldn't he have been better off if he was somewhere else at the time?"

Simon sighed. "But the risk was that whoever was Luca's sous chef would eat them too. The only way he was able to stop that from happening was to be there on stage and make sure Luca did all the tasting."

Perry gasped. "And he didn't taste anything himself, remember? Fitzwilliam was at pains to point that out to Bea and I yesterday. Although she made a good point, that it was only a rehearsal, so Seb wouldn't have bothered to check Luca's food for him."

Simon propelled himself up straight. "It's a valid comment. The main issue for me with Seb as the killer is motive. Why would he want Luca dead? They were good friends and about to start filming a lucrative television show together. Luca was also Seb's most senior chef at his most prestigious restaurant, so I can't imagine he would want to lose him, unless—"

The beeping of his phone interrupted him. He took it out of his pocket.

Is that Bea? Perry turned to him expectantly.

"It's Fitzwilliam. He says he's just got my message, and he's back at the security offices if we want to talk to him."

49

MEANWHILE, TUESDAY 6 OCTOBER

"I'm sorry I shouted, *bella*. Please forgive me." Sebastiano Marchetti looked contrite as his blue eyes stared into hers. "It's Marta... I cannot accept she killed Luca, but..." He shook his head slowly from side to side and lowered his gaze to the temporary office's grey-flecked floor.

Lady Beatrice smothered a sigh. Only a few minutes ago, she'd wanted to give him a piece of her mind. *And now I feel sorry for him.* She glanced down at Daisy standing by her side, her tail straight and her ears slightly back. *I'm not sure Daisy will be so easily swayed.*

Seb moved towards the desk now littered with boxes. He dropped the sacking he'd been gripping in his hand into a wicker basket and added it to a box already half full of papers in front of him.

"So you think they've got the wrong person, do you?" she asked.

Seb glanced up and frowned. "No. I'm sure if the police said she did it, then she did."

"But you just said—"

"They know what they're doing, *bella*." Seb smiled. All

traces of his earlier sadness about Marta had vanished. "Coffee?"

She shook her head as she walked towards the desk and stopped short of it. He scooped more paper out of an open drawer and piled them on the desk. *Come on, Bea, say what you came here to say.* She took a deep breath in, and a few seconds later, she let it out slowly. "So about this interview you did with *The Daily Post*, I—"

Seb stopped moving papers around and held up his hand. "It wasn't an interview, *bella*. I was on my way into the restaurant last weekend, and one of their reporters collared me by the back door. He caught me unawares and started firing questions at me. I hardly remember what I said." He shrugged and gave her a tentative smile.

"You don't remember saying that we were getting married?" she asked incredulously, her voice rising. *Does he really expect me to believe that?*

———

"So, Lattimore, what can I do for you?" Detective Chief Inspector Richard Fitzwilliam rose from his chair and walked around the desk.

Perry looked around the cramped room for DS Spicer, but she was nowhere to be seen. *That's a shame.* She was usually more receptive to what they had to say. As Simon told Fitzwilliam what Klara had said, he stared at the floor. Why hadn't they heard from Bea yet? He'd hoped they would bump into her on their way here… He picked up his phone.

Perry: *Bea, where are you?*

. . .

He stared at the screen and watched *Delivered* appear underneath the message. Waiting for a response, he looked around the shabby room. Boxes full of paperwork were piled by the sides of the desks, while the whiteboard that had been up against the wall the last time he'd been here and covered in scribbles had been wiped clean and now stood on its end. It looked like they were getting ready to leave. *They must be sure they've got their killer.*

"Perry?"

He spun around to face Simon.

"I was just saying to Fitzwilliam that Lord Fred texted you with some information about the financial status of Luca and Seb."

"Can I see it, please, Mr Juke?" Fitzwilliam moved forward as he reached his arm out towards him.

Perry quickly glanced at the message to Bea. No three dots to say she was responding to his message or her image in the corner to say she'd read it. *Come on, Bea, where are you?*

He closed the text and scrolled through the list of previous messages until he found the one from Bea's brother. Opening it, he passed his phone to Fitzwilliam.

Fitzwilliam studied the screen for a few minutes, then returned the phone to Perry. "Thank you, Mr Juke. That confirms the information we already have."

Perry nodded as he looked into the man's drawn face. *He looks exhausted.* He must have been up all night questioning Marta, he imagined.

Perry liked Marta and understood how fond of her Simon had become during the time they'd worked together at the show. *Poor Marta.* "How's Marta?" he asked the chief inspector as the man leaned back and perched on the front of his desk.

"We still have her in custody," Fitzwilliam said, folding

his arms across his chest. "We'll need to decide whether to charge her soon or let her go."

"And will you charge her?" Simon asked.

Fitzwilliam let out a long sigh. "We don't have enough evidence. It's all circumstantial, and our theories are merely supposition at the moment."

"But I thought you found Luca's laptop in her room?" Perry said.

Fitzwilliam's brow creased, and the gaze from his brown eyes seemed to bore into Perry's soul. *Oh my giddy aunt! Did I just get us into trouble?*

"And why would you think that, Mr Juke?"

Perry glanced away from Fitzwilliam, towards Simon. *Help!*

"It's what everyone who's staying at the hotel is saying, Fitzwilliam," Simon jumped in. "Isn't it true?"

Fitzwilliam looked from one man to the other and huffed. "Yes, it's true."

Perry gave Simon a quick smile. *Thanks, love.*

"However," Fitzwilliam continued, addressing Simon, "there are no fingerprints on it, not even Luca's. Someone wiped it clean, which seems suspicious to me. Almost as if someone else planted it there to implicate Marta."

"And was there anything interesting on it?" Simon asked, keeping Fitzwilliam's attention.

But we already know someone erased the hard drive? He frowned, then he realized. *Ahh... I see what you did there...*

"The tech guys can tell that someone deleted a load of files, and they're working on recovering them. Marta claims she knows nothing about it." He shrugged. "But then she would, wouldn't she?"

"So you see, it was all a misunderstanding, *bella*." Seb walked around the desk and moved towards her, his arms outstretched before him. As Daisy emitted a low growl, Seb stopped, glaring down at the little terrier.

Misunderstanding? You mistakenly told them we were getting married, did you? Lady Beatrice sighed. "You told them we were getting married, Seb. That's why they're making so much fuss. Why did you do that?"

He dropped his arms. "I didn't tell them that, *bella*." He gazed at her with wide eyes, pleading. "Please believe me."

She didn't know what to think anymore. "The press is ruthless, Seb, but they wouldn't have jumped straight to wedding bells without at least some foundation to it."

He shrugged. "I vaguely remember he asked me if wedding bells were on the horizon."

"And you said yes?"

"No, of course not. I don't recall I even answered the question."

She stared into his blue eyes, the single central light from the office reflecting in them. *I should believe him.* She wanted to believe him. But… they stood opposite each other, their gazes locked.

Then a slow smile crossed his handsome tanned face, his white teeth slowly showing as it widened. "Would it really be so awful, *tesoro*? We make a great team, you and I…"

No! You're not getting out of this so easily. She remembered what her mother had told her. "But you were telling the press where we were, Seb. Even on holiday. How can I ever trust someone who does that?"

He shook his head. "No. No. You've got it wrong."

He sounded insincere. Like a man who, deep in his heart, was aware the game was up but was not willing to admit it just yet.

"And you lied to me about not knowing anything about mushrooms on the estate. You told the police you saw Marta in an area where there were death caps. Were you foraging on Sunday?"

"No!" he cried, his smile gone. "I was just out walking and saw her."

"So where were you on Monday morning, Seb?"

"I was with Malcolm."

"At what time?"

"Why are you interrogating me, *bella*? That is a job for your detective friend," he sneered.

Why isn't he answering the question?

Her mind whirled. Was Fitzwilliam right? Was Seb *actually* Luca's killer?

No, surely not. Luca was Seb's friend. She didn't want to believe it. But more and more, he was behaving like he had something to hide. Snippets of what they'd found out started invading her brain — Seb not tasting the mushrooms during the rehearsal, Seb telling her he'd not had a chance to look around the area to forage when he clearly had, Seb not telling her or the police about what Luca had said to Fay when he'd been dying.

A wave of nausea threatened to overtake her. *What if, rather than telling Fay he wanted to talk to Seb, Luca was actually trying to tell her that it was Seb who had killed him?*

"You ask too many questions, bella," Seb said as he inched towards her.

Daisy jumped up and made a low rumbling sound.

"Well, thanks for your help, gentlemen." Detective Chief Inspector Richard Fitzwilliam uncrossed his arms, and using his hands, he levered himself off the desk. "Where's Lady Beatrice, by the way?"

He asked them casually, but it didn't fool Perry. He'd seen that look of concern on Fitzwilliam's face twice before, and both times it had been just before rushing off to try and save her from danger. *I don't care how much she denies it. He has a soft spot for her.* Perry quickly amended that to add, *when she isn't interfering in his cases.*

Perry glanced at Simon, and he nodded. "She's gone to find Seb. She's not happy about what's being said in the press today."

Fitzwilliam gave a wry smile. "I'm not surprised. He's completely the wrong person for her. He's too smarmy by half, if you ask me."

Perry raised an eyebrow. Fitzwilliam suddenly found the floor interesting. Perry contained his grin. *He's wrong for her, so you would be what? Right for her?*

Fitzwilliam cleared his throat. "Er, anyway. She needs to be careful around him. I'm still not convinced that he's not involved in all of this. He told us he was with Mr Cassan on Monday morning, but clearly from what Miss Damas has told you, there's a gap that he's now unaccounted for. He had the opportunity during that time to add the mushrooms. I'll need to interview him again."

Simon nodded. "I've texted her, but she's not responded."

"So have I," Perry added.

Fitzwilliam frowned. "Do you know where they're meeting?"

As both men shook their heads in response, a phone in the middle of the cluster of desks rang. Fitzwilliam hurried over and grabbed the handset. "Fitzwilliam," he barked as he held the receiver up to his ear.

Perry felt a tug on his sleeve and twisted to face Simon.

"We should leave and find Bea," Simon whispered.

Perry nodded, and with a last glance at Fitzwilliam, who seemed totally absorbed in his call, he followed his partner out of the door.

Sebastiano Marchetti stopped a few metres away from Lady Beatrice and glared down at Daisy, then scowled at Lady Beatrice. "Can't you do anything about her? Put her outside or something?"

Lady Beatrice glanced down at the little white terrier standing next to her. It was as if Daisy was vibrating. Her tail was up straight, and her lips were pulled back, exposing her teeth in a menacing grin. A throaty growl grumbled from her.

"She's just being a little over-protective," she told him.

He huffed and threw his arms up. Lady Beatrice flinched as his hands flew within only a few inches of her face.

"I wouldn't do anything to hurt you, *bella*. Why do you need this little dog to protect you from me? I—"

He stopped as a beep came from her person. She reached into the back pocket of her jeans and retrieved her phone. Glancing down at it, she saw two text messages. One was from Simon, but the notification gave no detail. *I must have missed that coming in.* The other one was from Perry. She pressed the message to open it up, but suddenly, Seb leapt towards her and snatched the phone from her hand. *What the heck?*

She jerked her head up to see Seb standing before her, holding her phone. "What do you think you're—"

"We need to talk, *tesoro*. And we can't do that with interruptions." He peered down at the screen.

Lady Beatrice felt like her blood was boiling in her veins.

How dare he! "You've no right to take my phone away from me like—"

"It's okay, *bella*. I'll just put it here."

He touched the side of the phone, then placed it on the table face down. *What's he doing?*

"And now we can talk."

Ring, ring, ring.

Walking along the gravel path framed either side with yew hedging, his mobile plastered to his ear, Perry sighed.

Ring ring, ring.

He pressed the red button and cut the call. *Where is she?* He stopped and turned to Simon. "There's still no answer."

They turned the corner, coming to a halt where the path split in two. Simon scanned both paths ahead of them. "Where would she go to meet him?" He frowned.

Perry shrugged. "The catering tent is closed now, so not there. Would she take him to the Garden Cafe, do you think?"

Simon shook his head. "Too public. She'd want it to be somewhere she could speak her mind and not be photographed doing so."

Perry opened the text he'd sent her earlier, then scrolled up. "We can't even be sure she's at Fenn House. She said she was on her way but was going to—" A loud *crunch, crunch* came from behind them. Perry spun around and was almost bowled over by Richard Fitzwilliam, who'd come running round the corner, heading straight for them.

He skidded to a stop. "Have you got hold of her yet?" he demanded.

"Who?" Simon asked.

"Lady Beatrice!" Fitzwilliam barked. "You said she was with Sebastiano Marchetti. Where are they?"

What's wrong? It was clear from the look on Fitzwilliam's face that all was not well. Perry's stomach turned over, and he reached out to grab the bush by his side. *Is Bea in danger?*

"We were just trying to work it out. The last we heard from her, she was on her way here, but she said she would be late as she wanted to find Seb and confront him."

Fitzwilliam groaned and ran his hand through his hair.

"Is she at the hotel?" Perry suggested.

Fitzwilliam shook his head. "Spicer is on her way back from there now. She went to look for Seb but was told he was at Fenn House packing up."

"The production offices!" Simon cried and began running towards the right-hand fork in the path. But Fitzwilliam was faster. "Come on, let's go," he shouted over his shoulder as he sped past them.

50

AT ABOUT THE SAME TIME,
TUESDAY 6 OCTOBER

Her heart beating fast, Lady Beatrice watched her phone move around as it vibrated on the table. *Who keeps ringing?* She wanted to reach forward and grab the mobile, but Seb stood in front of the desk, his arms folded, his blue eyes flickering as he tried to catch her eye.

"Bea, I don't want it to be like this between us. I want you to trust me."

She took a step backwards, but Daisy held her ground between her and Seb. *My little bodyguard!*

"Well, you should have thought about that when you told the press our whereabouts every time we went out," she snapped.

His eyes narrowed. "You're obsessed with keeping the press out. You need to embrace them, *bella*. They could make us the most powerful couple in the world."

Is he mad? She studied his face and noticed that blood vessel sticking up on his forehead again. Her stomach churned. *I need to calm him down so I can leave.* She would forget about asking him to make a statement to the press. She would talk to Malcolm Cassan instead. He could handle Seb for her. She took a deep breath. "I—"

"Bea. My *tesoro*. We could be so good together, you and I. Please, *bella*. Can we try again?"

Puffing behind Simon, who in turn was chasing Fitzwilliam, Perry Juke regretted his choice of footwear this morning. His brown Church's double monk strap brogues looked amazing (*if I say so myself*) with his blue Burberry slim two-piece suit. Understated and ultra-smart. But they were not made for running in.

In fact, none of Perry's shoes were made for running. Perry didn't run. But right at this minute, he had little choice. Simon was gaining on Fitzwilliam, and Perry was falling behind them both.

Come on, Perry, dig deep. Bea could be in trouble!

He inhaled deeply and pushed on.

"Look, Seb, why don't we have this discussion some other time? I'm supposed to be meeting Perry and Simon, and they'll be wondering where I am."

As if to make her point, her phone vibrated again, and Seb grabbed it off the table and looked at the screen.

She moved forward and reached out to take it from him. But it was clear he wasn't going to hand it over that easily. *Why's he acting so strangely?*

"Fitzwilliam?" He glared at her, clearly rattled. "Isn't he that policeman? Why is he ringing you?" He dropped the phone back on the table and ran his fingers through his spiky brown hair, mussing it up. It gave him a slightly wild look.

Lady Beatrice's throat was dry, and she swallowed. *Why is Fitzwilliam ringing me?*

"Well?" he prompted, his voice breaking.

"I don't know," she replied, trying to appear nonchalant by shrugging. But she felt far from calm. Simon and Perry had both texted her. Someone had rung only a few minutes ago, and now Fitzwilliam was ringing. *Is something wrong?*

Suddenly, a cold wave crept into her bones, overtaking her whole body. Perry and Simon knew she was with Seb. *What if they are trying to warn me about him?* The cold reached her brain, and she stood there, frozen.

What am I going to do now?

———

Simon tried to regulate his breathing as he caught up with Fitzwilliam. "What's happened?" he shouted to the man running parallel to him.

Fitzwilliam looked over, his face contorted with effort, his breathing laboured, and he noisily gulped in some air. "They've found something… on Luca's phone… a recording. Luca thought… it was Seb… who poisoned him."

Oh no. Bea!

———

"Can I have my phone back, please, Seb?"

She kept her voice low and calm, even though she was trying to suppress a scream.

Surely Seb isn't Luca's killer? Not the man I… Another

wave of nausea hit her. Her gaze darted around the temporary office. *How can I get out?*

Seb was only a few metres in front of her, swaying slightly as if he was on a boat at sea. He and the desk he was in front of were blocking her escape route. *If I can move backwards, maybe I can run sideways and take him by surprise.*

She shifted her gaze to Daisy, still standing by her side, her eyes fixed on Seb. Then she remembered her other option. *Send Daisy!* Although she'd been lax at keeping up to date with Daisy's training recently, she still had every confidence the little dog would remember the *Daisy, get help* command Sam had taught her last year. After all, it had worked back in April when she'd faced Alex Sterling's killer. *Even better, I can do both at the same time.*

She ever so slowly moved her left leg backwards and shifted her weight onto it. As Seb glanced at her phone on the table, she rapidly lifted her right leg to join it.

She took a deep breath as he turned back and shook his head.

"No, *bella*. We need to talk without your friends interrupting us."

He looked around the room and frowned.

He's noticed I've moved. Rats!

Perry slowed down as he saw Simon and Fitzwilliam stop ahead of him in front of a woman who looked like a square of turf. *Is that Klara Damas?*

Not far to go, Perry, then you can take a rest.

"So where's he most likely to be?" Fitzwilliam, his hands resting on his knees, asked the woman in the green dress as

Perry approached. Simon, his hands on his hips and breathing deeply, looked over and gave Perry a thumbs up.

"As far as I know, he's in the show production office. He told us all to go back to the hotel and pack. He said he would finish up here."

"Thanks," Fitzwilliam said, taking a deep breath. Then he straightened up and, looking at Simon, said, "Come on, Lattimore." He set off again, heading towards the cluster of temporary cabins in the distance.

"Perry, try texting her again," Simon shouted over his shoulder as he followed Fitzwilliam. "Seems like she's in danger."

Hands on his sides, trying to get his breath, Perry pulled his phone from his pocket.

Perry: *If you're with Seb, get out of there as soon as you can. He's probably the killer. We're on our way!*

Giving a worried-looking Klara an apologetic shrug, he began to run.

51

MEANWHILE, TUESDAY 6 OCTOBER

Seb moved a step closer as Daisy bared her teeth at him. He ignored her.

"You see, *bella*, my business is in a little trouble. I have big loan repayments due next month, and I am —how you say— strapped for cash. It's just a temporary situation. But if you and I were to reunite and stay together for maybe six or seven weeks, the people I owe money to will back off, and I'll have time to deal with it."

Is he joking? He wants me to agree to get back with him to get his creditors off his back!

The fear and panic she'd been feeling was replaced with a massive surge of anger.

Is he mad? Does he really think I'll act lovey-dovey with him to cover for his poor business management?

Glaring at him, she hissed, "I've never heard anything so ridiculous in my life. No, Seb, I will not pretend to be your girlfriend while you work out how to pay your debts."

"But, *bella*—"

So is this what this has all been about? And there she'd been, worrying he'd killed Luca. And all along…

"How dare you use me like this!" she yelled.

She was about to barge past him, grab her phone, and storm out, but a quick glance at his face stopped her in her tracks. Distorted with rage, it was a reddish-purple colour and almost puffy, as if he was having an allergic reaction to something.

Oh my goodness. If looks could kill!

"Stop!" he bellowed. "You don't understand, bella."

What was there to understand? He'd used her; that was all she needed to know. Her courage rose again. She wasn't interested in his excuses anymore.

"Oh, I understand perfectly," she shouted back.

He stared at her, then taking a deep breath, he seemed to calm down. His eyes met hers. "No, *bella*, you don't. There are things about me you don't know." He shook his head. "Nobody knows. Only Luca. But if those things get out, then I'm a dead man."

Only Luca? *What did Luca know about him?*

She held his gaze. "Luca? What happened with Luca, Seb?"

His eyes widened and then tears began to well up in them.

Oh my goodness. He killed Luca! Blind panic felt like it would overtake her again as she backed away from him. A trickle of sweat ran down her back. She needed to get out. She looked over again towards the door. If she took him by surprise, then maybe she would just have time to make it out before he realised. It was her best hope.

He reached out his arm. "*Bella*, please…"

She managed to take one step forward before he lunged at her.

Fitzwilliam desperately tried to get enough air into his lungs to keep running, his vision fixed on the group of cabins ahead of him.

A car was parked by the side of one office, and he recognised it as Seb's.

Thank goodness he's still here.

Simon, not far behind him, shouted something to Perry.

Just let her be all right.

He narrowed his eyes and drew on all his remaining energy as he sped up.

Hang on, Lady Beatrice, I'll be there soon.

Feeling her whole body shaking, she instinctively jumped to the side, hoping to evade his grasp. But she was too late. The pain of his fingers as they dug into the flesh at the top of her right arm made her gasp. For a second, she froze, her brain struggling to accept that the man who had lovingly touched her arm in the past was now snaring it in his hand, oblivious to the hurt he was causing her.

He pulled her towards him. His warm breath fanned her face as he murmured, "This isn't how I wanted it to be, believe me. But I had no choice, *bella*."

Her arm began to throb, and she felt like her heart would burst out of her chest. She struggled to get out of his clasp. But it was no use. He was too strong.

She was vaguely aware of a growling noise coming from below her as he continued, "And now I have no choice again."

She took a deep breath in as she racked her brain for a suitable move she had learned on her kidnapping awareness course. But Seb was taller and stronger than anyone she'd been shown how to tackle. *Maybe if I bite...*

Suddenly, there was a yelp and her arm was released. She fell backwards with so much force she felt as if she'd been hit by a truck. She automatically put her hands out to steady herself, but she couldn't find anything to hold on to. She hit the low cabinet behind her hard, producing a loud *thump* as her back made contact. Pain washed over her as she crumpled down the front of the unit.

Sitting on the floor winded, she opened her eyes to see Seb jumping up and down, holding his lower leg, a series of what she assumed were Italian expletives tumbling out of his mouth.

Standing a little away from him, her teeth bared and still emitting a low growl, was Daisy.

What happened?

She placed her hands on the floor and tried to scramble up. Wincing as a sharp hot pain shot up her back, she slouched back against the cabinet, her legs giving way, her head spinning.

Seb jerked around, hopping on one leg, his voice shaking with fury as he looked down at her. "Your stupid dog bit me!"

A large dark-red patch of blood seeped through his jeans. *Serves you right!*

His lips curled like flames as he turned and swooped towards the little dog.

"Daisy!" Lady Beatrice cried out in alarm. *Don't you dare hurt her or...* She desperately tried to move again, but as she twisted to put her weight on her hands so she could get up, she felt as if a red-hot poker was being stabbed into the base of her back. Her vision blurred, and she felt the urge to cry. *Get a grip, Bea!* As she slumped backwards, she frantically scanned the room. Seeing Daisy dart away from Seb and run behind his desk, she breathed a sigh of relief. *Wait there, Daisy. I'm coming.*

She breathed in deeply. *It's only pain,* as Fred, her brother, would say. As she slowly let her breath out, Seb staggered after Daisy. Lady Beatrice placed her hands in front of her and bent forward, gritting her teeth as pain sheered through her body. Now on all fours, she looked up just as Seb looked around.

He hesitated and turned to gaze at her. The manic look in his eye made her gasp in a large gulp of air. *Will he come after me now? I must get up.* Using her hands, she pushed herself backwards onto the balls of her feet, her eyes fixed on the man limping towards her. Her heart turned somersaults. *Is he going to kill me?*

Suddenly, he stopped.

Her legs went weak.

He wheeled around as Lady Beatrice's mobile phone, still sitting on the edge of the table, vibrated again. He lurched forward and seized hold of it. His brow furrowed as he read the message, then his face turned pale. Throwing the mobile back onto the table, he muttered, "*Cavalo!*"

From her crouching position, Lady Beatrice saw the light glinting off his forehead, which was beaded with moisture. Seb looked around the room, feverishly muttering, "*Fuga,*" then returning his gaze to the table, he grabbed his car keys and hobbled from the room.

Barking, Daisy ran after him.

———————

"Look!"

Detective Chief Inspector Richard Fitzwilliam slowed down slightly.'

Simon Lattimore, just a shoulder length behind him, shouted, "Isn't that Seb getting into his car?"

A man limped towards the blue Mercedes the width of a football pitch ahead of them. "Looks like it," Fitzwilliam shouted back. *But where's Lady Beatrice?*

He shifted his gaze towards the office to the right of the car just in time to see (and hear) Daisy come charging down the stairs, barking.

Where is she? Why isn't she following Daisy?

He took a deep breath and sprinted towards the cabin, shouting to Simon as he pulled away. "Get the number plate and ring Spicer."

I must get my mobile and ring Fitzwilliam.

As Daisy dashed through the door after Seb, Lady Beatrice pushed her heels down firmly on the floor, and keeping her back still, she straightened her legs. Wobbling, she pushed her hands backwards to grab the back of the piece of furniture, but it was no use. Her knees buckled, and she slid down the cabinet again into a heap at the bottom.

Reaching Daisy a few minutes later, Richard Fitzwilliam looked to his left to see the back of the Mercedes disappear around the corner in a cloud of dust. *He won't get far.*

Coming to a standstill in front of the little terrier, he rasped, "Where's your mum, Daisy?" Daisy wagged her tail, then ran towards the cabin steps.

As they burst into the office, Fitzwilliam's heart still pumped heavily. Frantically scanning the cabin, he followed Daisy as she scuttled across the room and disappeared around the side of a large desk.

Hands on his hips, he stooped down to see where she'd gone. His stomach flipped over when he saw, poking out from behind the back of the desk, two black jeans-covered legs lying on the floor.

Lady Beatrice! He launched himself towards her.

Please let her be okay!

It's only pain! Perry gritted his teeth as the back of his shoe gouged out another layer of skin on his right heel. *Keep going. It's not far now.*

Ahead of him, Perry watched Fitzwilliam vanish into one of the offices, following closely on the heels of Daisy.

Perry had been relieved to see Daisy appear a few minutes ago, barking at Seb as the chef had dived into his car and sped off. But concern had quickly replaced that feeling. *Where's Bea?*

Still focused on the door to the cabin, hoping she would appear any moment, it took him a few seconds to realise that Simon, who had been right behind Fitzwilliam, had stopped and was now shouting on his phone. *What's going on?*

Puffing, Perry took a deep breath in, and with one last enormous effort, he hurtled towards his partner.

"Lady Beatrice?"

There was an urgency to the shout. She recognised the northern accent of DCI Richard Fitzwilliam. *What's he doing here? Have they caught Seb?*

Before she had time to reply, Daisy came haring around the side of the desk and flung herself at her mistress, landing a wet, soppy lick right on her nose.

"Get off!" Lady Beatrice whispered as the terrier continued to nuzzle her face. Thank goodness Daisy wasn't hurt. Lady Beatrice swallowed as the back of her eyes prickled. *If anything had happened to her…*

"Lady Beatrice… Are you all right?" The voice was broken and getting closer.

She sniffed, and fighting off Daisy, she replied in a weak voice, "Yes, I'm fine."

Come on, Bea. You don't want him to find you on the floor!

Gently pushing Daisy away, she gritted her teeth, took a deep breath, and flipped herself over onto her knees. The pain hit her in a wave, and she thought she might be sick, but it passed quickly, and reaching up, she grabbed the top of the cabinet and heaved herself up.

"Are you hurt?" Fitzwilliam appeared just as she got to her feet but was still hunched over the set of drawers. He breathed heavily, and his face had a healthy glow.

"I think I'm okay," she said as she took another deep breath and slowly straightened up. The pain had dulled somewhat, and as she steadied herself on the furniture, she looked up and smiled into the concerned face of DCI Fitzwilliam. "I'll live. Did you catch Seb? I think he killed Luca."

"Don't worry, he won't get far… Now come and sit down," Fitzwilliam said, still breathing heavily, and offered her his arm.

She hesitated for a second. *I need to tell him what Seb said.* The base of her back was now throbbing. *Okay, I'll sit down for a minute.* Slipping her arm in his, she hobbled alongside him as he steered her over to an office chair by the door. "He said Luca knew something about him that no one else knew. I think that's why he killed him. He told me that if anyone found out his secret, then he was a dead man."

"Let's not worry about that now. I need you to sit quietly and recover." As she let go to sit down, he continued, "Now can you waggle your toes for me, please?"

She moved her toes. "Yes, they're working. Honestly, I'm fine."

He still looked at her with concern in his eyes, but before he could say anything more, Simon and Perry burst through the doorway.

"Bea, are you okay?" Simon cried as he rushed towards her, Daisy dancing around his feet.

"Are you hurt?" Perry shrieked as he followed behind him.

She held up a hand. "I'm all right. Just a little sore. Where's Seb?"

"He drove away before we could stop him," Perry replied, his face bright crimson and his breathing uneven.

"But we've told Spicer and CID. He won't get far," Simon added, sweat dripping down his forehead.

She looked up at Fitzwilliam standing over her. "Do *you* think Seb murdered Luca?"

Fitzwilliam returned her gaze, then slowly nodded as he took in a long breath. "I believe so." He shifted his weight and took another breath in. "We found an audio file on Luca's phone a short while ago. I've not heard it myself yet, but it seems Luca had worked out that it was Seb who had added the mushrooms to the demo dish."

Luca had known it had been Seb while he'd been dying. *How awful.* She raised her hands to her face and rubbed her forehead with her fingers.

"He said it must have been to stop him from revealing Seb's secret," Fitzwilliam continued.

"What secret?" Perry asked, his eyes wide.

Lowering her hands, she opened her mouth, but Fitzwilliam got in first. "Mr Marchetti told Lady Beatrice here before he did a runner that Luca knew something about him that no one else did. Hopefully, he can throw some light on that for us when we find—"

Daisy moved to the desk and stood in front of it, barking.

I forgot about the bag and basket. "There's a basket in the box on the table, Fitzwilliam, with a hessian bag inside," she told him. "Daisy retrieved it from the back seat of Seb's car. I don't know if it's any help."

Fitzwilliam walked over to the desk and bent down in front of Daisy, who had now stopped barking. "Well done, Daisy," he said as he patted her on the head. He peered at the items, then stood up. "I'll get Forensics on it."

Lady Beatrice nodded and rose slowly. The pain was subsiding now and being replaced by a dull ache at the base of her back. She rubbed it with her hand and winced. *Ouch!* She inched towards the desk just as her mobile phone vibrated its way an inch closer to the edge.

Fitzwilliam snatched it before it fell off. "Is this yours?" he asked her, holding it out towards her.

"Indeed. Thank you." She reached him and took it. Glancing down, she saw four missed calls and five unread text messages. But one notification was still on the screen. She gasped. *Seb!* She felt dizzy and grabbed at the desk to steady herself.

"What is it?" Perry cried, rushing over.

She turned to face the three men in the room. She swallowed. "It's a message from Seb."

"What does it say?" Fitzwilliam asked gently.

With shaking fingers, she tapped the message.

Seb: *I'm so sorry, bella. xx*

52

EARLY AFTERNOON, TUESDAY 6 OCTOBER

"Are you sure you're okay, Bea? Maybe you should get a doctor to look at you. Just in case." Simon leaned over the table in the Breakfast Room at Francis Court and dabbed her right arm. She flinched. *Ow!*

The adrenaline that had kept her going since they'd left Fenn House seemed to be running out. She wanted to close her eyes and sleep for a week. And the aches and pains had returned with a vengeance. Her back ached, and now her arm was throbbing again.

"What's wrong?" Perry leaned over, his eyes full of concern.

Lady Beatrice stroked the top of her arm and smiled. "It's fine. Seb grabbed me, and it's a little sore." She was relieved when the server arrived and delivered their food and drinks. She suddenly felt ravenous and dived on her brie and cranberry panini as if she hadn't eaten for days.

"So why do you think Seb sent you that message?" Perry asked as he picked up his club sandwich. "Bearing in mind that he was probably being chased by the police at the time."

She'd been wondering about that herself. *Sorry for what?*

Hurting her physically? Betraying her trust? Or for killing Luca? *Did Seb really murder Luca?* She was still trying to get her head around the idea that Seb could kill anyone. And what was this secret? If it was the reason Luca had had to die, then it must be a fairly big deal.

She shook her head as she finished chewing and picked up a napkin. Wiping her mouth, she replied. "I really don't know. It all seems like a bad dream now. I can't believe that Seb would kill anyone. I really can't."

Simon nodded. "I agree. But the evidence against him seems to be stacking up."

She sighed. "Do we know anything more about the recording on Luca's phone?"

"Not at the moment. I'll try to talk to Steve later. It's possible Seb will have an explanation for it all when they interview him."

I really hope so.

Daisy, who had been sitting next to Perry, her eyes wide and pleading as he tucked into his food, jumped up and dashed off towards the door. Lady Beatrice turned to see Fitzwilliam's tall frame walking across the almost empty restaurant and heading towards them. Her scalp prickled. *Have they caught Seb?* Fitzwilliam's shoulders were slumped, and he was looking down at the marble floor while Daisy trotted beside him. *Something's wrong. Did Seb get away? Have they found out he's not the murderer?* She shifted sideways in her chair as he sat down next to her.

"I have news," he said, rubbing the stubble just showing on his chin.

Perry and Simon, sitting opposite him, leaned in.

"Did you catch him?" Perry asked eagerly.

He shook his head. "Not exactly."

53

LATE AFTERNOON, TUESDAY 6 OCTOBER

The Society Page online article:

<u>BREAKING NEWS Sebastiano Marchetti Tragically Died in Car Accident</u>

The police have now confirmed that Sebastiano Marchetti (38), known to his army of fans as Chef Seb, died earlier today in a car accident in Fenshire.

They have released no further details at this time, but we understand the chef was driving on the Fenshire coast road when he lost control of his car, and it went over a cliff. Emergency crews scrambled to the scene, but sadly, Chef Seb couldn't be saved.

An eyewitness told The Daily Post, 'A blue Mercedes came speeding along the road at about eighty and didn't turn in time at the corner. The car left the road and plunged about seventy feet down the side of the cliff. He didn't stand a chance'. It is not known if Sebastiano was wearing a seat belt or not.

His fans are left devastated by the news and have taken to

social media to share their shock and grief. One fan wrote, 'RIP Chef Seb. I have no words right now. My thoughts are with your family and friends', while another wrote, 'First Luca Mazza, now Sebastiano Marchetti. Two amazing chefs taken too soon. I only hope they are in heaven right now cooking up a storm. RIP Chefs'.

Tributes have also flooded in from the chef's friends and business contacts. His agent Mal Cassan released the following statement: 'Words cannot describe how devastated I am to have lost my great friend, Sebastiano Marchetti. He was not just an incredible chef, he was an extraordinary man who will be greatly missed'.

The Italian chef, who until recently was romantically linked with Lady Beatrice, the Countess of Rossex, was best known for his television appearances on shows such as Get Your Cook On, *the BBC's* Sunday Roast *and* Cook Italian. *He was also a regular guest judge for the cooking competition,* Elitechef.

Sebastiano also owned and was the executive chef of three of London's best restaurants, including the two-Michelin-starred celebrity haunt, The Flyer in Mayfair, and Nonnina, the three-Michelin-starred fine dining restaurant in Knightsbridge.

We will bring you more details as they emerge.

54

EARLY EVENING, TUESDAY 6
OCTOBER

"Darling, my advice is to get it over and done with now, while his death is still all over the press. If you leave it more than a few days, it will become a much bigger story in its own right. Right now, there are so many people having their say about him, it will get lost in the general tributes." Her Royal Highness Princess Helen leaned back on the teal sofa in her daughter's sitting room and crossed her legs, holding her cup containing Earl Grey tea steadily with one hand and resting the other on her *Valentino* silk printed trouser-clad knee.

Sitting on the sofa opposite her mother, her back to the large windows dominating the room, Lady Beatrice frowned. *I'm sure she's right. But what do I say?* She felt nothing at the moment. The initial shock of finding out Seb had killed Luca had been compounded when Fitzwilliam had told them that Seb was dead. *A dead murderer!* She'd dated a murderer who was now dead. *How did that happen?* She was still numb around the edges. *I just can't believe this!*

Earlier, Perry and Simon had escorted her to her apartment and fed her copious amounts of coffee. Her head had only just stopped buzzing. After she had convinced them she would be all right on her own, she had sat where she was now, shaking from head to foot. Then the tears had begun. Streaming down her face, fat tears had covered her lips, their saltiness invading her mouth. She hadn't been able to fathom out if she had been crying for Seb, whose life had been tragically cut short, or for herself, who had been duped by a handsome, charming murderer. One who may well have killed her too. At least that's what the boys and Fitzwilliam had been concerned about.

She wasn't so sure. Admittedly, when she'd confronted him, she'd been afraid when he'd lashed out at her. And she'd been fairly sure given half a chance, he would have willingly harmed Daisy. But kill *her*? She shook her head. Seb was all about appearances, about living up to the image he'd created. He wouldn't want anyone to know he was capable of murder. Not at that stage anyway. Of course, once he'd realised the police had been on to him, he'd fled. She assumed because he'd believed he would be in danger if the truth came out.

And, in a cruel twist of irony, he was certainly getting all the press attention he could ever have dreamed about right now.

She suppressed a sigh. It was still hard to believe Seb was gone. And yet as more information had come out about Seb's accident, the more she could imagine what had happened. The police had recovered his phone, and the last text he'd sent had been the one to her. *How many times did I warn him about texting while driving?* The emergency services had also told Fitzwilliam that Seb's seat belt hadn't been fastened when they'd recovered his body, but his arm had been hooked through it. *The number of times I had to remind him to fasten it before setting off, not while he was driving!* Upset, afraid, and unfamiliar with the twisty coast roads, trying to get his seat belt on while texting her, not looking where he was going… There was a tightness in her chest. *Oh, Seb, you must have been in such a panic.* She took a sip of her green tea.

"Darling?"

"Sorry, Ma. If I'm honest, I don't know what to say right now. I'm still in shock. And I don't want to lie about my feelings either. After all, it's only a matter of time before everyone finds out he killed Luca."

Princess Helen leaned forward and placed her empty cup of tea on the low wooden coffee table between them. "Do we know for sure he killed Luca?"

"According to Fitzwilliam, there is very little doubt, even at this stage. Plus, he had means and opportunity. And of course, once he read the text from Perry to me, warning me that he was the killer and they were on their way to rescue me, he hightailed it away. Why would he run if he wasn't guilty?"

Her mother nodded slowly. "And what do you think, darling?"

Lady Beatrice shook her head. "I think I have poor taste in men and I'm better off alone."

"Aw, darling." Her mother rose elegantly and joined her on the sofa opposite. Putting her arm around Lady Beatrice's shoulders, Princess Helen pulled her tightly into her side and kissed the top of her head. "You just haven't met the right one yet." Princess Helen moved her hands to Lady Beatrice's arms and twisted her around to face her. "They say that every relationship we have teaches us something new about ourselves. Even the wrong ones, Bea, teach us something to prepare us for the right one."

"So next time, don't get involved with a murderer. Is that what you mean, Ma?"

Princess Helen dropped her arms and patted her daughter's hand. Her tone shifted from gentle to stern. "I know you like to make a joke of things, Bea, but do try to learn something from this. You have good instincts. No, in fact, you have excellent instincts. There were red flags all over the place during your relationship with Seb that had nothing to do with the murder. You ignored them. Don't make the same mistake next time."

Well, that's me told!

Her mother sighed. "And I'm sorry, darling, but you still need to make a statement to the press about his death."

She's right. She's always right!

Lady Beatrice suppressed a sigh while she tried to assess how she felt. *Sad.* Yes, that's how she felt about Seb's death. *I'm sad.*

"All right, Ma. How about if we keep it short and sweet? Say that I am saddened by his sudden death and my thoughts are with his friends and family at this difficult time. Is that enough?"

"Yes, that will do. I'll talk to our PR team now and get it issued."

Her mother nodded and rose, a smile playing on her lips. "And next time you meet a handsome and charming man, darling, get Daisy to vet them. They say dogs are an excellent judge of character."

55

MEANWHILE, TUESDAY 6 OCTOBER

"Will Bea be all right?" Perry Juke walked over to the armchair overlooking the garden at Rose Cottage and, having placed his tea on the side table next to it, plonked himself down.

"She'll be fine," Simon shouted from across the open-plan living space, from the kitchen area where he was stirring a butter sauce on the stove top. "She's much tougher than she —" He stopped as his phone beeped. Picking up the mobile, he opened the message. "Perry, can you come here, please?" he hollered.

Perry jumped up, concerned by the urgency in Simon's voice, and hurried across the room. "What's wrong?"

"This sauce is at a critical stage, and if it's not stirred continuously, it will split. Can you take over while I make a quick call?"

Perry huffed. "I thought it was something important."

"If you want my cod in butter sauce for dinner, then yes, it's important."

Fair point. It was one of Perry's favourite fish recipes. "Okay, I'll stir it gently, as required."

Simon grinned and pressed his phone screen.

I bet it's CID Steve with some important inside informa-tion about Luca's murder or Roisin telling us about Seb's autopsy. Perry wondered if they'd found out what this secret was that had made Seb kill Luca. It still seemed like a bit of a mystery to him, and with Seb dead, how would they ever know the truth now?

"Sam? How are you, mucker?"

Sam? Perry frowned. Who was Sam? Someone at Simon's book publishers, maybe?

"Yes, she's coming over for dinner in about—" Simon looked at his watch. "Twenty minutes."

Perry was even more confused. Why would someone at Simon's publishers be interested that Bea was due for dinner shortly?

"We only left her an hour ago, and she was going to talk to your grandmother. She's doing fine. There's no need to worry, Sam…"

Perry mentally slapped his hand to his head while stirring the rich yellow sauce in front of him. *Oh,* that *Sam.*

"… yes, milk poached cod in butter sauce with chard and a beet tops pesto. And probably an endive and rocket salad…"

Perry smiled. He loved that Simon and Sam could talk food together.

"… okay, we can cook it together when you're next home. So how are you feeling about the whole Seb thing, buddy?" A slow smile spread across Simon's face as he listened to the boy at the other end.

He's so good with him. Perry's smile faded, and cold suddenly flooded his body. *Simon would make such a great dad.*

"… well yes, he was preoccupied when you met him…"

Why can't I see myself being like that? Perry shivered, remembering the incident a few days ago when Simon had thought he'd been feeding Sam alcohol at the gin stall. *He worries I'm not responsible enough. And he's right to worry.*

"... no, I've never seen Daisy take a dislike to anyone like that either..."

Perry swallowed and looked down at the sauce, just bubbling at the edges of the saucepan. *I couldn't cope with the mess for a start.* All their friends who had children seemed to have piles of various brightly coloured toys stuck in the corner of every room in the house. *How do you live like that?*

"... yes, I expect Ryan and Finn will do more television work now. So you're cool with it all, are you?"

Simon looked over Perry's shoulder at the sauce and gave him a thumbs up. Removing the saucepan from the heat, Perry placed it on the warming plate. *And what about holi-days?* You'd not get Perry at an all-inclusive hotel with a kid's club if you paid him. *The wine selection in those places is appalling!*

"...it is sad, you're right. But he wasn't really that old, Sam. He was only thirty-eight. I'd hardly call that ancient." Simon caught Perry's eye and winked, a smile on his face.

And they're more of a financial drain the older they get. Perry recalled his aunt recently complaining to him about how she'd had to bail out his twenty-something cousin who'd run up a credit card debt while studying to be a doctor in London. "Well, it's just so hard for them to afford to go anywhere or do anything on a student loan," she'd explained. Perry enjoyed spending his own money too much to want to waste it on funding his children's drunken nights out at the latest 'in' club. *And they seem to get away with going out in tracksuits and trainers these days!* Perry shuddered.

"… well, when you get older, you'll change your mind. Okay, then, mucker, you need to do your homework. And don't worry about your mum, we've got her, okay?… Yes, we'll give her a big hug from you when she gets here."

Simon cut the call and turned to look at Perry. "Thanks for that. Sam's worried about how Bea is holding up." He shook his head. "It's funny how sensitive thirteen-year-old boys can be sometimes, isn't it?"

Perry nodded. *Maybe Bea is right.* He should subtly tell Simon that he was worried about not wanting children. He took a deep breath in and let it out in a rush.

"I don't want children. Please don't leave me," he blurted out, heat rising up his neck as Simon's brown eyes met his gaze.

A smile tugged at the corners of Simon's mouth. "I know you don't. And you'll have to try harder than that to get me to go."

Perry thought he would pass out. He licked his dry lips. "I, er, what? So you're okay with it?"

Simon's smile turned into a grin. "Perry, do you really want a screaming child stopping you from getting your eight hours of sleep a night? Who will then turn into a toddler with sticky fingers messing up the house? And then it will go to school and probably bite some other child, and we'll get told off for being terrible parents. And of course, just when we hope it's all over and they become adults, we'll need to buy them a car or be prepared to be permanent taxi drivers. Oh, and that's also the point when they will go on holiday abroad for the first time, get completely drunk, and end up either in hospital or in jail, and we'll have to fly out to rescue them." He shook his head.

He gets it! An enormous smile split Perry's face. *I love this man so much.*

"All I can see in our future if we have children is tantrums and arguments."

Exactly!

"And that's just from you!"

Aw, he knows me so well! Perry threw himself into Simon's arms and held on tight. "Thank you, love."

After a few minutes, Simon detangled himself and held Perry at arm's length. "Perry. I love you just as you are. And although I think you'd make a great dad, I totally get that it's not for you, and I'm fine with that. You're enough for me." He leaned in and kissed Perry gently. "More than enough," he whispered.

Cheeky! Perry swiped at the love of his life as he pulled away and threw his head back, laughing.

56

SLIGHTLY LATER IN THE EVENING, TUESDAY 6 OCTOBER

"This is scrumptious." As she took another mouthful of the flaky cod coated in the rich buttery sauce, Lady Beatrice was aware she was running out of adjectives to describe Simon's food.

"I helped with the sauce," Perry told her proudly as he scooped up another forkful.

She raised an eyebrow at Simon. "You let Perry cook? I thought his job was to chop vegetables and select wine?"

"Rude!" Perry tried to suppress a grin as he threw her a look. "I'll have you know I can also assemble a mean salad."

Lady Beatrice laughed. *I needed this.* She needed the light and effortless banter she had with her two friends to chase away the gloom that had surrounded her earlier as she'd contemplated her part in the events that had led to Seb accidentally driving off a cliff. The sadness and disbelief she'd felt when talking with her mother had now been replaced with a combination of guilt *—if only he'd not been texting me* — and anger *—how dare he drag me back into the spotlight again.* Some of the popular press were now comparing Seb's death to that of James's fourteen years ago, just because they'd both been killed in car accidents. As if losing the man she'd loved and had expected to spend the rest of her life with could compare to losing someone she had barely known and, if she was totally honest, had begun to go off even before he'd turned out to be a murderer. One newspaper columnist had even suggested that she was a bad omen and now no man would want to date her. *Good!* That suited her just fine...

"How are you holding up, Bea?" Perry leaned over and touched her hand as he pushed his empty plate away.

She smiled. "I'm still finding it hard to take it all in, but I'll be fine."

He nodded. "Yes, I wish we knew a bit more about why Seb killed Luca. It must be something to do with this 'secret' Luca knew about him. I wonder if we'll ever find out what it was." He stood up and gathered the used plates. "I'll take these and then put the coffee on."

"Thanks," Simon said, smiling at his partner.

As Perry disappeared into the kitchen, Lady Beatrice was surprised when Simon leaned across the table and, grabbing her hand, whispered, "I need your help."

"Of course. What's wrong?"

"Nothing. In fact, it's just the opposite." He grinned.

Intrigued, she raised an eyebrow. "Go on."

"I want to ask Perry to marry me."

Somehow she managed to suppress the *squeal* she so wanted to make, and instead, a huge smile engulfed her face. *Oh my goodness.* "Oh my goodness, I'm so happy for you both." She kept her voice low, although the noise of Perry crashing and banging around by the dishwasher reassured her that he couldn't hear them.

"So I was thinking, what better place to do it than in a castle in Scotland?"

Lady Beatrice's pulse quickened. "So you'll come with us?"

She and Perry had been trying to persuade Simon to accompany them up to Drew Castle in January, but he'd been worried about his early February deadline to submit the draft of his next book to his editor and thought the trip would be too distracting for him.

"You and Perry have convinced me I can write as well up in Scotland as I can at home. Is the offer to find me a room or office I can use still on the table?"

"Of course," she replied, squeezing his hand. "And the sunsets from the front of the castle are amazing." She sighed. "Maybe you could ask him on the balcony of the Upper Drawing Room with the sun setting in the background."

"Hey, don't go all Barbara Cartland on me." He grinned. Then his smile faded. "He will say yes, won't he?"

She chuckled as she let go of his hands. "Yes. Definitely. Without a doubt. Totally."

57

SHORTLY AFTER, TUESDAY 6 OCTOBER

Perry placed the coffee pot and cups on the table. "What are you two up to?"

"Nothing," Lady Beatrice replied, putting on her best 'innocent' face.

"Actually, I have some news," Simon said as Perry sat down.

He wasn't going to tell him, was he? *That's not how you do it, Simon!*

"Oh, love," Perry said, lifting his hand to his chest. "I'm not sure I can cope with any more news today."

"It's okay. It's good news."

"All right. Good news I can do." He nodded as he picked up the pot and poured a steaming black coffee into a cup and handed it to Lady Beatrice.

"I'd love to come to Drew Castle with you both in the new year."

Thank goodness!

Perry put done the coffee pot and clapped his hands. "That's brilliant news!" He turned and hugged Simon. "We promise we'll let you write, won't we, Bea?"

She nodded. "That's what we were just talking about. I'll find the perfect room for Simon to work in so he doesn't get disturbed."

"Yay," Perry cried. "I'm so excited now. Scotland with all my favourite people..." He paused. "Daisy is coming too, isn't she?"

Lady Beatrice smiled as she glanced over at Daisy curled up on her preferred armchair in front of the bifold doors leading to the garden. She nodded. "Of course. As my mother pointed out, she's a better judge of character than I am. So from now on, she goes everywhere with me."

"Oh, Bea." Perry returned her smile. "He fooled us all, hun."

"Except Fitzwilliam. He thought it was Seb right from the start," she said, grimacing. She hated that he'd been proven right.

"Oh, that reminds me," Simon said, adding cream to his coffee. "I had a text from Roisin just as I was serving up. They found traces of death cap mushrooms on the hessian sack Daisy found in the back of Seb's car."

There's no doubt then. Seb had killed Luca.

The doorbell ringing made them all start. Daisy jumped out of the chair and ran across the open-plan kitchen diner as Perry got up and followed her out into the hall.

"Sorry," Simon said. "I fear I may have killed the mood."

She gave him a wry smile and shook her head. "We can't avoid the truth when the evidence keeps mounting up like this."

A movement behind them made her turn just as Daisy trotted back into the room, followed by DCI Richard Fitzwilliam and Perry.

"The chief inspector is here, Bea," Perry said and winked at her. "Coffee, Fitzwilliam?" He held out an arm and steered the detective over to the large dining table. "Please sit down."

"Yes, coffee would be great, thanks," Fitzwilliam said as he took a seat beside Lady Beatrice. "My lady, Lattimore. Sorry to disturb you, but I have some new information to share with you."

Perry handed him a cup of coffee.

"No problem, Fitzwilliam," Simon said. "Fire away."

"Well, first, the results on the sack Daisy found have come back, and it contains traces of death cap mushrooms, as did the basket they were in when we recovered them."

Lady Beatrice and Simon nodded while Perry murmured, "Oh, really?"

Fitzwilliam didn't seem to notice their combined lack of surprise and carried on. "So as she found it in the back of Mr Marchetti's car, they will now check the recovered vehicle and see what else they can find in there."

Lady Beatrice frowned. "Simon, didn't Klara Damas tell you she'd seen Seb getting something from his car before she'd watched him head to the demo tent for the rehearsal?"

Simon nodded. "Yes, well remembered. Maybe he picked the mushrooms earlier that morning or even on Sunday evening and then kept them in his car until he could use them?"

"You could be right," Fitzwilliam said, taking a sip of his coffee. "Secondly, the PaIRS IT team have been working on Luca's laptop and have come across some files that may indicate what the secret was that Luca knew about Seb. We need to do more digging, I might add, because it seems extraordinary if it's true."

Come on then, tell us! Lady Beatrice twisted around in her seat while Perry and Simon leaned across the table.

"Luca had a directory titled *Autobiography* on his laptop.

It seems he gathered information and made notes ready for him, or more likely a ghostwriter, to use for the book. Along with birth and death certificates of various family members and a career timeline, there was a sub-directory called *Seb.* Inside were some old newspaper cuttings that had been photographed and uploaded."

On the edge of her seat, Lady Beatrice gripped her coffee cup, her lower leg bouncing off the tiled floor. *Come on. Get to the point...*

"The articles all refer to an incident that took place twenty years ago in Calabria, an area in Italy that, at the time, was heavily controlled by the local mafia. However, there was a power struggle going on between the local gang headed up by the Brambilla family and the Cosa Nostra, the Sicilian mafia you may have heard of, who wanted a slice of the action. Anyway, on this one particular night, there was a violent confrontation between the two groups. People on both sides were killed and injured. One person who was shot dead was a leading member of the Cosa Nostra organisation called Pietro De Santis and another was a young boy of eighteen, Franco Brambilla, son of the leader of the local mob. Eyewitnesses claimed it was Franco who shot Pietro first, then one of Pietro's brothers in turn killed him."

He took another sip of his coffee and continued, "Luca had reports not only of the actual fight but also of the funeral of the young boy, Franco, who was buried only a few days later at a private funeral attended only by close family. He also had a copy of Franco's obituary from the local paper. In it was highlighted in green the section about Franco having attended a catering college called Pesah Academy from the age of seventeen. His father was rumoured to have pulled him off the course after only six months when his eldest son, Franco's brother, was killed in a hit, believed to have been instigated by Pietro to intimidate the Brambilla family into giving up their stronghold in the area."

Why are you telling us this?

"But what has this got to do with Seb?" Perry blurted out, unable to contain his frustration any longer.

Indeed.

"I'm getting to that, Mr Juke."

Perry, colouring, mumbled, "Sorry."

"When the PaIRS officers looked at the timeline document Luca had written, low and behold, Luca Mazza had also attended the Pesah Academy at the same time as young Franco Brambilla, and by the side of those dates, Luca had written 'Franco - scar on left hand injured when killing lobster.'."

Lady Beatrice gasped and raised her hands to her mouth. *Oh my goodness.*

"Lady Beatrice?" Fitzwilliam's voice cut through her shock.

She swallowed and in a shaky voice whispered, "Seb had a scar on his left hand!"

58

A FEW MINUTES LATER, TUESDAY 6 OCTOBER

"Bea?" Perry Juke broke the silence following the revelation that Sebastiano Marchetti could have been Franco Brambilla —son of a mafia gang leader, killer of the regional head of the notorious Cosa Nostra, and supposedly buried twenty years ago.

"I appreciate this has probably come as a bit of a shock to you, Lady Beatrice." Detective Chief Inspector Richard Fitzwilliam shifted in his seat next to her.

A bit of a shock? What a good old British understatement that was! Lady Beatrice smothered a desire to giggle.

"Indeed," she responded, her voice sounding muffled in her own ears. *Could this possibly all be true?* She tried to recall what Seb had told her about his childhood, but he'd told her very little. He'd talked about his love of cooking coming from his beloved Nonna, who he'd later named his first restaurant after. Lady Beatrice couldn't recall him mentioning a catering school, although he had talked about being in New York as a young chef and how that had been where he'd learned his trade. Remembering how he'd told her that his parents hadn't been around anymore, she asked, "What happened to Franco's parents?"

"They died in an explosion at their home six months after Franco's supposed death. It was reported to be a revenge killing by Pietro's family."

It all seemed so fantastical. But deep down, she knew it was true. Because of the scar. "Seb told me he got the scar when he was first training as a young chef, preparing a lobster."

"Oh my giddy aunt!" Perry raised his hand to his mouth.

She had a sudden thought. "Wasn't lobster one of the words Luca cried out to Fay when he was dying?"

Fitzwilliam frowned. "I don't have my notes with me, but, yes, I think it was. I remember thinking the recipe was very fishy." He gave a wry smile. "No pun intended."

"So it seems like Seb really could be Franco," Simon said, shaking his head. "How extraordinary."

Fitzwilliam nodded. "And had a compelling motive for wanting to keep it quiet."

Of course! Luca could have blown Seb's cover, and Seb would not only have lost everything, but presumably not only the Italian police but also the surviving Cosa Nostra would have been after him for the murder of Pietro De Santis. No wonder he had been so scared he'd run away.

She turned to Fitzwilliam. "But Luca and Seb were friends. They worked together for years. Luca was Seb's right-hand man. So why now?"

"We're not sure, but Marta told us that Luca was hoping to open his own restaurant soon, and Seb was going to back it. Bearing in mind that we know Seb's business was in trouble financially, it's possible that Seb couldn't find the money. Perhaps he thought Luca would reveal his secret if he failed to fulfil his promise to set him up with his own restaurant?"

That would explain why Seb was so keen to put off his creditors.

"Is it possible that Luca was blackmailing Seb?" Simon asked. "I know from listening to the chefs gossip that everyone expected Finn Gilligan to get the executive chef job at *Nonnina* when it came up a few years ago, but Seb gave it to Luca, who was less experienced. Perhaps Seb had no choice?"

"It's an interesting theory. There's no evidence from Luca's bank accounts that show he was receiving cash payments from anyone, but yes, it's possible that payment was being made in the form of support and promotion within Mr Marchetti's restaurants." Fitzwilliam placed his empty cup on the table and sighed. "And that leads me nicely to my second piece of business."

The three of them looked at him expectantly.

"It's a request, really. From Luca's family. As you probably know, they've been adamant that Luca wouldn't have made a mistake of accidentally picking and eating death cap mushrooms. Clearly, an assertion now backed up in fact because we know he didn't. Their major push all along has been to clear Luca's name. However, now having been told the truth, they have done an unexpected U-turn and asked us to not make it public that we are investigating Seb for Luca's murder."

What? Why would they want to leave Luca's public image as that of a chef who'd died having made such a silly mistake? Lady Beatrice frowned. *There has to be more to this...*

"But why would they do that?" Perry asked.

Fitzwilliam shrugged. "Officially, they've said Seb is

dead now, and they don't think they will gain anything by dragging it all up again."

Simon raised an eyebrow. "And unofficially?"

"They seemed very concerned when we shared with them the possibility that Seb was, in fact, Franco Brambilla. Luca's brother in particular was suddenly very keen to let sleeping dogs lie."

Perry's eyes widened. "You mean they think the mafia might come after them?" he whispered.

"Let's just say, read into that what you will."

"So can you do that? Can you keep it quiet?" Lady Beatrice asked, not sure how she felt about Seb getting away with it as far as the press and public were concerned.

"We have to complete the investigation, of course, but unless Luca's family pushes it, then there is no need for the results to be made public." He rubbed his chin with his hand. "Although we have some evidence to support the case that Mr Marchetti deliberately tried to kill Luca, without being able to interview him about it, then what we have would probably not be enough to prosecute. And when it comes to motive, although we have what he said to you, Lady Beatrice, which could be considered open to interpretation, we don't even have a statement from Luca confirming that he believes Seb is Franco, just the articles in a folder on his laptop. Making it public would be irresponsible even if we suspected our conclusions are true and fit what we know."

"So you want us to leave it now and not say anything to anyone?" she asked.

"I think it would be for the best. We will complete our investigation and hand what we know to the coroner in both cases. My guess is they will record an open verdict on Luca Mazza's death and an accidental one in the case of Sebastiano Marchetti."

Lady Beatrice slowly twisted the rings on her right hand as they sat in silence for a few minutes, contemplating the unexpected turn of events.

Her mind was jumbled, her back was aching, and her arm, the bruises from Seb's fingers now slightly purple, was still sore. *I'm done. I need to go home and sleep.*

59

NOT LONG AFTER, TUESDAY 6 OCTOBER

"Are you sure you want to walk, Lady Beatrice? I can have a car brought around?" Detective Chief Inspector Richard Fitzwilliam blew into his hands. "I'm not sure what happened to our Indian Summer, but it seems to have turned on its tail and left us for good."

"I'm fine, thank you." Lady Beatrice, snug in her Moncler quilted parka, was glad she'd swapped it out earlier from her usual suede jacket. She looked down at Daisy, who trotted between them. Lady Beatrice had even remembered to put a fleece on the little terrier. She glanced up at Fitzwilliam in his suit jacket and grinned, not sure if he could see her face with only the low lights lining the pathway from the village to the north side gate of Francis Court providing illumination. "Unless you're too cold, Fitzwilliam?"

"No, no. I'm warm enough, thanks," he said, wrapping his arms around his chest.

Of course you are!

"So how are you feeling, my lady?"

About what? Finding out I've been dating an ex-mafia murderer? Or that he's now dead and everyone is treating him like he was a saint? She sighed. She'd been part of the decision to keep Seb's involvement in Luca's death under wraps, so she couldn't really complain, could she? Had she done the right thing? Her overriding thought had been of Sam and all youngsters like him who had been inspired by Seb as a chef. Could she shatter their illusions? *No, it would serve no purpose.* She sighed. It just meant she would have to continue to grit her teeth through the tributes flooding in for Seb. Although, admittedly, they were mostly about his abilities as a chef, and that had never been in doubt.

"Lady Beatrice?" Fitzwilliam stopped as the security light above the north gate picked them up and flooded the surrounding area with light. He reached out and touch her arm. "I'm sorry. I didn't mean to upset you."

She stopped and turned to him, smiling. "You didn't, Fitzwilliam. I was just trying to figure out an answer to your question, but my feelings are confused. Mostly, I'm just angry with myself for failing to see that Seb was a credible suspect until it was too late." She looked down at the ground. *I closed my mind and refused to believe he could be the murderer simply because of how it would reflect on me.* She wasn't proud of her behaviour. *What must Fitzwilliam think of me?*

"Don't be so hard on yourself. He didn't have an obvious motive, and at one point, it seemed as if he had an alibi for Monday morning."

"But *you* knew right from the start."

He dropped his hand from her arm, and stretching it out in front of them, he said, "Shall we?" Approaching the gate, Fitzwilliam held his hand up to the security officer on the other side of the metal side gate. A *click* sounded as the gate sprung open. Fitzwilliam held it open for her and Daisy to pass through.

"Evening, my lady, chief inspector." Jeff, the lead security guard, leaned his head out of the open glass window and raised his hand.

Lady Beatrice waved. "Evening, Jeff."

Fitzwilliam nodded, and they followed the pathway lit by floor LEDs towards the main house.

"I have a confession to make, my lady." Fitzwilliam stared ahead as they rounded the corner, catching their first glimpse of Francis Court lit up in all its glory in front of them.

A confession? This sounds interesting...

"I didn't *know* that Seb was the murderer. Not really. It wasn't until Lattimore came and told me that Klara had seen Seb that morning and, most importantly, that he'd instigated the bringing forward of the rehearsal, that I truly thought he'd done it. That was something we'd missed. We had accepted the producer's explanation that they'd been concerned about running out of time, so she'd brought the show forward."

But you argued Seb was the one from the beginning...
"But you—"

"I know. But I didn't really think it was him. I just wanted it to be him, so—"

"Why?"

He shrugged, still looking at the ground. "And..." He trailed off. She turned and grabbed his arm.

"And what?"

He twisted around and met her gaze. "I wanted you to see that he wasn't to be trusted."

She dropped her hand. "But how did you know he couldn't be trusted?"

In the semi-dark, she could just make out a smile tugging at a corner of his mouth. "Woman's intuition?"

She laughed. *After all the times he's teased me about my woman's intuition!*

He grinned at her.

He has a nice smile. It was a shame she got to see it so infrequently.

Daisy, who was a little ahead of them, stopped and sat down, looking back at the two of them standing and grinning at each other. She gave a low woof.

"I should have known something was wrong when Daisy took such a disliking to him."

"I tried to warn you."

"And, of course, that made me want to defend him even harder."

He nodded, still smiling, and started to move forward again. Lady Beatrice followed, and they caught up with Daisy. As they continued towards the house, the only sound was their footsteps as they hit the gravel.

'You're as bad as each other.' Had it been Perry or Simon who had said that recently? *I wonder what it would be like if we worked together rather than against each other.*

"So you'll be okay then?"

She nodded. "I'll survive." *And I'm giving men a wide berth for the foreseeable future!* She wanted it to be just her, Sam, and Daisy from now on.

"Well, if it helps, I think you've handled it very well. *TSP* seems to be on your side too, which is lucky."

He was right. With her mother's help, they had consistently played down her relationship with Seb to the point where even the popular press no longer referred to him as her ex. *Should I tell Fitzwilliam about Ma's relationship with* The Society Page*?* She thought he would probably find it intriguing and quite funny. *But can I trust him with the information?* While she pondered on that key question, she suddenly remembered the donation James had made to Lady Jane's donkey sanctuary.

"Fitzwilliam, do you remember back in April when I checked James's bank statement after Alex Sterling's death and found James had taken out ten thousand pounds in cash shortly before he'd died?"

"Yes." He hesitated. "Why?"

"Well, I made the assumption that he'd given it to Gill Sterling so she could buy tickets for her flight to Mexico and anything else she needed."

"Yes, I remember." They were approaching the bottom of the stone stairs leading up to the north side door. Fitzwilliam slowed down.

She stopped, and the security light flooded them and the surrounding area with light. She turned to him. "Well, I don't think that's what happened."

He stopped too and returned her gaze. "Why?"

"I found out a few days ago that James made a ten-thou-sand-pound donation in cash on the day he died. He handed it to Lady Jane Vickers for her donkey sanctuary in Cyprus at the charity committee meeting he attended that afternoon."

Fitzwilliam raised an eyebrow. "Really?" He began to amble up the stairs, following an eager Daisy.

Lady Beatrice nodded as she followed them up. "So if that's where the money went, then what about the money Gill Sterling had in her bank account? If it didn't come from James, then where did she get it from?"

Fitzwilliam turned and frowned. "Good question."

She'd expected him to be more animated. *Maybe he's not as interested in James's death as I am?* Was she becoming obsessed? Did any of it matter anymore? James was dead. He had been for almost fifteen years now. Why couldn't she let it go? Was it because she still didn't want to accept the contents of the letter James had written telling her he was leaving her for another woman?

"And," she continued, "why would she even need James's money if she already had plenty of her own? Don't you see? It blows my theory out of the water completely."

Fitzwilliam shrugged. "Not really. It just means that she didn't need him for his money."

"So then why fake bruises? Why tell James that Alex was abusing her if she didn't need his help to escape?"

Had Fitzwilliam forgotten she'd found the makeup while she'd been searching Alex's cottage as part of their investigation into Gill's husband's death? The professional makeup stash suggesting that the physical signs of abuse hadn't been real.

"My entire theory was based on her needing James's help to escape. Or more precisely, on needing his money to start a new life. We know she wasn't in love with him because she wasn't planning to go to Mexico with him as he believed she was. Instead, she bought a train ticket to Scotland and left her passport at the cottage. So why try to persuade him to help her? *And* where did she get all that money from?"

Reaching the top of the steps, they stopped in front of the large wooden door studded with metal fixings. She turned and looked into Fitzwilliam's brown eyes. There was something there, but what? *It's as if he already knows.* Did he?

She frowned. "You already know all of this, don't you?"

He broke her gaze and sighed. "Yes and no."

What the devil does that mean? She shifted her weight to one side and crossed her arms.

Fitzwilliam grabbed the sides of his thin jacket and pulled them together.

He's cold, is he? Good! She'd thought she could trust him

on this. Now it turned out he had information he hadn't shared with her. "Well?"

He wrapped his arms around himself. "I didn't know about James making a donation to Lady Vickers. But I had access to Gill's bank account back in April, as you know, and there was more than ten thousand in there. A lot more."

"Why didn't you tell me?"

He shook his head. "I don't know. You were coming to terms with what you'd discovered after Alex had died, and I thought your theory made sense."

She threw her hands up. "Except it doesn't, Fitzwilliam, because she wouldn't have needed his money if she had that much of her own!"

"But maybe she still needed his support to be brave enough to make the leap?"

With money behind her, why not just leave Alex? It made no sense.

Fitzwilliam shook his head. "But now that we've discussed it further, I must agree with you. It doesn't really make sense, does it? We know she wasn't being abused by Alex, and we know she had more than enough money to leave if she wanted to. So why not leave?"

"And why involve James?"

They stood in silence for a few seconds. *Wasn't there something else that I was going to tell him?* She struggled to pull it from her over-worked brain. "Phones!" Lady Beatrice suddenly blurted out.

Fitzwilliam tilted his head to one side, his brows furrowed.

"Did you know Gill had two phones?"

Fitzwilliam shook his head. "I'm fairly sure we only found one on her when she died."

"Well, Ellie Gunn told me she had two. Alex had thought

it meant she'd been having an affair, but when he'd challenged her about it, she'd told him it was an Irish mobile she'd been using to call her mother. He didn't believe her, according to Ellie."

"I wonder what happened to it. You didn't find one at Alex's cottage, did you?"

She shook her head. "No."

Fitzwilliam bounced on his feet.

He really looks cold now.

As if sensing his discomfort, Daisy scratched at the door.

Fitzwilliam grinned. "I think Daisy wants to go in."

Lady Beatrice removed a key from her pocket and opened the door. Daisy ran in, but Lady Beatrice stood on the doorstep, facing Fitzwilliam. "I suppose it doesn't matter really, does it? It's just that I hate not knowing. It's stupid, isn't it?"

"No, it's not stupid. I feel the same. After we spoke about it in April, I contacted someone senior who, like me, hadn't necessarily been happy with the end inquiry into your husband's death, and told him about the money in Gill's account. He was going to do some digging for me."

What? Her head buzzed. Had Fitzwilliam just said he hadn't been happy about the outcome of the investigation into James's death? Her stomach lurched. What did that mean? "You weren't happy that it was an accident?"

"No, no. Sorry, I may have unintentionally misled you. What I meant was I wasn't happy with the way the investigation was handled at the end. There were some inconsistencies that were never followed up and some background checks, especially on Gill, that weren't done to my satisfaction. I'm not questioning the ultimate conclusion. I just would have liked to have seen a more thorough job done, that's all."

Inconsistencies? Lady Beatrice frowned. "What inconsistencies?"

"I'm sorry, my lady. I didn't mean to alarm you. Nothing sinister, I assure you. Just some witnesses who were seen near the site of the accident but were not chased up, and a few irregularities that I wanted to look at further but didn't get the chance."

"Why?"

"PaIRS, Fenshire CID, and Gollingham Palace wanted the investigation wrapped up as soon as possible so they could arrange your husband's funeral and smother the press speculation around Gill being a passenger in your husband's car."

So they rushed through it without doing a proper inquiry?

Fitzwilliam raised his hand as she opened her mouth. "And before you ask, that's perfectly normal. They wanted to spare you and the rest of the family any more pain than was necessary. And not for one minute, did anyone believe the earl's death was anything other than an accident."

She took a deep breath and sighed. "Not even you?"

"Not even me, my lady." He smiled slowly.

"And did your contact come up with anything more about Gill and where she got all that money?"

Fitzwilliam's smile disappeared, and he shook his head. "No, he didn't. And I've been meaning to chase him about it, but I haven't got around to doing so yet."

"And will you now?"

"Yes. I don't like loose ends. I'll also ask if they found a second phone at the scene or in Gill's belongings. It's certainly possible. I was only a DS at the time, after all, so Reed may not have shared everything with me."

"Is Inspector Reed the other person who wasn't happy about the way the investigation was handled?"

Fitzwilliam sighed. "No. Reed was very focused on facts

only. As he pointed out to me frequently back then, he had no interest in 'could haves' or 'maybes'. Just what we knew and what the evidence told us."

"And I bet he was also the one under the most pressure to reach a speedy conclusion?"

Fitzwilliam raised an eyebrow. "You've got it."

There was movement at the door, and Daisy poked her head out and looked at them both.

Lady Beatrice grinned. "I think I'd better go in."

Fitzwilliam nodded. "And please don't let what I've said disturb you. I will let you know if I find out any more about what we've discussed. But—"

"I need to move on, right?"

He gave her a wry smile. "Enjoy Drew Castle, my lady. And try not to get into any trouble."

———

Fitzwilliam started the engine and set the temperature to twenty-five degrees. He rubbed his hands together as the car warmed up. *Should I have told her about the holes in the investigation into her husband's death?* He'd not intended to share his concerns with anyone else. *So why did I?* He sighed. *Those eyes!* Those big green eyes staring into his soul, begging for answers. *How could I resist?* He hoped she wouldn't worry about what he'd said. Thrusting his hands in front of the air vent the feeling returned to his fingers. *I should call him.*

He slid his mobile into the holder attached to the dashboard and selected the number.

"Richard." The voice at the other end sounded surprised. "It's been a while. What can I do for you?"

"Hello, sir. I rang to see how you've got on with investigating Gill Sterling after our conversation back in April."

"Sorry, Richard, I've been meaning to ring you. In short, there isn't much to know, it would seem. Gill Sterling moved to Scotland in her early twenties and worked in the marketing department at Drew Castle. She met Alex Sterling not long after, and they got married about a year before they moved to Francis Court. And that's it. Oh, and there's no criminal record for her, either here or in Ireland where she was raised. So nothing of any interest to us."

Richard sighed. "So no idea where she got all that money from then, sir?"

"No. We can only go back so far with bank accounts. All this data protection stuff means that information gets deleted after a time. She had a healthy balance on the account when she first arrived at Francis Court from Drew Castle. She spent some of it, but nothing new came in until four months before she died. That's about all I can tell you."

"And no luck tracing where that money came from?"

"No. They were all cash deposits."

Fitzwilliam rubbed his chin. *An inheritance maybe?* But that would be one lump sum, surely? And during the investigation, her husband hadn't mentioned that anyone had died and left her money. But then, had he been asked? *Not by me.* Had she been blackmailing someone? Nothing they'd found out had suggested she'd been the type. But then, they had known from what Lady Beatrice had found out in April that Gill had been manipulative and had lied to James. *Was she blackmailing James?* Had she been threatening to reveal their relationship to the world? But then, there had been no money other than the cash donation that had gone from his account. And that wouldn't explain the letter either. *Unless someone forced him to write it?* He sighed. *Maybe*

James had another account? At the end of the day, it was clear that Gill Sterling had been up to something, but what? *What was she being paid for and by whom?*

"Fitzwilliam?" There was a trace of impatience in the man's voice now.

"Sorry, sir. I'm just trying to work out why Gill Sterling had so much money and where it came from."

"Er, yes, it's a confusing one, that's for sure. But I'm not sure we'll ever know. The trail has gone cold, I'm afraid."

He's right. It would be hard to prove anything after fourteen years. *What was the other thing Lady Beatrice told me?* Phone! "How many phones did we find belonging to Gill Sterling, sir?"

"Phones? From what I can recall, there was just the one phone. Why do you ask?"

"Someone recently told Lady Beatrice that Gill had two phones. I can only remember one as well. But I *do* remember that the earl had a call on the night of his death from an unidentified number that was traced to a pay-as-you-go mobile. Could that have been her second phone?"

"Well, if so, she couldn't have had it in the car with her on the night she died. I'm not sure it's important."

"Yes, you're right, sir. I just dislike loose ends."

"Me too, Richard. But I think we're both going to need to accept that this all happened a long time ago, and although we would have liked to have insisted on a more thorough enquiry at the time, it doesn't change the outcome."

He's right. I don't like the way it was done, but is there really any point in pursuing this further? He closed his eyes. *I can't fix this for her…*

"Well, Richard, if that's all…"

"Yes, sir. And thank you for your time."

"No problem. And Richard?"

"Yes, sir."

"I think it's time for us all to move on, don't you?"

"Yes, sir. Goodnight."

The line at the other end disconnected. Fitzwilliam stared out into the darkness. *Yes, we all need to let it go now.*

He selected a Simon Lattimore audiobook from his phone, put the car into drive, and started the long trip home.

60

MID-DAY, SATURDAY 28 NOVEMBER

The Society Page online article:

Lady Beatrice Attends Charity Dinner in Fenswich

Last night, Lady Beatrice, the Countess of Rossex, attended a fundraising dinner for Friends of Fenswich Cathedral, along with her mother Her Royal Highness Princess Helen and her sister Lady Sarah Rosdale. The countess looked stunning in a Jenny Packham embellished cuckoo gown with Christian Louboutin black patent sandals, while the princess was resplendent in a midnight-blue Celine evening dress with silver Manolo Blahnik satin pumps. Lady Sarah, elegant as always, wore a cream Roksnda draped-sleeve gown with multicoloured Alexandre Vauthier slingback heels.

It's the first time Lady Beatrice has been seen in public since the death of Sebastiano Marchetti, better known as Chef Seb, who tragically died seven weeks ago in a car accident aged 38. A consortium of investors has recently purchased the late chef's business Marchetti Restaurants Limited, which includes the London restaurants: The Flyer in Mayfair, Nonnina in Knightsbridge, and Squisito in Piccadilly, in what is believed to be a debt restructuring deal.

A memorial service is being held for the chef next week in London. Expected to attend are Ryan Hawley, executive chef at Nonnina, and Finn Gilligan, executive chef at The Flyer. Ryan and Finn are currently filming for a new BBC television show, Two Chefs in a Camper, in which they are travelling around the British Isles in a campervan, cooking at country food shows. A royal spokesperson said that a long-standing prior engagement will prevent Lady Beatrice from attending.

Lady Beatrice and her business partner Perry Juke have completed phase one of the five-year project to update the interior of the king's private country house, Fenn House, in Fenshire. Phase two is due to start in the summer. In the meantime, the design duo are planning on overseeing the refurbishment of another of the king's private residences, Drew Castle, in Scotland, with work due to start in the new year.

If you enjoyed this book then please write a review on Amazon or Goodreads, or even both. It helps me a lot if you let people know that you recommend it.

Want to know more about the investigation into Lady Beatrice's late husband's death fourteen years ago? *An Early Death* is a prequel and in it you'll meet all your favourite characters in the series for the first time. You can pre-order it now on Amazon.

.   .   .

Will everything go to plan at Drew Castle? Not likely! Look out for Book 4 in the A Right Royal Cozy Investigation series *A Dead Herring*. You can pre-order it now on Amazon.

Want to know how Perry and Simon solved their first crime together? Then join my readers' club and receive a FREE short story Tick, Tock, Mystery Clock at www.subscribepage.com/helengoldenauthor_nls

You can also find me on Facebook (www.facbook.com/helengoldenauthor), Instagram (www.instagram.com/helengolden_author) and TikTok (www.tiktok.com/@helengoldenauthor)

A BIG THANK YOU TO...

I still have to pinch myself when I realise that writing is my life now. I still can't get used to telling people I'm an author when they ask me what I do. But none of it would be possible without the support of my friends, family and you, my readers.

As always my fabulous husband Simon continues to encourage and support me, and I love that he is so proud of me. Thank you for being by my side.

To my girls Ellie and Emma, who are always there cheering me on, and my parents Ann and Ray, who continue to be with me through each of my books, providing the best feedback. You all help me believed that I can do this. Thank you.

To my beta readers, Lesley Catterall-Price, Lissie Morgan and Lelia Wynn, thank you for your constructive comments, you help me find the best book I have in me.

To Peter Boon (the author of the Edward Crisp murder mysteries - check them out; you will love them) and Hannah (Bound by Crime on instagram), thank you for loving my characters almost as much as I do.

To my editor, Marina Grout, whose exceptional editing skills make my books the best they can be. It's always a great to work with some who just gets you, and she does. Working with you is a pleasure.

To my lovely friend, Caroyln Bruce, my final pair of eyes.

Thank you for all you do to buoy me up when I'm unsure my books are good enough.

To my ARC readers, thank you for being part of my team, your reviews and feedback are invaluable to me.

To you, my readers, thank you for reading my books and taking the time out to review them. I hope we can continue to enjoy Lady Beatrice, Daisy, Perry, Simon, and Fitzwilliam together as the series continues.

And finally, thank you to my little furry best buddies, Alfie and Margot. Sometimes you drive me crazy when you start barking for no apparent reason, but most of the time I love that you curl up with me while I write and keep me company.

As with my previous books, I may have taken a little dramatic license when it comes to police procedures, so any mistakes or misinterpretations, unintentional or otherwise, are my own.

CHARACTERS IN ORDER OF APPEARANCE

Perry Juke — Lady Beatrice's business partner and BFF.

Lady Beatrice — The Countess of Rossex. Seventeenth in line to the British throne. Daughter of Charles Astley, the Duke of Arnwall and Her Royal Highness Princess Helen. Niece of the current king.

Luca Mazza — Executive Chef at Nonnina, Seb's fine dining resturant in Knightsbridge. TV chef.

Simon Lattimore — Perry Juke's partner. Bestselling crime writer. Ex-Fenshire CID. Winner of cooking competition *Celebrity Elitechef*

Sebastiano Marchetti — Famous chef. Italian. Lady Beatrice's new beau. Luca Mazza's boss.

Fay Mayer — Luca's girlfriend and food critic.

Ryan Hawley — Head Chef at Nonnina and TV chef

King James and Queen Olivia — King of England and his wife.

Finn Gilligan — Head Chef at The Flyer in Mayfair, Seb's fine dining resturant.

James Wiltshire — The Earl of Rossex. Lady Beatrice's late husband killed in a car accident fourteen years ago.

Daisy — Lady Beatrice's adorable West Highland Terrier.

Sam Wiltshire — son of Lady Beatrice and the late James Wiltshire, the Earl of Rossex. Future Earl of Durrland.

Lady Sarah Rosdale — Lady Beatrice's elder sister. Twin of Fred Astley. Manages events at Francis Court.

Richard Fitzwilliam — Detective Chief Inspector at *PaIRS (Protection and Investigation (Royal) Service)* an organisation that provides protection and security to the royal family and who investigate any threats against them. *PaIRS* is a division of *City Police*, a police organisation based in the capital, London.

Marta Talaska-Cowley — Head Chef at Squisito, Seb's brasserie in Piccadilly.

Malcolm Cassan — Seb's agent.

Klara Damas — Malcolm's PA.

Ambrose Weir — Luca's agent.

Alex Sterling — the late Francis Court's estate manager.

John Rosdale — Lady Sarah's husband.

Charlotte (Lottie) Rosdale — Lady Sarah's daughter.

Characters In Order Of Appearance

Mr Stevens — Sam's housemaster at Wilton College, Sam's boarding school.

Mike Ainsley — Detective Inspector at Fenshire CID.

Eamon Hines — Detective Sergeant at Fenshire CID.

Carol — DCI Fitzwilliam's PA at *PaIRS*.

Nigel Blake — Superintendent at *PaIRS*. Fitzwilliam's boss.

Elise Boyce — Richard Fitzwilliam's sister

Rhys Boyce — Elise's husband. Richard Fitzwilliam's brother-in-law

Hayley Carroll — Richard Fitzwilliam's ex-girlfriend

Steve/CID Steve — ex-colleague of Simon Lattimore at Fenshire CID.

Tina Spicer — Detective Sergeant at *PaIRS*

Charles Astley — Duke of Arnwall. Lady Beatrice's father.

HRH Princess Helen — Duchess of Arnwall. Mother of Lady Beatrice. Sister of the current king.

Roisin — Simon Lattimore's friend who works in Forensics at Fenshire Police.

Nicky — server in the Breakfast Room restaurant at Francis Court.

Mrs Dunn — Cook at Breakfast Room restaurant at Francis Court.

Alfie — The Duke and Duchess of Arnwall's five-year-old border terrier.

Matteo Mazza — Luca's brother.

Archie Tellis - Sam's best friend from school.

Gill Sterling — the late wife of Francis Court's estate manager. Passenger in car accident that killed her and James Wiltshire.

Lady Jane Vickers — Friend of Lady Beatrice's grandmother, Queen Mary The Queen Mother

Ellie Gunn — Francis Court's catering manager

Pete Cowley — gardener at Francis Court. Ex-marine. Rumoured new beau of Ellie Gunn.

Mr Hutton — executive chef at Francis Court.

Frederick (Fred) Astley — Earl of Tilling. Lady Beatrice's elder brother and twin of Lady Sarah Rosdale. Ex-Intelligence Army Officer. Future Duke of Arnwall.

Dylan and Janet Milton — landlord of the pub The Ship and Seal in Francis-next-the-Sea and his wife.

Jeff Beesley — late shift lead security officer at Francis Court.

Made in the USA
Las Vegas, NV
30 January 2023

66501668R00204